The Seven Bosses of Honey Malone

JULI A. HERREN

ISBN-13: Print 979-8-218-50349-9
eBook 979-8-218-56885-6

Cover design by Roderick Brydon

DEDICATION

For women in business who'd rather laugh than cry

THE SEVEN BOSSES
OF HONEY MALONE

ACKNOWLEDGMENTS

My grateful acknowledgment to readers Helen Patterson, Margo Wickersham, Lisa Daffy, Nancy Collins, Lori Janies and Peggy Benson. Their support was invaluable.

Table of Contents

Meet our hero

Honey Malone's brain worked just fine. During her final semester as a double-major honors student at a State college in Florida, her English Lit professor had pleaded with her to pursue a PhD—and two days later, so did the Linguistics mentor she'd been crushing on. But Honey had to say no. This 23-year-old had a secret plan.

Our girl wanted to give business a whirl.

She'd never taken classes in it. But her father was a businessman, a powerful man, and he'd explained it to her.

A massive, fast-moving river of money hurtled directly overhead, blasting forward with such momentum that all a business had to do was siphon off just a bit of it, just sluice the proper straw up there into the stream, and their coffers would be flooded with wealth. Some just knew how to build bigger conduits.

It sounded so exciting, with all that momentum blasting about, and she was a capable person, upbeat and detail oriented. Certainly, it would be easy to add value in American business. Surely, if she put forth the effort, Honey would make Dad proud.

1

Her family had moved every two or three years—Honey was a "corporate brat." As Dad climbed the ladder, the states flashed past: Virginia. Ohio. Texas. Colorado. Florida. All the cities, all the schools. She didn't make many childhood friends.

But Honey did develop an advantage: she learned how people were different from each other. And even better, she learned how people were the same. Dropped into any social situation, she could engage in a genuine way with complete strangers. It was easy to do, if you cared about the stories that people tell, and why.

Where will the business world take our secret striver as she steps away from academia?

Let's examine one woman's career and the people who shaped it.

Let's take a look at the seven bosses of Honey Malone.

BOSS 1: MR. MELOSO

Honey's title: Executive Assistant, Ramrod Real Estate Development

In Tampa, it turned out, a BS in Linguistics was just about as appealing to hiring managers as a BA in English Lit. Honey's father had made it clear that once she graduated, she was on her own financially—and because she was Broke Girl, she had to stay local.

Determined to make her way in the business world and armed with a documented typing speed of 75 words per minute, Honey scored an administrative position at a new commercial-real estate development company, reporting to the owner. This job would pay the rent, with some left over for partying, cute shoes and takeout.

I won't be doing this forever, Honey thought. *Everybody has to start somewhere.*

~ ~ ~

Meloso means sweet. This guy was decidedly not. A middle-aged, olive-skinned man of about 5' 5", he and Honey were on eye level.

His suits were tailored, his nails buffed to a shine, and his brand-new offices bare of furniture. His native tongue was Castilian Spanish, but the boss was quite capable of getting his point across in English.

"You can call me Mr. Meloso," he told her. "Or sir."

Okay, Honey thought. *Here we go with this.* But she wasn't caught unaware. After all, he'd named his company "Ramrod." He'd proclaimed that brand, and she'd signed on. The gig paid 30% more than similar jobs, and she could get there in 10 minutes from her studio apartment—an important consideration for a girl who drove an unreliable beater car. This was business at its most basic. Just supply and demand.

~ ~ ~

Her friend Nicole helped celebrate Honey's first job with dinner and drinks. So many drinks. Luckily the TGI Fridays was within walking distance of Honey's apartment, so the two friends were able to make their way back there on foot, weaving and giggling through the darkened streets of Tampa's Hyde Park.

"You ought to stay the night," Honey said as they approached her door. "I've got an air mattress."

"Oh, could I? There's no way I can drive." Nicole looked up at the moon. "I'm so blasted."

When they entered the apartment, Honey closed the front door—the only door—and reached for the portable security bar. She fitted the V-shaped slot of the steel bar up under the doorknob, then kicked the other end, to make sure that it was snugged up tight against the floor. Now the door was firmly braced against outside entry. Honey turned and saw that Nicole had been watching the whole process.

"You're pretty security-conscious there, girl."

Honey knew that Nicole didn't live alone. Since she'd left high school, Nicole had lived with a big broad-shouldered husband and a big mean-eyed dog, both of whom had a hair trigger for strangers. So Honey just said *Better safe than sorry*, and crossed over to the fridge to pour two glasses of orange juice.

They talked for another two hours, chugging vitamin C and laughing at their urgent drunken stories that started strong but then seemed to peter out into nothing. They were too inebriated to set up the air mattress even if they'd found it—Honey had just moved in, and there were bags and boxes everywhere. At two in the morning, Honey shut off the lights. Both women fell across Honey's bed, and were instantly asleep.

BAM! The front door shook with a violent blow from outside, and the women jerked upright in bed. Nicole screamed, and then **BAM!** again. Whoever was outside was determined to get in. Nicole clutched at Honey and burst into tears.

The clock read 3:25. Somebody was out there, throwing their weight against the door. In the dim light from the kitchen, Nicole and Honey could see the lock on the doorknob turning. The stranger had a key.

BAM! They watched the security bar shimmy and shake with the force.

BAM! But it held firm.

It always had. Honey's father had subsidized her rent when she attended college, and she'd lived alone. She was accustomed to slimy landlords using their key to try to get into her place at night. At that point in her life, at her rental price point, it was unusual to find a landlord who *didn't* try it. These men were always surprised when her door didn't open with their master key. They weren't accustomed to encountering a security bar. Honey's had been a gift from her parents, when she first left home.

5

When Dad said she was on her own, he was serious.

It was Honey's habit to find a new place to live, when a landlord attempted to enter her space. She could move in a single day, as had been proven, and 100% of her rental deposits were returned voluntarily without question, in case she was considering calling the cops. Like they could buy her off, that way. Honey had several friends with pick-up trucks who would respond within the hour if she was in need, and Bobby helped her most often. The third time he'd helped her load his truck and unload it, he looked over at her and said, *I love it that you're confident, Honey. But there's such a thing as too confident, you know?*

After she cashed the refund check for her rental deposit and signed the lease for a new—and hopefully less slimy—apartment, Honey picked up the phone. Our girl called the cops every time. In case it mattered, for the next single woman who came along.

~ ~ ~

The Ramrod job duties had seemed realistic, in the interview. Mr. Meloso's first order of business was to get the office furnished and staffed. He'd be hiring three salespeople—"But only the professional. That is what I desire." Honey would be responsible for following up on the furniture orders, orchestrating its timely delivery, and placing calls to interested business-development candidates, to set up time on his calendar.

Honey was excited to start this phase of her life, and got up extra early on the day that her career in business would begin. Our girl felt confident in her appearance, which is easy to do when you weigh 90 pounds. She made sure that her navy suit was perfectly crease-free. She put her hair up in a bun, and then took it down. She kept her makeup minimal, but then when she looked at herself in the mirror on the way out the door, she realized that she looked too breezy, too surfer-girl. She twisted her hair back up into the bun.

On the short drive to the office, Honey looked around at the other cars and realized that she, too, was a commuter. She was adulting, big-time, and it made her feel more proud than scared. She thought, *If Dad could see me now.*

By the time she pulled into the parking lot at the office complex that housed Ramrod Real Estate, Honey was feeling quite empowered, and shook her hair free of its restrictive bun. At the perimeter of the lot, she was able to find a parking space in the shade—an important consideration for a car without a working air conditioner that would sit in the Florida sun all day. Walking away from that little spot of shade, sweating already in the humid heat, our girl felt like she'd scored a victory already. Perhaps this was a sign.

~ ~ ~

Or perhaps not. Her first day on the job, Honey discovered that Mr. Meloso was a particular man.

"Let me explain the expectation here," he said to her. "Come into my office."

Mr. Meloso's office was the only room in the suite that was fully furnished, with an expensive Persian rug laid down across the carpet tiles, and a heavy mahogany desk. Two upholstered client chairs faced the desk, so when the boss sat down, Honey started to sit, too.

"You are not invited to sit," he said.

Honey changed the trajectory of her velocity, mid-sit. Her recovery was awkward, but she regained her footing and stood across from him. Waiting, for what would come next.

From his place in the comfy executive chair, Mr. Meloso pointed to his office door. "You will have a key to this door. Only you and me. No other."

He was looking at her, and Honey realized that she was supposed to respond. Maybe she'd try *awed*.

"Wow," she said, and he smiled. He slid a key across the desk, and she took it.

"Every day is what you do," Mr. Meloso said, and thinking that he was making a metaphysical observation, Honey nodded.

"Unlock the door," he said, "then check the chairs."

They both looked at the two upholstered chairs.

"What am I checking them for?" she asked. *Critters? Don't tell me there's mice.*

He threw up his hands and chuffed a breath toward the ceiling, then opened a desk drawer. He withdrew a retractable tape measure, stalked past Honey and stopped in front of the nearest chair. Like an expert measurer, without even bending his knees, Mr. Meloso extended the tape from the front of his desk to a leg of the chair.

"Twenty-eight," he said.

He stepped to the next chair, and measured its distance from the desk.

"Twenty-eight." With a snap, he retracted the tape. He looked at Honey. "See?"

"I sure do," she said. *Yeah, I see it all.* Honey said, "Thanks for explaining."

With a flourish, Mr. Meloso handed her the tape measure, which was engraved with the priapic spear of the Ramrod logo. She looked down at it. *An honor*, she thought. *Such an honor.*

"Now," the boss said, "this is just the start of expectations."

Somehow, Honey wasn't surprised.

~ ~ ~

Mr. Meloso personally demonstrated how she should dust the surface of his desk each morning, and Honey wondered how it was possible for a person to keep their nose that close to the wood, without leaving smudges of skin oil. She'd have to practice. Her boss showed her which drawer in the credenza held the proper cloths for desk-dusting.

Honey learned that she was to check the seam in the lampshade, to make sure that it faced the wall. *We're not going to get a lot of earthquakes here in Florida*, Honey thought. *Won't be much to jar that lampshade out of place, my man.*

"This is daily," he said. "I must be clear. Will you make notes now? To write this down?"

"Nope. I think I got this."

"Then here is the pencil test," Mr. Meloso said. "Important." He indicated a leather box on his desk. It held a dozen identical pencils, eraser-end down, lined up like soldiers in uniform rows. The boss pulled out a sheet of paper, folded it in half, and laid it across the sharpened points of the pencils. Then he stooped, so that he could gauge whether all the pencil tips touched the paper.

"Equal," he said. "All the same, for height."

Just shoot me now, Honey thought.

"You will attend to sharpening each day before my arrival. Precision is key."

Honey struggled to keep her expression passive. Her eyebrows kept trying to rise. She cleared her throat and asked, "Can I expect access to a specially-designed pencil sharpener?"

"But of course!" He was delighted, like he'd found a kindred spirit. He touched the credenza's second drawer. "In here."

Mr. Meloso pulled the sheet of paper away from the pencil tips, and they stood looking down at the leather box of perfection. Honey could hear the click of the wall clock, soft as a bullet sliding into its chamber.

The boss asked, "What have you learned?"

That your OCD is not well-managed? That I need to find another job fast?

Honey said, "I've learned that the shortest pencil dictates my action."

His eyes looked hopeful. "You will go well here."

"That is what I desire," Honey said.

~ ~ ~

Honey called home to deliver the news that she'd scored her first real job. Her mother answered, so our girl asked, "Is Dad home?"

"You know better than that," her mother said. "It's after dark."

And of course she was right. Honey's father had a habit of staying out late after a day at the office.

"Well, I have good news. I got a job. Full-time, with benefits."

"That's wonderful, sweetheart."

Now that Honey had a little distance from her foundational home life, it was beginning to dawn on her that it was her Mom who was always there. Mom had never wavered in her celebration of Honey's successes.

"Tell me everything!" Mom said. "Oh, I just can't wait to hear."

~ ~ ~

Two months later, all the well-dusted furniture was in place in the Ramrod sales offices, and Honey had completed her morning duty of replacing every pencil in Mr. Meloso's leather cup with brand-new ones, from the case of factory-sharpened pencils she'd stashed in the supply closet. She'd never used the special sharpener that waited in the second drawer. And he'd never questioned the office-supply budget.

That morning, Honey was eager to review the resume of a salesperson who was interested in what Ramrod had to offer. Trevor Bankhead was smooth. She'd seen him at the clubs. He'd run a political campaign at one point, and his chiseled visage was often in the press. He even knew the Cuban community of Ybor City, which was a hard nut to crack for developers—his connections were highly prized. Honey realized that while Trevor was unquestionably tall and undeniably buff, he also had one hell of a resume. This was the professional that the business needed, right then, and Mr. Meloso seemed to sense it, too. On the day of the Bankhead interview, the boss wore his special tie.

Honey peeked out the window to see what the job candidate was driving—and it was a perfectly restored 1953 Pontiac Chieftain, with wide whitewall tires and a bumpersticker that read:

When cryptography is outlawed,
bayl bhgynjf jvyy unir cevinpl.

I like this guy already, Honey thought. She reached up and pulled her hair out of the bun.

Honey had fluffed her curls and was seated at her reception desk when Trevor strode in, looking absolutely dapper, his wide smile bright, his beautiful suit tailored snugly around his broad shoulders. Our girl sighed with delight.

"Wait," he said, "I know you."

She stood up, and extended her hand. "I'm Honey Malone."

They shook hands professionally, though Honey's heart was pounding, to be so close to him. His eyes. That smile.

"I think we've seen each other in Ybor," she said. "Let me tell Mr. Meloso that you're here."

~ ~ ~

But after Trevor Bankhead left that day, Mr. Meloso came out of his office, folded Trevor's resume twice, and dropped it into the trash can next to Honey's desk.

"Schedule more candidates," he said.

"Oh, no," Honey blurted out. "I had such hopes for this guy. What happened?"

"Come, this will tell you."

Honey followed the boss into his office. He pointed down. And when she looked closely at the nearest chair, Honey could see that all four legs were out of their customary divots on the Persian rug.

"He moved his chair," the boss said.

Then both businesspeople were very sad, but for different reasons.

~ ~ ~

It was Christmastime at the most-recent Malone family hacienda. Honey's parents had moved to an upscale neighborhood in Tallahassee, into a spacious rancher on the northeast side of town, so that Dad had easy access to the State Capitol. He'd become a lobbyist by then, though he was unclear in his communication about which entity he represented. Dad had never talked with his family about his job. Maybe he assumed they were too dense to grasp the full gravity of his position. Or maybe he was just tired of talking—he no doubt did plenty of that, during his long hours at work. He was, as her mother often reminded her, a good provider.

The day before Christmas, Honey drove up from Tampa and waited outside the quaint little Tallahassee airport for her brother Max, who was flying in from Colorado. Max was three years younger than Honey, but he'd skipped two grades in middle school because his excellent brain produced excellent test scores. Max had graduated from college the same time Honey had—and then went on to pursue a Doctorate in Accountancy at the University of Colorado. Max had always been the quiet one, more likely to observe than to interject, whereas Honey had been the one to showcase her strong verbal skills ad infinitum, like their dad.

She spotted her brother coming out the doors at baggage claim, a tall, handsome fellow walking with a stoop, dragging his feet as he pulled a wheelie bag toward the curb. She tooted the horn, and when Max looked up, Honey saw that his face was filled with dread. Max hated holidays with family. He always had. But he always showed up.

Honey began the next leg of her route: their parents' new address.

"So you're working now," Max said. "Do you like it?"

"It's—um—okay, I guess."

Her brother gave her the side-eye. "Not real positive, there, sis. I

13

always said you're a great singer. Why not try that?"

"There's no money in that."

Max nodded. "True enough. Well then, what is it you don't like about the job?"

"Well, the boss is obsessive-compulsive, so that's no fun. Like, every tiny little thing has to be perfect, or he locks up and can't function."

Max smiled over at her. "You are the ideal person to keep him on track, then."

"I'm not OCD."

"If you say so," Max said. "Let me ask, how many times did you change your hairdo, your first day on the job?"

"Four," she muttered. "But that's not being obsessive. That's just being a girl."

~ ~ ~

Their mother was waiting on the front porch when they pulled up, looking trim and perky in a tomato-red sweater, eyes alight, with a big grin on her face. *How can she stay so positive?* Honey wondered. *Maybe it's in her genes, or something.*

As soon as the car's tires came to a stop, Mom rushed to the passenger door and threw it open. "Max, oh my goodness, how handsome. Look at you. Oh, Honey, oh sweetie, I love your hair. Are those highlights? Come in, come in, let's get you settled."

She hugged them both. A petite woman just five foot two, she smelled like cinnamon, no doubt from the home-made pies, cakes and cookies that awaited them on the groaning board that was the kitchen counter. Mom baked for days before Christmas, even though she didn't much enjoy it, because: "tradition."

Their mother claimed to value tradition, but Honey never sensed a fire in her belly about that. Mom had been a paralegal when she met her mate, and hadn't worked outside the home since. Samantha Malone's whole job had been her house and her children—and now her kids were out on their own, not exactly flourishing, in Honey's case, but self-sufficient.

~ ~ ~

The siblings unloaded the car and rolled their bags through the front door of a home they'd never seen. They were used to new houses, having moved every two years, and both of them had grown accustomed to the fact that each residence their father purchased would be larger and more imposing than its predecessor. Dad was big into curb appeal, but relegated the interior of each house to their Mom.

Their father had no interest in furnishings, draperies or decoration. As long as he could say he had the biggest place on the block, in the nicest neighborhood in town, Dad was happy. Mom had explained it once: "He wants people to drive past and say, 'Look, that's where Mitchell Malone lives.'"

"Nice place, Mom," Max said.

"Oh, isn't it? I like the high ceilings." Mom led them down a broad hallway, past the pies in the expansive kitchen toward the bedrooms in back. Honey saw that a row of paintings had been hung on the wall: three angry-looking medieval burghers. She hadn't seen those before.

Mom said, "I hired a decorator this time. An interior design firm from Thomasville. They were on HGTV."

To Honey, the space had the vibe of an unused airport concourse—clean, echoing and empty, with occasional artwork.

She pulled her suitcase past a statue of Pan that rested atop a marble pedestal. They'd never had statues in the house. This one seemed to be holding a goat over his head, like a fuzzy hat descending.

"I'm not sure I'd get a decorator again," Mom said, looking up at the statue. "It's the designer's style, more than mine."

"You can say that again." Max indicated a monumental tapestry that was hung on the wall, dripping gold fringe. A hunting scene, with wild-eyed baying hounds straining against the leash, men on horseback, and clouds roiling in the woven sky. "But it's impressive."

"That's what your father said."

Max rolled his eyes to the ceiling. "Oh, I bet."

"Now Max," Mom said, "don't start."

Their mother turned and started walking, and they followed her down the concourse. She'd picked up speed, her heels clicking against the marble.

"Where is he, anyway?" her son asked.

"Working."

"On Christmas Eve?" Honey asked.

Max shot a glance at his sister. "What, was there some kind of lobbyist emergency?"

"He'll be home for dinner," Mom said with finality in her tone, and the siblings knew then that the time for snark was over. Mom stopped midway down the hallway and opened a door.

"Max, we'll put you in here. And Honey, you're right across the hall."

"Bathroom?" Honey asked. It had been a long trip from Tampa.

"Oh, all the bedrooms are *en suite* here," Mom said. "I don't want to sound snooty, but that's just the fact. You two get settled, and I'll go start dinner. I just—I can't tell you how nice it is to see you. I'm so excited that you're here!"

She grabbed them both for another hug—right there in the hallway, which wasn't on script—and when they broke from the clinch, Honey saw that her brother stood taller. His eyes were shining.

"You're the whole reason I came," Max said, "you and Honey. I love you guys."

"We're a team," Mom said. "The three musketeers."

~ ~ ~

Their father arrived late, after the table had been set, the wine poured, and the hot items arranged on the buffet, steaming in their chafing dishes. The three of them waited for him at the dining-room table, catching up.

"I must say, Honey," Mom said, "you're looking very chic."

Our girl was wearing a navy shell over navy slacks. A yellow-and-blue striped sweater. A simple belt, embroidered flats. Before Honey could say "thanks" for what she considered a totally unremarkable outfit, Max contributed to the conversation.

"She gets her good taste from you, Mom."

"Well, goodness. That's nice to hear."

"You taught her well." Max inclined his head toward his sister.

"Honey doesn't buy anything that's not linen or cashmere."

Honey could not contest this, because it was nearly true. She'd rather have a few good things than chase the latest fashion. So she just looked over at him and said, "Look who's talking."

~ ~ ~

The three of them had been discussing Max's desire to join the academic staff at Colorado State, but all conversation ceased when they heard it: the resolute hum of the garage door opening. The musketeers waited in silence, listening to the tinny jingle of a chafing-dish lid, looking to the door.

"Well, Merry Christmas!" As always, Dad's voice was loud, like he was projecting to an audience, and as always he was dressed in a crisply tailored dark suit. His shirt was the same color as his eyes, slate blue. His salt-and-pepper hair was perfection. Mitchell Malone, the powerful businessman, was a natural at taking center stage.

"Honey. My girl. So good to see you."

Honey stood up and embraced him. He smelled like soap and leather with a high note of sour mash bourbon. He smelled like he always smelled, and she rode the familiar little rollercoaster that instantly transported her back into childhood. Not a bad feeling, if you liked rollercoasters, which are, after all, a legal, generally safe and relatively cheap means of experiencing a natural high. Hearing Dad say her name always got Honey's blood pumping, her adrenaline flowing. She came to anticipate the build-up of potential energy on the hills, kinetic energy on the drops, and g-forces on the loops and turns of life in Mitchell's sphere.

She was lucky. Some people didn't even know their dad.

Her father slipped out of his suit jacket and laid it across the back of a chair. He did that thing where he took a few seconds to survey the room. Then he smiled. Like he was thinking, *I got this covered.*

Dad looked over at his son and said one word: "Max."

From his seat at the table, Max nodded in perfunctory greeting, then raised his wine glass to his lips and chugged.

Mom was beaming, to see them all together. "Let's sit," she said. "I made pot roast. Dad's favorite."

As Honey sat next to Max, he whispered, "I thought YOU were Dad's favorite," and then they had to come up with a joke real quick, as an excuse for busting out laughing just as their father was preparing to say grace.

~ ~ ~

During the night, Honey dreamed of a resolute boy playing the flute, but the sound that came out was the hum of a garage door.

Christmas morning followed the regimented annual plan. The Malones traditionally slept until nine, then convened in the kitchen for coffee. That morning, Mom was dressed in a pants suit of robin's-egg blue, wearing full makeup topped off by her signature bright lipstick. Dad appeared, wearing a bathrobe over pajamas that still had creases in them, they were so fresh out of the package. Honey watched as he sweetened his coffee with a strong shot of whiskey, and they all turned to leave the kitchen. As they'd done for decades, the four members of the clan took their beverages into the living room to begin the primary festivity that brought them together just once a year: opening gifts.

As they followed their parents, Max put a hand on Honey's arm. Their steps slowed as he said, "What time will he make his escape this year? I say noon."

"I say two. He's gonna want lunch."

"It's a bet," Max whispered. "Winner gets the statue of Pan."

Honey wrinkled her nose at that idea, and the two siblings were snickering together as they entered the Room of Many Gifts, where acoustic Christmas music played at low volume. They were greeted by a tree standing 18 feet tall, covered in glittering ornaments recently purchased to make a statement, its thousands of professionally arranged twinkle lights aglow. A mound of identically wrapped packages supported the color scheme, and surrounded the base of the tree for three feet in every direction.

This will take a while, Honey thought. Their Mom always overdid it, at Christmas. It was almost like she could keep everybody together longer, if there were more presents to be opened.

To further extend the experience, they didn't tear into their gifts willy-nilly, like normal families. The Malone method was to sit at full attention while a single person unwrapped a single gift, so that all the *oohs* and *aahs* could be properly tallied. As each individual box was opened, Dad was as surprised as anyone to see what had been purchased. He had no interest in choosing gifts, so Mom did it. Every item that came out of a box on Christmas Day was a total revelation to their father.

As was customary on Christmas morning, Mom was the first to open a present—and it would be marked *From Mitchell*. This one was tiny, like it might contain jewelry.

"Ooh, look at this," Mom exclaimed. She held up a heavy golden bracelet made of interlaced links. "A charm bracelet starter. Just what I've been wanting."

She turned to her husband. "Thanks, sweetheart."

"You're quite welcome," Dad said. "Glad you like it."

Max launched himself off the couch and stomped over to the window, where he stood with his back to them, looking out. Dad shifted his eyes to the door and took another sip of coffee whiskey.

"I will love this," Mom was saying, "I can add little charms along the way."

Now I know what to get her for her birthday, Honey thought. *A little charm or two.* But then Honey wondered, *What are her actual hobbies and interests, though? Other than me and Max?* Maybe it wouldn't be so easy to find the right charms for the woman who seemed to have everything except a life of her own.

Dad opened a gift next. He peered down at the tag and said, "Oh, it's from Honey. I wonder what this could be."

It was the standard joke, of course. The package either contained a necktie he'd never wear, or a book he'd never read. That's all Honey ever purchased for her father, and those two options had been her go-to gifts for years. Her brother's evergreen Dad Gift was gimmick socks, those imprinted with phrases like *Florida Man* or *I ♥ drag*, or sometimes socks with Mitchell's face repeated in a pattern across them, like that year when Max found a photo where Dad looked irate. This year, Honey knew, the socks would read *Kick this day in its sunshiny ass*. Her brother had tipped her off to that lucky find.

"Max, you're next," Mom called over, and her son returned to his spot on the couch.

Max seemed surprised by the weight of the box when Mom handed it to him. He looked at the tag. "From Mom and Dad," he read. He opened the carton and pulled out two heavy onyx blocks that were felted on the bottom.

"Bookends!" Max said, and his delight was obvious. "Mom, how did you know?"

Their mother's eyes shone bright. "You said something on the phone back in June."

"Damn," Max said, "you're good."

Mom had never looked happier than she did in that moment. *I love her smile*, Honey thought.

"Yeah, good luck getting THAT back on the plane," Dad said.

"Oh, I can ship it." Mom pulled an oversized box from the pile. "Honey, this is from me and your father."

It was Honey's turn for the slo-mo reveal on Gift 1 of 20. She untied the bow, ever so slowly, and then turned her attention to the wrapping paper, taking care to pull back with her thumbnail on each little snippet of tape, because she knew it drove Max crazy. When he started to whine like a high-pitched puppy, Honey took pity on him. She stripped away the paper and popped the box open.

"Wow. A desk set." She pulled out a large desk blotter that was trimmed in leather, and a squat leather-cloaked clock. And, Honey soon discovered, a leather pencil cup exactly like the one she touched every weekday at the office. Now she had one of her own. *Maybe I'll put PENS in mine*, she thought. *Or Twizzlers.*

"I really like it," Honey said. "Thanks so much. This is far too fancy for me. But that doesn't mean I won't use it."

"How IS your job going?" Mom asked.

"Her boss is nutso," Max volunteered, and everybody laughed except Dad.

Their father set his empty cup on the table. "Let's get this show on the road. Who's next?"

~ ~ ~

As Max predicted, their dad left at noon on Christmas Day, as he always left: with no apology. Just a brief hug for Honey, and a whisper in her ear: *Call me anytime. Really. I worry about you.* Our girl felt her heart do a sideways turn, like it was moving beneath her ribs, when she heard those words from her father, whose attention had usually been elsewhere, seldom trained on her. But then there were moments like these.

Her Dad wasn't perfect, obviously—but he obviously cared. Calling back *Merry Christmas* to his other two family members, Dad was out the door to the garage, where his immaculate black sedan waited. He seemed to be always hurrying, stoked to get to his next appointment, dressed in his dark suit, carrying his briefcase. Maybe he was off to ink a time-sensitive contract with the Governor, or a middle eastern sheik.

Honey and Max had lunch with Mom and helped with the dishes. The siblings made three trips each carrying plastic bags of crumpled wrapping paper out to the bins. The rest of Christmas Day was much more pleasant, when it was just the three of them, like back in the old days.

When everybody in your world is brand new to you except your mom and your sibling, it's comforting to know that at least two other people in the world know who you are. Conversation flowed easily without Dad around, and they laughed themselves silly at the silliest things. They scoffed when Honey suggested Scrabble.

"I'm not playing with you," Mom said. "You make up words."

"I do not. I just know more Scrabble words, that's all."

"You're a cheater," Max said. "Either that, or linguistics spoiled you as a Scrabble player, forever. It's possible to know too much about words, Honey."

"Never," she said. "Listen to yourself, that's just wrong."

The women were pleased to hear that Max was beginning to date again, after his last long-term relationship went down in flames.

"You'll find somebody," Mom said.

"I guess. It's not easy, finding somebody nice."

Mom leaned over and put her hand on his arm. "You're a fine man, Max. I'm proud of you."

"Well, thanks," Max said, flushing red. "That means a lot, coming from you."

When the siblings transported their armloads of new possessions back down the concourse to their rooms, they approached Pan on his marble pedestal, and their pace eased. The Christmas visit home was coming to a close—Honey would be taking Max back to the airport in an hour, and there was so much left to say. They stood side-by-side, silently considering the statue. If Pan had looked down, he would've seen a brother's eyes slate-blue, and a sister's green, gazing upward from faces that looked much the same. Honey took a deep breath and spoke.

"Good luck getting THAT back on the plane."

~ ~ ~

At the office in Tampa, Honey discovered that Mr. Meloso was in extraordinarily good spirits after his return from a holiday trip to Panama. He went there for a few days every month, in spite of— or maybe because of—continuing political unrest in the country. Honey never knew the purpose of these journeys, but this time he came back all pumped about something, wearing a brand-new pair of exquisite shoes. She could swear they were Prada. The boss couldn't sit still in his office that day, and his comfy chair sat disregarded as Mr. Meloso busied himself by repeatedly re-dusting the desk. She could actually hear him humming, in there. He normally wasn't a humming kind of dude.

As always, at the end of the day, Honey stopped by his office door to say goodnight. But this time, the boss held up his hand to stop her. "I brought you something."

He handed her a soft package wrapped in tissue and encouraged her to open it. Honey unfolded a colorful piece of intricate hand-made textile art. Layers upon layers of cloth had been overlaid, sewn, then meticulously cut away to form detailed designs.

"It's called *mola*," Mr. Meloso explained. "Made by indigenous women of Panama. Every finished *mola*—like the woman who builds it—is different from all others."

"It's beautiful," Honey said, and she wasn't shining him on. She loved everything about it. *Whose hands made this?* she wondered.

"What a nice surprise," Honey said. "Thank you so much."

~ ~ ~

When she wrenched open the screechy door of her ancient Hyundai in the parking lot, Honey tossed the package on the passenger seat. *What a cool gift*, she thought. She remembered the way Mr. Meloso had described women's uniqueness and creativity. *What a nice guy.* Maybe she'd misjudged the boss. Maybe there was a normal human being in there, after all.

But that night Honey did some research on the piece he'd brought her, which came with a tag that revealed the artist's name. The *mola* was worth $30,000. This piece of cloth was worth more than all of Honey's other possessions put together.

What kind of man gives his assistant a gift this expensive? Will he expect something in return?

Honey's mind was swamped with overwhelming implications. She was way out of her depth, and she knew it. So our girl sought counsel. She called her dad, but he didn't pick up—maybe he thought she was looking for money. She called her girlfriends, and her brother, and her mom, walking around the apartment soaking up their advice as she searched for a hiding place for the most valuable item in her life.

By the time she went to bed that night, the *mola* was safe, tucked into a big envelope that was taped behind her bureau, and a consensus had been reached on Honey's next, best action.

She would bide her time, to see if her boss expected favors.

If he didn't, then she could keep the gift.

If he did, then she would quit the job and return it.

~ ~ ~

Mr. Meloso's behavior toward her never changed, though he did ask her once when she planned to marry.

"I'm thinking never," Honey said.

He drew back in shock. "Why would you say this?"

"Because the wife always gets the short end of the stick. That's why."

Then Honey spent ten minutes explaining what *short end of the stick* meant, while her boss struggled to absorb the nuances of the idiom. Many questions were asked, many examples given. When they'd gone through that exercise, neither of them said anything. The silence lingered. *Mr. Meloso looks sad*, Honey thought.

"You are perceptive," he told her. "That much I will say."

~ ~ ~

Things got interesting when the salespeople were hired. Two men and a woman, all with proven experience in commercial real estate, moved into their new offices at Ramrod, and waited for permission from Mr. Meloso to proceed. That permission, Honey learned, was slow to come.

The saleswoman, Patrice, was first to reach out. A seasoned professional, Patrice was a no-nonsense woman, one whose approach was unerringly direct and clear. She walked up to Honey in the breakroom one day and said, "Let me ask you something. Mr. Meloso told me not to take any action until I got specific instruction from him. But it's been three weeks. Should I be worried?"

"Hm," Honey said, stalling because she wanted to be helpful. But Honey had no clue whether Patrice should worry. "I'll ask you this: did Mr. Meloso tell the guys to wait for instruction, too?"

"Yeah. But we're on straight commission. We'll never have any income if we just keep sitting at our desks doing nothing. Sometimes these deals take months to close."

"I can see that you're concerned," Honey said. She racked her brain, searching for a way to add value somehow. "Maybe he's working out the territories, or something. Maybe there's a method to his madness."

"Or maybe it's just madness."

Now you're closer to the truth. Honey gave her a sad smile. "I wish I could offer advice. But I can't. I just don't know."

Patrice sighed and sipped her coffee. She seemed to be staring across the room, at the wall that separated them from Mr. Meloso's office. "I'm tempted to disregard him entirely." She adjusted her grip on her coffee cup and darted a quick look at Honey. "I'm tempted to just get out there and start drumming up business. What could be wrong with that?"

So much could be wrong with that, Honey thought.

She said, "I guess you could try that approach."

"You're not giving me much here, Honey."

"I know. I'm sorry, there's just not much to give."

~ ~ ~

At that time in her life, Honey had a new boyfriend. She often spilled her guts about the freakish atmosphere at Ramrod to the person who was most convenient—and most motivated to listen: Joe Stecher.

He was a big, laid-back guy, and Honey had been drawn to the fact that he was handsome, well-endowed and preternaturally frisky. He was a sought-after partner in a sought-after circle of friends. Joe had ticked a lot of Honey's boxes, back then.

Joe was four years older than her, had served in the Air Force, and held a high-paying job maintaining electronics for industrial machinery throughout the Southeastern United States. Check, check, check. But he talked funny. The way he used words was sometimes slightly wrong. *A small price to pay*, Honey thought, gazing across at him in the restaurant that night. He looked fine in that blue shirt she'd bought him. She squirmed in her seat. She grasped his hand.

"I enjoyed talking with your mom earlier," she said. Joe had encouraged the two women to engage, which to Honey indicated that he might seek an exclusive relationship with her. She felt a little thrill move up her spine. "I felt like I've met her already, even though it was just over the phone."

"I knew it!" Joe said. "I think the two of you are surrogated sisters."

That was the moment when Honey began to document these Joe-isms, jotting them onto a note in real time, or scribbling them on a napkin. Never once did he notice.

"HE HANDLED THAT KNIFE THE WAY A SURGEON HANDLES A SCAFFOLD."

"SHE WASN'T DEAD. SHE WAS JUST UNCONSCIENTIOUS."

"WE LIKED THE NEW JOB CANDIDATE. YOU COULD PROBABLY SAY HE PASSED MUSTARD."

~ ~ ~

The Ramrod salesmen approached Honey next. Rodolfo and Rich came in early one day, before the boss arrived. They stood at Mr. Meloso's open office door, watching Honey as she hunched over the desktop, massaging it with the special cloth. Neither man came into the room. Like dogs wearing shock collars, they sensed that they must not cross the threshold.

"You have to dust his desk every day?" Rodolfo asked.

"Yes."

"Why is your nose so close?" Rich said.

Honey asked, "Do you really want to know?" and Rich put out his palms. He shook his head.

They watched her cross over to the floor lamp.

"Do you have to dust the lamp, too?" Rich asked.

"Not yet. Right now, all I have to do is make sure the seam in the shade is still facing the wall."

He put a hand to the back of his neck. "No shit? That seems super strange."

Honey smiled over at them and shrugged, but didn't speak. *It is what it is.*

"We're thinking this guy has a problem," Rodolfo said.

"A control problem," Rich concurred.

Honey crossed back over to Mr. Meloso's desk to begin the pencil exchange. The two men watched from the doorway as she dumped the pencils out of the leather cup into a brown paper bag. Then they watched her pull out a new pack of pencils, unwrap the plastic, and arrange the replacements point-up into perfect rows.

Rich stared, wide-eyed. "Like I said. A control problem."

Honey stepped back to assess whether all the items on Mr. Meloso's desk were squared up.

"So, I gotta ask," Rodolfo said, "What do you do with the sack of perfectly good pencils?"

"I take them to my friend Stacy. She teaches at the elementary school down the street."

Honey lifted up the half-empty bag and shook it, for effect.

The men looked at each other, and Rodolfo heaved a deep breath. "You've been here longer than us. Any advice? Like, any words to the wise, about this guy?"

Honey looked over at the two professional salespeople who were caught in this Meloso madness, and she felt sorry for them. After all, they and Patrice had a lot more to lose than she did. They had careers, and house payments, and families. There was a lot riding on success at their new jobs, and Honey wanted to help them.

She pointed to the two pieces of furniture that faced Mr. Meloso's desk.

"Just don't move the chairs."

~ ~ ~

It was her little brother, not her mom, who had taught Honey the lesson about personal space. She and Max had been living in Ohio, and they'd been in line at the Sylvania library with Max's friend Danny, to check out books. The boys were nine years old. When it was Honey's turn at the counter, a nice-looking man in a nice-looking suit came up to her, threw his arm around her shoulders, and pulled her close as he said to the librarian, "Good morning, beautiful. My friend here will let me go ahead of her. Won't you, sweetheart?"

Twelve-year-old Honey had frozen when the man grabbed her like that. Nothing like that had ever happened before. She said nothing in response to the man's question.

Max and Danny exchanged a look, and then they both stepped forward. Max put both of his hands on the man's arm and pulled it away from Honey's shoulders. Danny pushed at the guy, who seemed surprised to be double-teamed by children.

"Keep your fucking hands off her," Max said, and the man stepped away. Honey had been shocked to hear her little brother speak the F-word out loud. In their mother's house, the rules about profanity were clear. The man in the suit recovered well. He shrugged at the librarian and walked off, like this sort of thing happened every day. Maybe in his world, it did.

After they checked out their books and were walking toward the library doors, Honey said to her brother, "Max. Where did you learn language like that?"

She saw the boys smile at each other.

Max said, "You can't just let people touch you like that."

"Right," Danny said, "not cool."

They pushed through the doors to a beautiful autumn day, and Max said, "You should've told him to go fuck himself."

"Well, I can't say that."

The boys' eyes widened.

"You have to say it," Danny said, and Max said *Right*.

Honey parroted her mother's rationale. "Girls don't use that language, though."

On the street, Mom's car pulled up. Max looked over at Honey. "You better use that language. Like, for when stuff like this happens."

"Yeah," Danny said. "Otherwise, they'll peg you as a sucker."

~ ~ ~

When she worked at Ramrod, Honey's lunch hours were the same every day. She was a creature of habit. Every weekday at noon, she'd climb into her superheated Hyundai, and then stop at the 7-11 near the office complex to buy two power bars and a bottle of Sprite—chosen because it had bubbles, and because if she spilled it, it wouldn't stain. There were usually rude men in the convenience store at that time of day, on that particular end of town, and Honey had grown used to their slack-mouthed ogling.

With regularity, some man at the store made a sexual suggestion, and she had to tell him to go fuck himself—and she always thought of Max and the library when she did. Back when she was twelve years old, Honey never could have imagined how many times that particular phrase would come in handy. But her linguistics training had taught her that if one's goal is clear communication, one must be able to speak the language of the audience. *Go fuck yourself* seemed to be universally understood.

Honey's lunch-hour destination was the parking lot near the airport that had a view of the bayou, and some shade. She still hadn't saved up enough to fix the car's air conditioning, so this was the perfect spot for Honey to spend an hour by herself. She sat with the windows open, smelling the salty breeze off the bay, sipping her Sprite from a bottle that dripped condensation onto the glossy magazine she'd brought to read. *Mademoiselle* had been her favorite, back then.

She flipped the pages. She imagined dresses made of silk. She dreamed of lunches at Le Bernardin.

~ ~ ~

"Mr. Meloso," Honey said one day. "If I wanted to learn about what's going on in business, what publications should I read?"

If her boss was surprised by this question, he didn't show it.

"In America?" he asked, and when she nodded, he listed them off: "The Wall Street Journal. The New York Times. Harvard Business Review. Fortune. Forbes. Business Week. The Economist. Not Quick Company, though—it is derivative to the point of plagiarism."

Honey hurried to write it all down, and when she looked up, Mr. Meloso was smiling.

"For this, you make notes," he said.

~ ~ ~

One day on the Howard Frankland Bridge, a seafoam-green car passed her, a big old Pontiac Chieftain with wide whitewall tires. Its bumpersticker bore this message:

**My daughter was inmate of the month
at Lowell Women's Correctional Facility**

BOSS 2: SUGAR MAN

Honey's title: Manager of the Executive Office, Deal Hipper Reybold Wealth Management

After eight tedious months working for Mr. Meloso, Honey got the chance to make a change. One of her friends had a mom who was a stockbroker—and her prestige firm was hiring an office manager. "The wealth management team," the mom told Honey, breathless. "The best of the best." Her bright eyes vibrated with possibility or maybe cocaine. She grasped Honey's arm. "Top floor. You'd be perfect."

Finance, Honey thought. *Why not?*

Her friend's mom had oversold the top floor—the third floor—of the chocolate-brown Deal Hipper building near the airport. That beige floor was home to the firm's Wealth Management suite, certainly, but it also housed a vacuum cleaner-repair business, a hypnosis practice, and the offices of a nonprofit that introduced at-risk kids to yachting.

~ ~ ~

When she took the job, Honey had no way of knowing how beige the third floor would be. That's because the Deal Hipper hiring

35

manager had scheduled her job interview across town at a legendary Tampa steakhouse, where the two of them had a $300 lunch in a cozy silk-lined booth under supremely flattering lighting. The man looked to be about 60 years old. His hair was grayish, his eyes grayish too, and his skin was moistly white, like an albino lizard that spent its life underground. His name was Thomas Featherston.

"Call me Sugar Man," he said.

Honey must have looked surprised, because he laughed.

"That's my nickname. Even my clients call me that."

Do they? Why?

She would've asked it out loud, but he was still laughing, projecting his gaiety, and Honey realized that he wanted the other diners—the other men—to see him having fun. In the booth. With her. She was decades years younger than anyone in the room, including the all-male serving staff.

Do they call you "Sugar Man" because you're so white? Or maybe it's a coke reference? There's nothing sweet about you, so that can't be it.

Honey's prospective boss continued to have a fine time there in the darkened restaurant, recounting tales of client capture in the wild, exhibiting his beautifully capped teeth in raucous laughter even when nothing was funny. Lunch stretched into two hours as he downed Scotch after Scotch from a crystal tumbler, and as time and table turnover provided him with a fresh audience. During those hours, he never broached the topic of the job, the responsibilities, or the pay.

This isn't a job interview, Honey thought. *This is the Sugar Show.*

He dropped names like confetti across the minuscule tabletop of the intimate booth. Her nose was 18 inches from his. It felt more like a date than an interview, and Honey didn't like it. So, when lunch was finally over and she watched him stumble ahead of her out the door toward the valet stand, our girl decided to speak frankly.

"I need to tell you, this job isn't for me."

Sugar Man blinked slowly, either because his opalescent eyes were shocked by the brightness of the sun orb or because it was occurring to him that *a job interview* was what he was supposed to be doing that day.

Honey said, "You can remove my name from consideration. Thanks for lunch."

"Whoa, wait." He was blinking faster now. "Where did this come from?"

She handed her ticket to the valet, using the opportunity to move away from Sugar Man.

"I bet you want a title, don't you?" he called over.

Honey turned her face to the sun. She could hear the sound of cars out on the boulevard, the patient purr of gridlocked Mercedes sedans.

"How about Manager?" he yelled. "Manager of the Executive Office? How's that sound to you?"

"Really," she said. "No."

That last word got his attention. Some people weren't accustomed to such flat rejection, and Sugar Man was one of them.

"Ah," he said, "so this is about money."

She shook her head. Down the street, she spotted her hooptie coming closer.

"Name your figure," Sugar Man demanded.

Honey was embarrassed at how loud he was. People were looking.

"Best of luck, though," she said brightly, "I'm sure you'll find the right candidate."

Sugar Man moved closer to her, close enough that Honey could smell the Scotch when he slurred, "How mush will it take? Just give me a number."

So she did. In the moment, Honey took her salary at Ramrod and tripled it, knowing that the figure was ludicrous, and whispered it in Sugar Man's ear.

"I get what I want," he said, and something in the way he said it made Honey jerk away.

"You're hired," he said. "That's what I mean."

You're not even going to remember this conversation, Sugar Plum.

As the valet opened Honey's dented car door, that familiar shriek of metal on metal, like the scream of a triumphant Pterodactyl. Honey called back "Put it in writing" as she headed for the Hyundai.

She was done with Sugar Man.

~ ~ ~

But a week later, when Mr. Meloso announced a new campaign that required her to use a wide-tooth comb on the fringe of his Persian rug each morning, and a Deal Hipper offer letter arrived at Honey's cramped apartment with her required salary figure displayed in black and white, she caved.

Even if I just do it for a year, she thought. *I could get into a nicer place. I could put money in savings.* For the first time ever, Honey speculated about what kind of air-conditioned car she might buy, with her own money. She felt a surge of excitement, to be having a thought like that. *Dad would be proud.*

~ ~ ~

Her boyfriend Joe had a habit of imagining their future. It wasn't necessarily Honey's idea of the future, however. His vision included a wife who stayed home and raised three children. Which wasn't going to happen, not with her. When she stated her feelings clearly, though, Joe had an odd response. He'd smile and change the subject.

This suited her. After all, she'd spoken her truth. Honey knew that the dichotomy in personal vision would prove the end of their relationship—but it wasn't ending now. Secure in the moment, and very much enjoying Joe's company otherwise, our girl discovered a sure-fire way to turn the conversation away from baby names: she'd ask him about his job.

"I'm so glad you're interested in this. My last girlfriend said it was boring." He'd sit on the edge of the couch, leaning forward, to describe in earnest detail the intricacies of the circuitry that challenged him.

"The machine was running slow. I think they contributed it to the belt being loose, but I knew better. It wasn't the belt, it was the flux capacitor relay, and when I went to run diagnostics, there wasn't even any documentation. None. I had to do it all on the fly, like really unpromptu. Let me tell you, Honey, I opened that panel, and right away I saw it: the red light was blinking on the cathode reverse-saturation attenuator. Something like that could really throw a klink into my plan."

"Wow! Did you get it fixed?"

"I sure did." Joe smiled broadly. "I tried transconductance source impedance, and then I was grueling over THAT decision for an hour, but sure enough it started running at full speed. It bothers me, though, that I never did find the root cause. We may never know what that stimulated from."

"WE'RE A REGULAR ROMEO AND JULIO."

"LISTEN TO THAT LIGHTNING! WE MIGHT BE IN INTIMATE DANGER HERE."

"YOU MOVED SO MUCH AS A KID—YOU'RE LIKE A SMELTING POT."

~ ~ ~

At the end of a narrow greige hallway, in a windowless space that was chilled to subzero like Antarctica or maybe the moon, Honey sat at her desk in the Wealth Management reception area. That desk held one item: A phone that never rang. The four walls were bare of decoration except for a big round clock. The horizontal file cabinet behind her held no files, and boomed like a mournful death drum each time her chair bumped against it.

During her eight months at Deal Hipper, no client ever walked through the door, wealthy or otherwise.

Honey was forbidden to eat or drink at her desk. She couldn't use her phone or read anything—not even Deal Hipper materials; she wouldn't be learning finance that way. Her only task was to brew the day's coffee in the giant industrial-sized machine outside Sugar Man's office door. He and the other three male wealth managers greeted her in the morning as they walked through reception, and then they closed their office doors. But they didn't speak to her as they went back and forth during the day. Honey came to realize that she served the same purpose as an expensive lamp, something attractive selected to sit motionless, just waiting, in case one of these important men needed somewhere pleasant to rest his gaze as he passed through on his way to the john.

They were willing to pay a lot for that. Supply and demand. Just business.

~ ~ ~

Nicole called Honey crying. Since the night of the attempted break-in by the slimy landlord, the two women saw each other regularly—but never at Honey's place. Now her friend was calling with bad news, the worst news. Nicole's mother, just 43 years old, was dead from a wreck on the Interstate.

Honey went to her friend's house, but Nicole could not be consoled. At the funeral, her father and sisters were equally distraught, the whole family operating in a daze of grief. After the service, when our girl approached her friend, Nicole grasped both of Honey's hands tightly. A grip like iron, surprising. And when she spoke, real urgency in her voice.

"Promise me you'll remember your mother smiling. Memorize every detail of how she looked. There's nothing more important."

Honey swore she would, and only then would Nicole release her.

~ ~ ~

Honey went through her photos but couldn't find what she wanted. She called Max.

"There are no pictures of Mom smiling," Honey told him.

"Well, hello to you, too," her brother said. "And, like, I'm sure there are."

"No," she cried, "I went through everything, and there's NOT."

In Colorado, Max must've muted the TV. She could hear him more clearly when he said, "Listen, I've got a bunch of pictures of Mom. And there's a box of prints in the closet, I'm pretty sure. Want to me look?"

"Yes," Honey sniffled.

"Are you crying?"

"I just—I'm upset," Honey choked. "Nicole's mother was in a car crash—and she's dead, Max, she's gone! And now I can't even find a picture of Mom smil—" She couldn't go on. She was sobbing too hard.

"Whoa, okay," Max said. "Settle down now, Honey. Really. It'll be fine. I'll look, all right? I'll find one—I'll find a dozen! I'll send them to you."

On the Florida end of the line, Honey wailed.

"Or," her brother said, "I could do it right now." This glimmer of hope gave Honey room to breathe. It was imperative that she see a smiling-Mom photo, so that she could memorize it. Nicole had been clear.

"Thank you," Honey blubbered. "Oh, Max."

"I know, I know. I had the same sort of thing happen last year, when Marco's mom passed away. I know it's tough. Hang on, let me look."

~ ~ ~

What does it mean when two kids remember a mother who never stopped smiling, but there is zero photographic evidence to back that up? Max seemed stunned to get through his entire selection of family photos without finding a single image of Samantha Malone with a smile on her face.

Some of the pictures in his carton dated back years, collected from the early days before digital, and Max obviously had felt confident when he began his search. He didn't think it would be difficult to quickly satisfy Honey's demand. She could hear him shuffling, searching for what he was so sure he'd find.

Our girl just listened as Max leafed through the printed photos, as she had with hers. She heard him mutter something about his phone, and then there was silence. Honey waited. Her cell phone was a starter model that didn't take photos, but Max embraced the latest tech. She felt a spark of hope—until she heard her brother whistle one slow, sad note.

"This is creepy," Max said. "Am I insane? Did I imagine that every time I've ever seen her, she's been smiling?"

"That's what I thought, too!"

"Weird. I can see why you called."

They sat in silence, trying to reason it out.

"We're trapped in an alternate reality," Max said. "Twilight Zone, or Truman Show."

"Seems legit."

Max had other theories. "Maybe she, like, turns off her smile when there's a camera. Right? Some people don't like being photographed."

"I guess."

Her brother proved determined to find a way forward through their twilight-zone conundrum. "Let's look at this as an opportunity," Max said. "When we see Mom at Christmas, we'll make damn sure we get a picture of her the way she really is."

"That doesn't help me now," Honey said. "I made a promise to Nicole."

"What exactly did you promise?"

"To always remember Mom smiling. To memorize every detail."

Honey could almost hear Max's gears turning. He had a knack for discovering truth—after all, he'd been the one to question Dad's persona pretty early on—so surely Max would find a way help. He also had a knack for keeping his somewhat emotional older sister calm when she went off the rails; he seemed a natural at it. Honey waited, and her brother did not disappoint. Soon enough, he posited a plan.

"We don't need a picture, to remember Mom smiling. All we need to do is talk about a time when she did."

"Hm, you're onto something, bro. I remember her face at Christmas, when she gave you the bookends and you said *Damn, you're good.* Remember that?"

"I do," Max said. "Good one! She sure had a smile on her face right then, didn't she? I saw gratitude, right? I saw affection. That's the face I want to remember. That's the face of love."

~ ~ ~

At Deal Hipper, Honey got 30 minutes for lunch, and treasured those precious moments. There was a canteen in the building across the parking lot, and at noon every day our girl showed up there, asking for a half a turkey sandwich, a cup of carrot sticks and a plain yogurt. She'd walk around the back of the building to sit on a low planter, dipping the carrots and then sucking off the yogurt before finishing off each veggie stick in four bites. Something about this rote action was supremely satisfying, when she could see the sky and feel the heat of the Florida sun blasting down. Thawing

44

her out, reminding her that she was alive.

On the other hand, Honey was the envy of her peers. She was making way more money than they were, despite similar academic backgrounds, so they were quick to remind her how good she had it. *And literally all you do is make coffee? This is officially the best job ever, Honey.* The admins who worked on the ground floor of Deal Hipper were in awe of her top-floor status, and gave her wide berth when she passed. When Honey complained of boredom to her friends, they scoffed. *You won't be bored with that paycheck on Friday,* they said. *I bet you're not bored when you're jetting around town in that new Audi convertible.*

And of course they were right. *I can take it,* Honey thought. *I can do this, the best job ever.*

~ ~ ~

Joe and Honey couldn't get enough of each other. They spent all their spare time together, and when he returned from a work trip, the occasion always warranted a dinner out at a nice restaurant, followed by Honey's very favorite dessert back then, celebratory sex.

Her after-hours life was so much better than her work life. She secretly hoped that she and Joe could move in together, especially after he bought a two-story house on the Hillsborough River—and sure enough, the invitation came.

"We'll be happy together," Joe said. "It's inedible." His mom sent flowers to their new address—she supported the arrangement, too. Honey was happy to help tote her lover's boxes up the stairs.

Labels on Joe's boxes

SUMMER CLOTHS

BEAD ROOM STUFF

SWEETERS & TROWELS

~ ~ ~

The months at Deal Hipper passed like a nightmare in which time crawled mercilessly into a beige slow-motion hell. It took every ounce of willpower Honey possessed just to get out of bed and drive down there, where the big round clock actively mocked her, like something from a frightful Franz Lang film.

Convincingly playing the role of a lamp all day, our girl came to understand precisely why some people consider drugs. Honey had a lot of time to dissect the compelling lure of pharmaceuticals—especially the numbing kind. *See a need and fill it*, a phrase she remembered vaguely as the capitalist's credo, kept ringing through her head. Big Pharma execs and drug lords probably knew that credo well. Maybe they all had matching *See a need and fill it* tattoos. Our girl's mind tended to wander, you see, as time expanded and the minutes felt like weeks felt like years. Really, is it possible to prove conclusively that a lamp *doesn't* have feelings? Who's to say?

Over time, Honey became inordinately aware of the sounds from the hallway, her ears growing increasingly sensitive to voices, to the ding of the elevator, like a prisoner in solitary confinement poised for the clank of the dinner tray that might deliver sustenance. Her only diversion was the game she'd created: count the holes in one acoustic ceiling tile, then count the holes in its neighbor, to see if the numbers matched. The game took hours to complete since she often lost her place and had to start over, but even if this occurred it didn't much matter, because she didn't much care.

Sometimes Honey fancied that she could feel her brain cells atrophy one by one, *ping pow*. She hated to see them go.

One morning on her way to the office, she spotted an antique car up ahead in traffic. A Pontiac Chieftain. Honey strained to make out the words on the car's bumpersticker.

Egrets? I've had a few.

~   ~   ~

Then came the day when one of the Deal Hipper admins from the first floor spoke to Honey in the elevator. This was a first.

"Call in sick tomorrow," the woman said. "It's Sugar Man's birthday."

Why? What? Honey's depleted brainpan scrambled to comprehend.

The admin looked her straight in the eye. "He always wants sugar on his birthday."

Then Honey knew. *This is the source of that nickname.*

"He'll be drunk when he comes in," the woman said. "Best stay home."

"Thanks for the head's up," Honey said.

But she didn't stay home. On some level, Honey knew that a confrontation with Sugar Man was exactly what she wanted, because maybe then he would fire her. Maybe then she'd be free.

And that's what happened.

BOSS 3: CASEY

Honey's title: Director of Manufacturing, Touchstone Business Magazines Inc.
~~Print Production Manager, Touchstone Business Magazines Inc.~~
~~Ad Production Manager, Touchstone Business Magazines Inc.~~

Honey had plenty of time to land her next job. As a result of what occurred in the Wealth Management office on Sugar Man's birthday, she'd been allowed to resign with a check for four months' pay, with the crucial signifier "would re-hire" attached for posterity to her personnel file.

Looking back on it, Honey was glad that the door to the Wealth Management suite always stood open. It had been easy for raised voices to funnel down the narrow hallway, easy for the hypnotist to hear *Get your hand off my ass, motherfucker* and *You little bitch you'll never work in THIS town again.* The hypnotist had intervened. The hypnotist had seen everything, so the Human Resources team at Deal Hipper thought it prudent to keep our girl quiet on her way out the door.

This time, Honey vowed to take a more strategic approach to job hunting. She'd had two jobs by this point, so she was getting a clearer vision of what she didn't want, and never would. As she scoured local job postings, she skipped over anything remotely secretarial or administrative. A career path, that's what she wanted. Honey sought a progressive, forward-thinking company, big enough to offer possibilities for advancement, and with some grasp of the fact that employees who were female could add business value, too.

~ ~ ~

Her boyfriend Joe had returned from a weeklong work trip in Georgia, where he'd investigated the electronics for a machine that printed miles of vinyl flooring at high speed. Over dinner at their favorite restaurant, he marveled over the luxurious Atlanta hotel that had been his home for six nights.

"This Swedish spa at this place was fantastic," he said. "For the massage, they used this long round thing like a hard white sponge. I tell you, babe, you haven't lived until you've had your whole body rubbed down with falafel."

"THE THING I DON'T LIKE ABOUT AIRPORTS IS THOSE DAMN LARRY KRISHNAS."

"I CAN'T GO ANY SLOWER. I ALREADY FEEL LIKE I'M MOVING IN SLOW COMMOTION."

"SHE SUFFERED FROM EARLY ONSLAUGHT DIABETES."

~ ~ ~

Honey was seeing press articles about *Touchstone Business*, a monthly magazine for Florida business leaders that had been in circulation for decades, and that had just become a wholly owned subsidiary of a local media conglomerate. Touchstone was staffing up with a higher caliber of writers and designers. They needed 20 creatives for the editorial side of the house. They also needed one advertising production manager, to oversee ad trafficking for the sales side. A bachelor's degree was required, and typing speed wasn't even mentioned.

~ ~ ~

"How do I look?" Honey stopped in front of Joe and turned slowly, so that he could take in her new suit for the job interview at Touchstone.

"I'd hire you." He came closer and drew her tight into a hug. "That skirt fits nice."

"Don't wrinkle me," she said, but man he smelled fantastic, and when he pressed himself against her just the way she liked, making it abundantly clear just how much he desired her, Honey could only respond with a moan.

"We can do it without wrinkling," he whispered. "Here, look."

Joe walked her backward two steps to the wall, until her shoulders were tight against it. Then he carefully folded her skirt up from the bottom, until it formed a panel around her waist. He dipped his fingers into her panties, and Honey inhaled sharply. He was so hot, so hard—Joe was irresistible.

Honey didn't want to be late to her important interview. She stole a look at the clock but then he was pulling her panties aside. Her eyes were on his as Joe thrust up to enter her, and our girl was lost in the building moment. *There's plenty of time.*

She'd never been interviewed while worrying that moisture from her panties was seeping through her skirt, never calmly answered questions about her background while so concerned about the funky smell of sex that seemed to rise around her. But Honey got the job.

~ ~ ~

Our girl stayed at Touchstone for ten years, in part because she could specifically describe how her work supported corporate revenue growth, every single day—and for somebody who self-identified as a businessperson, this was incredibly fulfilling. Honey also stayed for ten years because of the boss.

For nine of those years, her boss was the Publisher, Harvard MBA Casey Caruthers.

But it didn't start out that way.

~ ~ ~

When Honey took the job, she'd reported to the Advertising Manager, Hamilton "Cooter" McGee. Cooter seemed okay. After all, he'd hired a top-performing advertising sales staff that was 100% women, who also happened to be 100% knockout gorgeous. Honey did grow tired of hearing her male colleagues refer to the salesforce as "Hamilton's Angels." But she reminded herself that Cooter wasn't requiring her to comb carpet fringe. Cooter wasn't putting his hand up her dress demanding a little sugar. When it came to bosses, perspective was an important thing to retain.

Honey's first disappointment with Cooter as a manager came on a Wednesday in mid-April. He'd emerged from his office just before five o'clock to stand in front of his secretary Margo's desk. He pointed at Margo, and then he pointed at Honey, whose desk was nearby.

"Tonight," Cooter announced, "We're having celebratory cocktails. Just the three of us. I'm buying."

"Oh," Margo said. This was something different.

"Well, thanks," Honey said. *What's this all about?* She and Margo exchanged a look.

The three of them walked to the nearby bar, which was busier than usual. Once they got settled in, their drinks in front of them, Margo asked, "So what are we celebrating? Did you sign a big ad contract?"

Cooter beamed. He lifted his glass toward them.

"A toast," he intoned, "to the two best secretaries in town."

It's National Secretary's Day.

Margo lifted her glass and clinked it against Cooter's. Honey did not.

The boss was blindsided as this awkward shift in the mood reared up to bitchslap him. Cooter lowered his glass to the tabletop and focused his gaze on Margo.

"She's not toasting," he said of Honey, like she wasn't even sitting there.

"No," Margo said. "She isn't."

Cooter turned his palms up. "But why not?"

"Maybe because she's not your secretary."

He looked so confused. "Well, what is she, then?"

"She's your production manager."

"Well, Jesus," he said, "it's not like she's managing people."

It didn't take long for Margo and the boss to finish their drinks, since Honey's sat untouched. Cooter's celebratory cocktail experience didn't last long, and from then on, National Secretary's Day went unrecognized at Touchstone Business Magazines, Inc.

~ ~ ~

Four miles up the road from Joe's house was Tippy's Smokehouse, an open-air live-music venue that served good barbecue. A sprawling place right on the Hillsborough River, Tippy's could seat 200 people—and often did. The owners, who were reputed to be rich hippies, made an effort to bring all kinds of local musicians to the stage. Rock-and-roll bands from the area took the stage on weekends, or visiting headliners who had a desire to mingle with the beer-soaked masses in the Florida heat. Tuesday was country-western night at Tippy's, Wednesday night was gospel. And on Thursday, Honey's favorite: blues night.

Joe and Honey became regulars backstage on Thursdays. It started when they snuck back there and Honey found herself chiming in with harmony on some of the old favorites—and the artists didn't even mind. They'd motion for her to move closer. Honey felt like she might be adding something to the mix, which made her feel proud and surprised. Joe must have felt the same way. On her birthday, he gave her an acoustic guitar and a gift certificate for six weeks of personal instruction.

"It's fun to hear you sing," he said one Thursday night as they cuddled in bed. "I bet our kids will be musical."

"Don't start with me. You know how I feel about this."

Honey watched his dimple deepen as Joe smiled. "You're right, we shouldn't talk about it. We've come to an agreement. In Russia, that's called *periscopa*."

"YOUR GUITAR IS ONE WELL-MADE INSTRUMENT. I APPRECIATE ITS TUNAL QUALITIES."

"I GUESS YOU'D CALL IT PLOSH SURROUNDINGS."

"I WOULDN'T TAKE A JOB LIKE THAT EVEN IF I WAS DESTITUTE."

~ ~ ~

The event that caused the shakeup in Honey's chain of command occurred six weeks after National Secretary's Day. She'd just returned from New York City, where she'd attended a conference for practitioners of magazine print production. The trip had been Publisher Casey's idea, and Honey had embraced it. She was learning a lot about offset printing, the intricacies of paper, ink, and high-speed web presses, and she loved it. This job suited Honey's scientific bent just fine.

Now, sitting at her desk, thinking about New York, Honey's brain cells were back, and they were humming with possibility. She felt invigorated, to have spent time with people who were so successful in her new niche. She was pleased that these professionals considered her a peer. They'd even voted that Honey be a presenter at their next conference, to voice her strong opinion on proofing methodologies.

She looked up to see Casey approaching. He was young to be top dog, just 33, a compact Ivy League intellectual who seemed unconcerned with personal grooming or table manners. Sometimes that happened with insulated smart people.

"How was the conference?" Casey asked.

"Excellent," Honey said.

"Did you learn anything?"

"Oh my gosh, Casey, I learned so much."

That put a smile on his face.

"That's great," he said. "But did you learn anything that you could put to use here? Here at Touchstone?"

"A couple of things," she said. She described the first idea: densitometer readings for the film provided by advertisers for reproduction in the magazine. "The printing company sets the minimum and maximum density for each of the four film colors. And we provide those thresholds to the advertisers in advance. But if their incoming film falls outside those limits, we'd never know, because we don't have the proper tool for measurement. I learned that densitometer software could spot reproduction problems before they start."

Both Casey and Honey knew that advertisers often asked for a free re-run when they took issue with how their ad looked on the printed page. A "make-good" was money wasted.

"Densitometer software's expensive, I imagine," Casey said.

"Twenty thousand dollars," Honey said.

He blanched. "Well, I'd need to do a cost-benefit analysis, then. For next year's budget."

"Don't bother," Honey said, and when his eyebrows rose, she explained. "The company that bought Touchstone also publishes the local newspaper. So, I walked across the street to their press-prep department, and they said I could use their densitometer free, any time."

A slow smile spread across Casey's face. "You've caught problems already, haven't you?"

"Yes," Honey said, and then two businesspeople were smiling together.

"Tell me the other thing you learned at the conference."

Honey said, "There was this session on how to make ad production a profit center, by marking up the work we do when advertisers use our team as their ad agency."

"Nice," Casey said. His eyes twinkled at the prospect of a fresh revenues, as Honey's had. So she knew that it was now her job to squelch that sparkle.

"Yeah, well, it's not going to happen, though," Honey said.

"Why not? Didn't you bring this up with Cooter?"

"Cooter said no. He said that the approach is not for us."

Casey nodded and looked up toward the ceiling, as if one of his old MBA professors might be whispering from on high. "Did you ask why he felt that way?"

"I actually did. He told me to drop it."

"Really," Casey said, and he looked over at Cooter's office door.

That Friday, the Publisher made an announcement to the staff. Honey Malone would be reporting directly to him, from that point on. Honey had a new boss: Casey.

~ ~ ~

Joe and Honey were sitting on the couch, watching the evening news.

"In my opinion," he said, "the biggest problem facing the world today is the uprise in religious fundalism."

"It's a mess," Honey agreed.

"Religious leaders expect you to cow down before them," he said. "I guess they're all pretty inspirating speakers, though. They have to be."

An ad appeared on the screen, a plea for kids to stop bullying.

"In the TV business they call this a P.C.S. That stands for Public Service Announcement."

"THEN THIS VAN ALMOST HITS ME! IT WAS ONE OF THOSE FORD ARABSTARS."

"SHE WASN'T A FRESHMAN. SHE MIGHT'VE BEEN A SEMAPHORE."

"EMPLOYERS TODAY! BEFORE THEY HIRE YOU, THEY WANT YOU TO TAKE SOME KIND OF AMPLITUDE TEST."

~ ~ ~

Honey's new title was Print Production Manager. Casey told her that she was now in charge of print quality control for *Touchstone Business* magazine—and that she'd be attending press checks. There was no one at Touchstone to train Honey on how to do a press check, so she called her friend Milana, whose husband Francisco had experience at that sort of thing.

"Let me put him on," Milana said. "But don't hang up until you've talked with me. I've got some questions about this Joe guy."

Ruh-roh. Honey gulped. "Okay."

"Wear comfortable shoes," was Francisco's first tip. "And old clothes you don't mind ruining. Out at Exceptional, the magazine will be printed on a high-speed web press, in 16-page sections called a *form* or a *signature*, and once you okay the first form, they'll run it for a while. Expect to be out there, on and off, for two or three days. You'll be on call day and night, so sleep when you can. When you're signing off on a press approval, balance the beauty of the ad reproduction against the beauty of the editorial imagery, because sometimes one of them has to be sacrificed, if they're running in-line."

"What's 'running in-line'?" Honey asked.

He laughed. "Just ask the press guys. You're the client, their goal is to please you, and to educate you. Everybody's on the same side, really. Everybody wants to get up to quality fast."

"Got it. Thanks so much, Francisco."

Milana came back on the line to quiz Honey about Joe Stecher.

"He talks funny," Milana said. "Does he have some kind of problem?"

"No way. He's plenty smart. He just uses language differently."

"Yeah, I'll say. I could hardly keep from laughing last week when we were at dinner. He said his mom goes to that church because Reverend Brown is her favorite pasture."

Honey laughed, remembering the moment. "You did a fine job of keeping a straight face."

"I don't know how you do it," Milana said. "I'd be cracking up."

"It's endearing."

"You're just in love," her friend said. "Or in lust."

Good ol' Milana, a steadfast friend with a wicked sense of humor. She was one of our girl's favorite people. Honey said, "You know me so well."

"Which is it, then? Love or lust?"

"Yes," Honey said, and she expected her friend to laugh.

But Milana didn't let her off the hook. "So, fifty-fifty?"

"Well okay. Maybe more like 30/70."

~ ~ ~

Honey worried that the pressmen at Exceptional hadn't gotten the memo about everyone being on the same side. They'd literally never seen a woman on the press floor, because print production was traditionally a man's game. Even in her New York City meetings, Honey was always the sole representative in the room who didn't have a dick. In retrograde Florida, the masters of the web-press domain at Exceptional might not welcome a female client. There was no guarantee they'd be fans of the plan.

The night of her first press check, Honey was told to use the employee entrance at the back, since it stayed unlocked. She approached the stairs, stepping carefully through a thick carpet of cigarette butts, and climbed to the landing. She pushed the bar to open the back door. It didn't budge.

Is it jammed? Honey pushed harder. No go.

She took a step back and threw her whole weight against the bar. Still nothing, the door didn't even move—and now her wrist was hurting. Honey leaned back against the railing to reassess, and the slap of moths against the overhead light caught her attention. Then she saw a camera mounted up there. Had they locked the door? Were they watching, on some video feed inside, laughing at her?

Honey raised her hand, extended her arm, and shot the bird at the camera.

With a click, the door lock disengaged. When she stepped through into the roar of the presses, eight guys stood there laughing.

"You spunky, huh sister?" the biggest guy yelled over the din. He was an older man with a thick Southern accent and thick eyeglasses.

"I do my best," Honey shouted. She extended her hand. "I'm Honey Malone."

"Call me Pat. This here's Skippy, he's your QC guy tonight."

A man in his 50s stepped up to shake her hand. Skippy was barely five feet tall, wiry with unkempt gray hair, dressed in bright green coveralls. His cheeks were red, and his ears were oversized. He looked, Honey realized, like an ink-smeared leprechaun.

The assembled group went back to work, still chuckling and high-fiving at their prank—and at her response to it. Skippy handed her a packet of disposable ear plugs, and she put them in as he took her through the plant, toward the front offices. Honey soon understood why they called him Skippy—he walked with a strange jumping gait. They passed through a crevasse formed by rolls of paper stacked two stories tall, then walked between two Heidelberg presses that were thundering at full tilt. The noise was immense, and the hot-plastic smell of ink had already embedded itself deeply into Honey's coiffure.

Once they were inside a small client room with a window to the press floor, she could hear again. The proofs for the first form were laid out across a wide slanted table under a neutral-gray hood. Skippy reached up to activate the light, and the first 16-page signature was illuminated.

"You better get some coffee," he said. "It's going to be a long night."

He pointed at the big coffee machine, and Honey had to smile. It was exactly the same model that sat outside Sugar Man's office, back at Deal Hipper. *Look how far I've come.*

~ ~ ~

The fall meeting in New York City had gone well, and Honey had been pleased with her presentation on proofing methodologies. The sun was setting as she waited in the concourse at LaGuardia, dressed as usual in a navy suit and jaunty neck scarf—her nod to fashion, at the time—leafing through the most recent copy of *Forbes* and hoping for calm weather. A storm front threatened the entire East Coast, from Maine to Georgia. Everybody at Gate 12 was on edge, eyes glued to the Weather Channel on the monitors that hung overhead.

Sure enough, once she and the other 200 travelers got airborne, the pilot announced that their packed flight would be re-routed. No longer were they flying straight to Atlanta. They'd land in Cincinnati, where every soul aboard would be re-booked on new connecting flights. Honey listened to the men's groans and curses that accompanied this news. She was one of just a dozen women on the flight—and none of them were yelling *Jesus Christ* or *Fuck me.*

Honey settled in to read the article about diversity strategies. That morning's *Wall Street Journal* waited in her carry-on. *Good thing I brought plenty to read. I probably won't get home until two in the morning.*

Was she feeling a little empowered from her successful presentation earlier that day, to an audience of savvy businessmen from around the country? Had she been reading too many stories about corporate DEI initiatives in *Forbes*? For whatever reason, that evening Honey did something completely out of character.

She'd just left the plane's rear lavatory and was starting up the aisle to her seat. Suddenly, a man's hand reached out and gripped her forearm, twisting hard. If his intention was to stop her in her tracks, it worked.

"Get me my gate numbers." The man held up his ticket and was already turning away toward his buddy in the middle seat.

He thinks I'm a flight attendant.

Honey snatched the ticket out of his hand, and he released her. The interaction was over in four seconds, and she continued up the aisle to her seat far-forward.

The rest of the flight continued smoothly, with Honey gleefully awaiting the fireworks that would inevitably come. Whatever happened, she'd be among the first to disembark the plane, while bozo was stuck way in back. Our girl waited with a smile on her face and vindication in her heart. She was using the guy's ticket as a bookmark for the DEI article in *Forbes*.

She knew there'd be a ruckus, and she got tickled thinking about it. As she imagined what might happen, she started to snicker— and then she couldn't stop. The guy next to her leaned away, but that just gave her access to the armrest for the first time in two hours, so it felt like another win. Honey, it seemed, was on a roll. She had no plan about what she'd do, when bozo man found out that his ticket was missing. Honey had no plan at all—again, so unlike our girl.

It wasn't until the pilot announced that they were ten minutes out from Cincinnati did Honey's deception begin to have initial impact on the man who'd started everything. Soon, a voice was raised from the rear of the plane, and a flight attendant hurried past. A man was yelling *Well one of you took it* and the folks up front near Honey looked at each other, smiling and shrugging at the loud show from the rear of the aircraft. Then a male flight attendant from First Class made the long walk aft. When bozo yelled *What is your fucking problem* everybody could hear it, and 200 people had no choice but to listen to the string of choice expletives that bore witness to the passenger's Brooklyn roots. Efforts were made to calm the clown, and after much hushed conversation, there was a period of silence.

Then overhead, the public announcement system crackled to life.

"Would the passenger who has Mr. Rizzo's ticket please press your call button?"

She knew that the bozo was back there, watching for any movement. But the flight attendants were, too—and they were the ones taking the heat. For this reason, Honey prolonged the agony for only a moment longer than necessary. Then in the darkness of the cabin, her arm rose, her finger pressed the button, and everybody went back to their business.

Honey didn't have to return the ticket, of course, and had toyed with the idea of burying it in the trash after meal service. But she was afraid of what might happen. Would all twelve women on the flight be strip-searched in search of Rizzo's precious ticket, embarrassing her fellow females and causing further delay? She didn't want to go down that path.

A flight attendant reached her aisle, and Honey handed over the ticket. The woman was wearing a scarf much like Honey's—and like Honey, she was smiling.

"Well, that's a first," the woman said.

~ ~ ~

Honey earned grudging trust from the pressmen during her years of performing quality checks at Exceptional Press. The cast stayed the same—nobody ever left a job at Exceptional—and she got to know the key men on every shift. They were relieved that she was quick to admit her ignorance of their world, and glad she showed a willingness to learn. Press approvals came quicker, which suited everyone.

Once, when she questioned whether 50-pound offset stock was being used instead of the less-expensive 45-pound she'd budgeted for, Skippy stopped the press and took her back to point at the side of the enormous roll of paper, which was clearly marked "45." Honey thought that was the end of it, until somebody tested the paper stock itself. Sure enough, the roll had been mis-labelled. The client had been right. Honey's fingers had noticed the difference, when longtime pressmen's hadn't.

When she arrived for the next issue's press run, the crew made a big deal of presenting Honey with an elaborately designed paper-stock measuring gauge, with brass components fitted into a slim leather case. When she looked up to thank them, she saw the faces of the same eight guys who'd locked the door and laughed at her, on that first night.

~ ~ ~

Early in her tenure at Touchstone, Honey packed her bag and made the drive up to Tallahassee for Christmas. She picked up her brother at the airport, and on the drive out to their parents' house, Max said something that got her attention.

"I think Dad is getting worse," he said.

"Well, he couldn't get much worse."

Max looked over at her. "I hope you're right."

"Why would you say that, though?" Honey asked. Max was often the first to comprehend changes in the family dynamic. *What does he know that I don't?*

"It's just a feeling I get," he said. "Something's different. Like, now that we're both out on our own, he figures he can just do whatever he wants."

Honey was used to her brother's negative attitude about their father, but she knew that their situation with Dad wasn't abnormal. She'd polled her girlfriends, and everybody's dad was crazy. Max just needed to get over it.

She said, "Every dad is like our dad."

He frowned and sat back in his seat. "That's where you're wrong."

"Max," Honey chided, "Be realistic. Dad may not be a perfect man, right, but he loves us."

She turned into her parents' driveway, beneath the canopy of up-lit live oaks.

"Does he, though?"

~ ~ ~

Their mother stood on the front porch wearing an unfortunate Christmas sweater that involved reindeer antlers, waving wide. Smiling that big smile of hers.

"Let's get a picture of that," Max said.

When the car wheels stopped and Samantha Malone pulled open the passenger door of the Audi, she was looking into the lens of a cell-phone camera. Max pressed the button and captured her smile for posterity. Mom jerked back, surprised, and Max looked over at Honey.

"That's how it's done," he said.

~ ~ ~

The siblings followed Mom, walking down the wide hallway toward the bedrooms, pulling their suitcases. That's when Honey noticed that something was different, this year.

"Where's our buddy Pan?" she asked. Instead of a statue on a marble pedestal, Honey saw a small table that held an oversized bouquet of dark red roses.

"Oh," Mom said, "I got rid of him. Sent him on a trip to Goodwill."

"Why?" Max asked.

Mom shrugged. "Change," she said, "is good."

Max looked over at Honey, like *See? Something's different.*

Mom's statement was unusual, our girl knew. Their Mom had always been a diehard fan of the status quo. Change, from what Honey could tell, had never been Mom's friend. *Maybe something IS different*, she thought. *What's going on?*

~ ~ ~

Dad wasn't home yet, of course, on Christmas Eve, so the siblings helped their mom in the kitchen, where she was putting together the regulation pot-roast dinner, and preparing a special pie. Mom's hands were covered in flour as she rolled out the crust, so when the house phone rang, Honey picked up.

"Malone residence."

"Let me speak to Mitchell," a woman's voice said.

"He's not here right now. Can I take a message?" Honey looked around for a pen and paper.

"You can't keep him away from me forever," the woman said.

What? Honey was flustered. *Maybe this lady thinks she's talking to my mom.*

"Who is this?" Honey asked, and across the kitchen, her mother's head jerked up. Without even wiping her hands, Mom stepped away from the counter and marched across the room. She took the phone out of her daughter's hand and replaced the receiver, which was now covered with flour and piecrust tailings.

Max and Honey exchanged a glance.

"What was that all about?" Honey asked her mother.

"Nothing."

"Why is some woman calling for Dad?"

Mom smiled at her two children, but there was something shaky about that smile. Max stepped over to her, put his arm around her shoulder, and inclined his head toward hers.

"You're not in this alone," he said.

Honey watched her mom's face, which momentarily crumpled, like she was about to cry. But Samantha was a strong woman who didn't want her children to sense weakness. She of all people knew the value of a smile. Mom composed her face into the face that Honey knew and loved, and disengaged from her son's embrace. She walked back over to her piecrust.

"Everything's fine," Mom said. "Honey, check on that roast for me, see if it's done. Your father will be home soon."

~ ~ ~

But Mitchell was not home soon. His family waited in the dining room, with the Christmas Eve chafing dishes simmering on the buffet, and tried to make conversation. The phone call was on everyone's mind.

Mom seemed determined the change the mood. "Max, are you still seeing Peggy? That girl from the bookstore?"

Max smiled wide. "I sure am. She's a sweetheart."

"Oh, that's wonderful." Mom had always said that Max was "a catch," and Honey could not disagree. Any woman would be lucky to end up with a guy like Max, who was handsome and kind and had a bright professional future in front of him. He even talked about children, sometimes.

"Do you think she's—the one?" Mom asked.

Honey watched her brother's face, which was reddening. When he smiled like that, he looked just like Mom.

"I think she might be. I've never really met anybody like Peg."

"Well, this is the first I'm hearing about her," Honey said. "Do you have a picture?"

Max scrolled through his phone and held it out to her. Honey saw a handsome couple standing outside a restaurant, embracing. Smiling at each other in such a natural way.

"I think she loves you," Honey said. "It's in her eyes, bud."

Mom took the phone and looked closer. "Honey's onto something here. Do you love *her*, Max?"

"I do. She's pretty special."

"How exciting," Mom said, eyes alight. She lifted her wine glass. "Let's toast: To being in love."

They raised their glasses, and Max blushed even redder, to be the center of attention like that, to come out to his family as a man in love.

"And how about you, Honey?" Max asked. "You still happy with that Joe guy?"

"He's a cutie," Honey said.

"You always say how good-looking he is," Mom said. "Do you think we'll ever get to meet him?"

Honey looked over at Max, who gave her a thumb's up. He'd never met Joe, either. Maybe he was curious, too.

"Well, sure," Honey said. "One day."

"You should bring him up here," Mom said, and then she added something that changed everything. From their mother's mouth came the words, "Or I could drive down there."

Samantha hadn't driven on the Interstate since Dallas. There had been an incident one night, when the young mother was driving home alone from a bridge game. A truck had followed her, nosing up close at her bumper, pulling alongside so that a shirtless redneck could lean out of the passenger window to holler obscenities. She felt trapped as the truck raced to pull in front of her, then slammed on its brakes, so that she had to swerve to avoid a collision at high speed. Only when a police car glided past did the truck back off. Mom had been traumatized, and for the last 15 years she felt victorious if she just drove to the grocery store and back without panicking.

So now, when Mom suggested so offhandedly that she might drive to Tampa, silence greeted her statement. She lifted her glass to her lips and took a sip of wine, as if she'd anticipated that her children would be stunned speechless. The story of the menacing truck was family lore, after all. Max and Honey knew how scared she'd been—and Mom didn't talk much about her fears. They knew, even as little kids, that the story had significance.

Now, Samantha's kids responded quickly.

"Excellent idea," Honey said.

"Wouldn't that be something," Max said. "Wow, Mom."

"I've been practicing," she said, and Honey sensed something new in her voice. Like pride.

The children leaned toward their mother, craving more. And then: the hum of the garage door.

~ ~ ~

The hospital is a surprisingly festive place when your dad falls off the roof on Christmas Eve. Twinkle lights festooned the doorways as Honey accompanied the fast-moving gurney through Tallahassee Memorial's emergency department, and she saw orderlies in Santa hats exchanging gifts as they passed in the busy hallways. *Merry Christmas, homie!* they called out. *Merry Christmas!*

While her father was being X-rayed for cranial damage, Honey waited alone in a small, chilly room that held an examination table, a chair and a poster that explained proper hand-washing technique. Max was back at the house with Mom, and Honey wanted to give them a status report—but there was nothing to say, yet. She waited, wondering how she felt. *Will my dad die?* Right then, all she felt was numb—which was itself unsettling.

A man in a white coat entered the room and closed the door behind him. He was holding a clipboard full of papers. To show her respect for his station in life, Honey stood up from the chair.

"I'm Dr. Capelli." He stood across from her, a busy man who had no time for sitting. "I understand you're the daughter?"

Honey nodded.

"And it says here he fell off the roof?"

"Yes," she said. "He sure did."

"What was he doing up there? Hanging Christmas lights?"

"He said the gutters needed cleaning."

"Yeah, at nine o'clock at night?" The doctor looked down and leafed through the papers. "His blood alcohol is pretty high. Just sayin'."

Honey said, "That might explain it."

"Well," he said, opening the door, "hang tight. We'll get the X-ray results back in a few minutes, and then we'll know more. He'll need stitches. There's a soda machine by the elevator."

Dr. Capelli spotted somebody in the hall, and pulled a small, wrapped gift out of his pocket as he called out, "Hey Vincent, hold up."

That's Mom's gift wrap this year, Honey thought. She tried to breathe.

~ ~ ~

Mitchell Malone had come into the dining room like always that night—late and unrepentant—but there was no way for him to know that Mom had just rocked her kids' world with her offer of Interstate driving, and with the tantalizing suggestion that she might have been practicing at it. When the three of them looked up at him in that moment, Dad turned on his heel and walked back to the garage.

His abandoned family members postulated that he'd left his briefcase in the car. No one realized he was getting the ladder. They found out when he rapped twice on the dining-room window and shouted *I'll be cleaning the gutters if anybody cares.*

Now it was five in the morning, and Honey sat on the edge of a lounge chair by her parents' swimming pool, wrapped in a blanket and tapping her foot even as the adrenaline subsided. She looked up at the roofline of the house, and idly wondered why her dad had been up there in the first place. His drunken ravings about the gutters made no sense—he'd never cleaned a gutter in his life.

Max believed that as their mother grew stronger, their father felt that his spot at center stage might be threatened. *He just acted out*, Max had told his sister, while they'd waited for the EMTs.

Honey watched the dancing blue light in the pool. Max and Mom had given her a break, since she'd spent all those hours at the hospital. It was determined that Dad had a concussion, but nothing worse. After several hours of observation, he'd been released from the ER with instructions to keep his head elevated. He'd need to be roused every 20 minutes for 12 hours, so the three of them planned to take shifts, to monitor Mitchell in the recliner all night.

Shimmering reflections frolicked across the side of the house. Somewhere in there, Dad was the center of attention—like always.

A gleam on the concrete caught her eye. Honey walked across the pool deck toward the house, found the garden hose, and turned the spray nozzle to full force. It seemed important to wash away her father's blood before the Florida sun revealed it on Christmas morning. She heard the sound of the lawn sprinklers popping up, and the chirring of cicadas in the oaks. Soon her pants were soaked to the knee, but she never noticed.

She'd seen him fall.

~ ~ ~

The position of Print Production Manager at Touchstone suited Honey quite well, and she enjoyed it. What her boss Casey didn't tell her was that within three years, there would be four other magazines being printed, some of them with national subscriber bases, and that Honey would be promoted again, to Director of Manufacturing—responsible for hundreds of millions of print impressions annually, and a boss herself to a team of three.

She'd been moved out of her cubicle into an expansive office on a proper top floor, the twelfth floor, which held a comfy executive chair and a bank of 20-foot-tall windows through which Honey could watch sailboats skip across the blue waters of Tampa Bay. If she pressed her cheek to the glass and looked left, she could just see the building that had once housed Ramrod.

~ ~ ~

But all was not well in the paradise called Florida. Honey began to hear rumblings about revolt in the newsroom of Touchstone's sister company, the newspaper whose offices were across the street. Every time she went to use the densitometer, it seemed, she'd witness something surprising. Once it was a sit-in on the front steps, with only women sitting. The next time it was a big poster in the elevator that read "17% of front-page stories are by female reporters at this newspaper" next to a poster that read "71% of this newspaper's reporters are female."

Honey found a crumpled-up poster in the hallway one day. When she unfolded it, careful to avoid the dirty boot-print impression, she read "Why do male reporters earn more? Fight for pay transparency."

Because the media conglomerate that owned the newspaper was forward-thinking and progressive, it convened its crack crisis-management team, which soon recommended a way to provide solace. Leaders announced that they'd be putting into place a comparable worth study, organization-wide. And one day, a nice young woman from a management consulting firm sat down across from Honey to ask a few questions: *How big a budget do you manage? Do you negotiate contracts with outside vendors? Do your duties require you to work extra hours? Who is your backup when you're away?* The consultant wanted to learn who Honey interfaced with on a regular basis, internally and externally, and our girl was asked to describe in detail the skills that were required to do her job so well. *You're identified as a top performer*, the woman said. *But I guess you know that.*

Within weeks, the anger of the newspaper's female reporters seemed to dissipate. There were no more sit-ins on the steps across the street, no more posters. And about that time, Casey called Honey into his office. When she came in, he closed the door. That surprised her. He always left the door open—it was a big part of Casey's personal brand. Once she sat across from him, the boss got right to the point.

"You're getting a pay increase," he said. "Forty percent."

"Ha, it sounded like you said forty."

"I did say forty," Casey said. He didn't look particularly happy, but he delivered this amazing news in a level tone.

She sat in silence, stunned, as he explained that this magnificent raise would be phased in over the next four months. "It wasn't exactly in our budget plan," he said. "I'm sure you understand." That night, planning her own personal budget, realizing that finally, she could actually buy a house, and it could actually be close to the beach, Honey found herself feeling thankful to the newsroom reporters who had started the whole thing. She didn't know any of the women personally. She never knew their names.

~ ~ ~

Honey was interested in buying a house because her relationship with Joe had cooled, and then it ended when she discovered his deception. He'd been sleeping with somebody else. Probably somebody who wanted to raise three children, Honey conceded, so she really couldn't blame him for that part. It was time for their "inedible split." Joe was actually moving out of the house on the

Hillsborough River, boxing up his gear for shipment to his lover's house in Knoxville, when his cell phone rang.

"It's my mom," he said to Honey, looking down at his phone. His mother had been unwell, and he was worried about her. He hadn't told her about Knoxville. Joe stepped into the hall, but Honey could still hear him clearly.

"Well sure," he said. "She's here."

Honey didn't know if she should join him in the hallway, so she didn't.

"No, Mom, I told you. She's right here." Joe stepped back into the bedroom and held the phone out toward Honey. "Say hi to my mom."

"Hi, mom," Honey called over, trying for an upbeat tone even though she was surprisingly sad to see her man packing up his stuff, and surprisingly angry that he'd cheated.

Joe was silent then, the phone pressed tight against his ear. He didn't say much after that, because he was crying when he hung up. He stepped toward Honey and fell into her arms.

"It's cancer," he choked. "She's terminal."

And that's when Honey realized that Joe's mother had wanted to make sure that somebody was there for him when he got the news. His mom had put her faith in Honey, knowing that she would comfort her boy in that devastating moment. And Honey did, even though she had good reason not to. *Perspective*, Honey thought. *There's that word again.*

"GO AHEAD, TELL ME. I'M ALL EARDRUMS."

"I WON'T BE THE ESCAPE GOAT IN THIS, NO MATTER WHAT THE MIGRATING FACTS."

"THERE'S NOTHING WRONG
WITH MY LITERARY NOBILITIES."

~ ~ ~

At the office, boss Casey might not have noticed that with the impact of the comparable worth study, and with the accompanying shift in corporate acknowledgment of women's value, some of the male employees were displeased. To some, pushback felt natural.

Honey saw it first-hand, in her frequent interactions with the magazine's art director. Like all the creatives at Touchstone, the young man was exalted, and lived in the rarified air that only a high pedestal can provide. After all, *Touchstone Business* won national design awards because of the AD's prowess, and a certain sense of respect was expected, an undercurrent of power that was to be conceded even in the most casual of conversations.

She remembered when Casey taught her the cardinal rule: *Don't mess with the creatives. They're not like you and me.*

That spring, the art director had three new pieces of art installed on the wall opposite his desk. You couldn't see the enormous the black-and-white photographs from the hallway, but once you stepped inside his office, the artwork was very much on display: three extreme close-up shots of what appeared to be sultry naked vixens heaving themselves out of shallow pools of water. Any visitor to the AD's office conversed with him against a backdrop of glistening breasts and slick buttocks—all of them literally larger than life.

Honey never said a thing, because she knew that Casey could see it, too.

They're very much like you and me, actually.

~   ~   ~

The moment that Joe and Honey split, an alert went out via the gossip train known colloquially as the Palmetto Express. Faster than a hurricane-warning flag snapping at full mast, her cadre of Tampa Bay clubbers mobilized to get Honey matched up romantically.

Everybody knew that she was a one-man woman, an antiquated concept that held strong appeal for a number of guys who strategized to date her. This crew loved gossip as a matter of course, but business had been slow. They needed something meaty to sink their teeth into, and the Joe/Honey breakup sufficed. Friends were rocked by the dramatic developments.

I heard he moved to Nashville.
I heard he cheated.
I heard she left him when his mother was dying, who does that?

Several interested parties wanted to date Honey, and were very aware of which of their peers shared that desire. Honey's phone blew up with invitations, introductions, and intrigue. Different factions backed different candidates. As Honey waded back into the dating pool and eligible candidates emerged, it's a good bet that money was wagered.

~   ~   ~

SUITOR 1: ALISTAIR FORTHRIGHT IV

Honey was encouraged by some of her crew to consider a trust fund kid, the sole heir of the man who'd invented the pushpin. Alistair Forthright IV got mixed reviews, with his odds stuck solidly at 50/50 in the polls leading up to Date One. The fact that he had oodles of money did not tip the scales in his favor, which was a concern. This could be the sign of an aberrant personality, actually, but details were sketchy, because this aristocrat didn't date locally—Alistair preferred a more global pool of candidates, and he'd made an exception for Honey Malone. He was the first to step up when her status switched to "available."

Alistair wasn't the tallest man in town, but he was taller than Honey, and she imagined that she looked pretty good on Bayshore Boulevard the night he drove her to their dinner destination, when she let her hair free of its lamé scrunchy in his convertible Lamborghini, to let the blondness fly.

Drawing on the power of 600 horses, her suitor whisked her away in his acid-green carriage to dinner at the Columbia, a historic Cuban restaurant in Ybor City. It wasn't the fanciest white-tablecloth place in town, nor was it the trendiest. But Honey soon discovered something amazing: Alistair had reserved the entire place just for the two of them.

I can't wait to tell this story later, Honey thought. *Every woman has nights that go down in dating history, and this will be one of mine.*

Indeed. The hundred-year-old building was hushed and dim, with far-off candlelight luring a starry-eyed visitor down an arched hallway toward its fetching glow. His hand was on Honey's elbow as Alistair murmured compliments in her ear, some of them in French. A good-humored fellow, his toothy smile was balanced by sparkling brown eyes, and Honey had never seen a jacket more beautiful than the one he wore that night, woven of cloth that seemed to change color when he moved—but in an understated way, of course, just subtle shading from bisque to taupe. Honey felt certain that he'd spent more on his haircut than she'd spent on her shoes. He smelled exceptionally good, like his cologne had been flown in that morning from a stand of heirloom Côte d'Azur cedars.

It was all so dreamy. In a vine-draped central atrium ornamented with hand-painted tile, next to a trickling fountain topped by a comely bronze mermaid, a single intimate table waited. Honey's heart was aflutter with promise as she took in the scene. All around the columned court, candles flickered. At the end of the colonnade, a lone guitarist in a tux played softly. A flamenco beat, very old school. Very sexy.

I could get used to this, Honey thought. *I'm glad I went strapless, with the dress.*

Servers materialized from the shadows to pull out their chairs. Honey felt like royalty in that lavish setting, with a companion who seemed exceedingly attentive. Alistair kept complimenting her hair, which was validation for Honey, who'd invested major bucks in highlights and lowlights at the salon where she'd spent five hours the day before. She'd find another way to scrounge up the cash for her car insurance, which was due on the fifteenth. Queens, she was certain, had little time to worry about such things.

Her date looked across at her with his open, almost bashful grin, and then Alistair said something that got our girl's full attention: "This is where my great-grandfather proposed to my great-grandmother, in 1908."

Honey put her palms on the tablecloth and slapped it twice. "Right here?"

"This very spot."

Her spidey sense tingled. *That's a little presumptuous for a first date, bud.*

She asked, "So what's the message, then?"

Honey watched as he pulled an unopened bottle of Dom Pérignon out of its ice bucket. He shook it. Vigorously.

"The message is …"—**POW**—Champagne foamed up in a high arc—"Let's PAAAR-TAY!"

This was the cue for colored lights to flash in the colonnade, and the flamenco guitarist rushed forward, joined by a larger group of musicians, one of whom proved quite enthusiastic on the cajon drum, along with a fleet-footed flamenco dancer. Honey saw them coming through her bangs, which were soaked with Champagne, just like her face, where mascara ran freely. Liquid gushed down the front of Honey's dress, whose strapless bodice caught the torrent as effectively as the bucket of a Caterpillar front-end loader. She had bubbly on her boobies, and it was ice cold.

"Woo-hoo," Alistair called out from his chair, raising his fists high as the lights strobed to the Latin beat, and the flamenco dancer draped herself across him. Once she disengaged her cleavage from his aristocratic nose, Honey's date was able to light a big spliff, which was expertly constructed in dimensions similar to those of a traffic cone. From the left, cocaine appeared. From the right, poppers. Waving smoke aside, Alistair peered across at her.

"Hey, did I splash you? Sorry."

~ ~ ~

SUITOR 2: JOSH SIMMONS

The smart money was on Josh Simmons, another of Honey's suitors. She had to admit that she'd noticed him. Every woman notices a man who stands up from his chair when she approaches. That action instantly gets female attention, plus it instantly makes all the other guys present look like complete louche jerks. A man who takes that gentlemanly action in Tampa, Florida is a man who's fully prepared for the glowering disapproval of his kindred males—and he tends to be a loner. Understandable, really. No man in town wanted to be Josh's friend, in part because then he'd have to stand up every time, too.

Virtually all of Honey's friends believed that the union of Honey and Josh would be a match made in heaven. Over drinks at the bar one night, Nicole and Milana listed off his positive traits:

His manners are impeccable

He constantly works out at Gold's
His smile is nice
He's tall enough
He works in finance, which means he has a future

"Well, what's the flip side, then?" Honey asked. "What's the downside with this guy?"

Her friends looked at each other.

Milana said, "He's kinda old. He's 32."

Honey could see from their faces that they were hiding something else. "And?"

"And maybe he's not the most scintillating conversationalist," Nicole said, and Milana snorted out a laugh.

"He's boring, then?"

Milana waved the Hand of Dating Destiny. "You will be the judge of that. On Friday night."

~ ~ ~

Honey prided herself on her ability to draw people out. She was confident that down deep, Josh Simmons wasn't boring. He was a man with dreams and aspirations, a man of secret longings yet untold. Most men were. Most women, too. So when she left her house to get into his BMW that rainy Friday night, Honey's feet were sure—even in her new heels. She wouldn't be greeting her date over the console of the front seat, however. Josh had already jumped out, in the rain, to run around the front of the Beamer, and now stood next to the passenger door, his gracious hand extended, in case she needed help getting into the car.

He seemed quite fit under that raindrop-flecked shirt, and Josh's hair was exemplary, even in the humidity.

"You're too kind," she said.

And Josh said, "You're too beautiful."

Nothing boring about that, Honey thought. They exchanged a smile, and she saw him look at her legs as he closed the car door. *This feels promising.* Perhaps she had perfected the amount of thigh that can be exposed upon entry to a Beamer to ensure that the movement is simultaneously casual and titillating. She'd certainly had plenty of practice, over the years. Joe drove a BMW.

"I'm so glad we could get together tonight," Honey said.

She waited for him to say, *Me too,* but he didn't. Somehow, the instant he put the car in gear, her date had switched to Silent Mode. Josh accelerated into the drizzle, and Honey listened to the sound of the tires splashing through puddles on the road. She counted ten streetlights as the car progressed, hoping he would speak. Four more streetlights passed.

When he remained silent, she asked, "So where are we headed? Hugo's, did you say?"

He reached down to the console and handed her a menu for Hygge, a restaurant on the north end of town.

"Oh, I've always wanted to try Norwegian food," Honey said, trying for an enthusiastic tone. "Have you eaten there before?"

Josh shook his head. He kept his eyes on the road.

The *thump-thump* of the windshield wipers counted the moments of Honey's life that ebbed away, ebbed away, as eight more streetlights passed by her window in the misty gloom. The silence between them buzzed in her ears like low-grade static. She spent some time admiring Josh's perfect nose, handsome tresses and silky slacks.

The wipers said *thump-thump*. Honey understood that she had time, now, to try to remember the song lyrics that had eluded her for a week. Having accomplished that, she fluffed her hair.

Thump-thump. She adjusted her bra strap as a way to kill time.

Thump-thump. Thump-thump. Thump-thump. There was a nice rhythm to it, once you started noticing.

She pulled down the sun visor and checked her lip gloss in the mirror. *Thump-thump.*

"What a lovely night," Honey said, though the weather was dank. Still he didn't speak.

Thump-thump. Thump-thump. They waited at a traffic light, and the people in the cars around them were laughing, yakking, singing along to music. The two people in Josh's BMW were more like white people mannikins, propped up for show on the longest drive to dinner ever.

Can we at least turn on the radio, to liven things up? Maybe polka hour, on WMNF?

Honey was stymied by her date's lack of communication. His face was impassive. *What is going on with Josh? Is he always this way? But you can't be boring if you don't say a word—maybe that's his strategy.*

"Check it out," she said. Desperate to alleviate the tension of Josh's extended hush, Honey pointed to the menu. "Did you see they have Kjøttboller?"

He lifted an eyebrow. The light turned green. The BMW crawled forward, flanked by the cars full of talking people, people who were communicating, like natural people were born to do.

Okay, she said to herself, *this isn't working. Maybe I need a question that's more open-ended.* Even though the date was only 10 minutes old, she employed her secret weapon, the four words that acted as a magic spell on most humans.

"Tell me about yourself."

He did smile, and it was a cute smile, illuminated as it was by the reddish glow of the dashboard lights. *You little devil,* Honey thought. *You're not going to make this easy for me, are you?*

"Not much to tell," Josh said. His hands were relaxed on the wheel. Perhaps he was under the impression that the date was going well, or something.

"But I'm told that you work in mortgage-backed securities," Honey said. His eyebrows lifted and all the hair on his scalp moved back, like somebody in the back seat of the Beamer had tugged it from behind.

"Well, um, yeah. Yeah, I do, actually," he said carefully, like maybe it was a trick question somehow. He cut a glance Honey's way.

"But why mortgage-backed?" she asked. "You can pool credit-card deliverables. You can pool auto loans. Why mortgages?"

At this point she really hoped he'd take the bait, because she had just reached the sum total of her knowledge about the esoteric topic at hand. She hadn't expected to even get this far into it, to be honest, and Honey was glad that she'd prepared. The question was, had she prepared enough? Would she succeed in her crusade to unlock the silence of Josh Simmons, the world's most recalcitrant man?

His eyes flashed red in the dash lights as he accessed the GPS. They had 27 remaining minutes in the car together, according to the countdown, and she *had* outright asked.

"It's the CDOs I like," Josh said, and a gush of words at last bubbled up. Honey nodded thoughtfully from the passenger seat as the phrases splashed up in spurts, like the alkaline waters of a Yosemite geyser:

—the tranches themselves—
  —debt instrument pool creation—
    —consider the European option—

Be careful what you wish for was the refrain in our girl's head by then, and the streetlights couldn't pass fast enough. *It's all or nothing, with this guy,* Honey thought. He was talking so loudly and with such passion that his voice drowned out the sound of the windshield wipers. She missed that rhythmic sound.

Honey knew that if she'd been smarter, she could have gleaned some good information about the markets that night. At first, she'd interrupted Josh to ask him to define things, so that she might discern insider insight. Three streetlights in, she knew she was lost.

—speculate on collateral movement—
  —securitized structured products—
    —proactive puts are required—

He was still talking when they pulled up at the restaurant. Honey prayed that getting seated at Hygge would force a break in Josh's monologue, which had reached a crescendo of sorts as he explained the vast riches that awaited the type of people who took his business seriously. He seemed a little defensive about it, actually, and she intended to ask him about that, if he for God's sake would take one damn breath and just stop talking. *This isn't boring. This is torture.*

They waited at the front of the restaurant, which had low ceilings and was painted black, like the inside of a shoebox.

—the maturities, of course, and the yields—
  —first lien on the assets—
    —derivative collateralized debt—

The arrival of the black-garbed host boosted Honey's spirits, and she hurried ahead of Josh, who had flipped his switch to Silent.

Blessed silence, Honey thought. *I think I prefer him this way.*

At the table, the host placed their menus before them, making sure he caught their eye before saying, "Music starts at nine." The man rapped his knuckles on the tabletop twice, as if to seal a deal, then hurried away.

Did you know that the birthplace of black metal music was Norway? Honey hadn't been aware. Promptly at nine o'clock, amphitheater-ready subwoofers in the ceiling transported 30 diners into hell via Bathory, Venom and Mercyful Fate. Plus there was fish.

~   ~   ~

Honey had held high hopes for Josh Simmons—but they were not simpatico. She let him down easy when he called to ask for a second date, and when they ran into each other at the clubs, they could be cordial. Then, in the messy aftermath of a financial crash the following year, she began to see Josh's name in the local press.

He wasn't saying much.

~   ~   ~

One of the things that Honey learned at Touchstone was how to conduct herself in meetings. She listened more than she spoke, especially when she was a junior member of the team. But one thing our girl noticed right away was that when she did speak, men would routinely interrupt her. They'd totally talk over her. Honey didn't like that one bit. *It's only common courtesy*, she thought.

But sometimes it was more than lack of courtesy that prompted interruption. Sometimes, a man would be trying to preemptively address all aspects of her unspoken argument in real time. At one quality-review meeting held in the conference room at Exceptional Press, this behavior became painfully apparent to all.

Honey held up two items. In her left hand, an advertising client's proof, sent to her to set their expectation for reproduction, which showed bright color and crisp resolution. In her right hand, a copy of the magazine, where the full-page liquor advertisement looked muted, grainy and out of register.

She said, "Let's—"

"—You probably got that sheet before press approval," the quality manager interrupted. James was a new hire, and he and Honey, appropriately enough, were seated at opposite ends of the long conference table, with five men from Exceptional lined up on either side.

"As I was s—"

"—That's not indicative of the full run." James's voice was loud. "Really, there's no reason to be comparing an unknown sample to the client proof." And then he was explaining print-reproduction theory to professionals who had already acquired a strong grasp of it. Honey listened to the full harangue. When he finally stopped talking, the room was silent. But Honey waited, to see if James planned to stay quiet. He could erupt at any moment, as had been amply demonstrated.

When everyone was sufficiently aware of the awkward silence, our girl said, "From—"

"—Just a bad mix on the pH balance," James interjected. Again, Honey sat back as he launched into another long-winded description of a well-known variable. Everyone at the table watched James as he pontificated, offering a detailed explanation about how water was the culprit in the problem at hand.

Finally, he stopped talking, and Honey reveled in the silence that followed James' rant. Again, she let the moment go on too long, even though eleven sets of eyes were on her.

At last, Honey lifted the two examples. "If—"

"—It's a deficiency in the stock." James' voice was just a little too sharp, and Honey saw the Big Boss flinch. She lowered her exhibits and waited. Four minutes later, James was still talking about the substrate, still mansplaining Print Technology 101.

Everybody except Honey was staring at the tabletop. Honey kept her eye on James—but her gaze was mild. Welcoming, actually. *Come on, James, keep talking. Make an even bigger ass of yourself.*

Around Minute Five, James ran out of steam. He seemed to have exhausted his topic. Everyone in the room could hear the click-click of James' ballpoint pen as he repeatedly pressed it with this thumb. Honey waited an even longer time, now. Eventually, James seemed to notice that his clicking pen was the focus of attention. He put it down on the table. He put his hands in his lap.

All eyes were on Honey. She said nothing.

Nobody abides silence in a conference room full of men, Honey knew. The quiet went on too long, and became so uncomfortable that the Big Boss himself was forced to speak up.

"Honey, I'd be interested to hear how you feel."

"Oh, no," she said lightly, "I don't want to interrupt James."

"He's the one interrupting YOU," a press foreman burst out, and some of the men said *Yeah.*

The Big Boss flushed. He looked down the table directly at James as he said, "Gentlemen, let's agree: Honey has the floor."

~ ~ ~

SUITOR 3: ETHAN BURNS

After taking a pass on Alistair and Josh, Honey wondered if she'd ever date again. Her friends scoffed—they knew the level of interest, and that level was sky high. Assuming that Honey found Alistair too druggy and Josh too old and/or erratic, her buddies suggested another promising candidate who had expressed clear interest: Ethan Burns.

Ethan was relatively new to town, and he was exactly Honey's age. He was quick to buy a round of drinks. He was quick to throw a party. He worked with his dad, who'd made Ethan president of a residential-construction business that kept 600 people employed year-round. With a shock of blond hair and broad sun-kissed shoulders, Ethan had the demeanor of a fun demigod who'd just walked off the beach bearing umbrella drinks for all.

"He's having a house party Saturday night," Nicole said. "And we're invited."

She and Honey were talking on the phone, both moving through their respective spaces to turn out the lights and start the dishwasher, getting ready for bed.

"Perfect," Honey said. "That's way less stressful than one-on-one, and I'll get to see what his place looks like."

"A bounty of data for the curious," Nicole said. "You get to see how he lives, without even sleeping with him."

Then it was time to strategize what they would wear on Saturday night, an important consideration that warranted much discussion.

"It's going to be warm in there, with all those people," Nicole said. "You won't need a sleeve."

Honey mentally leafed through her closet. "I could go with that new tank top, the black one with the sequins."

"Nah. Wear the striped one, that tight one."

Honey rolled her eyes, hearing it. "You always want me to wear that thing. Why? I think it borders on sleaze."

"You're delusional, missy. With those boot-cut jeans of yours," Nicole said, "it borders on genius."

So, with that issue resolved, the two friends tackled Nicole's sartorial options for Saturday night.

"Jimbo doesn't like it when I wear something too short," Nicole said of her husband, who would also be attending the house party.

"Yeah, I seem to remember that." Honey didn't care much for Jimbo, but guess what? She didn't have to love him. "What about your racer-back midi, the emerald knit? You could wear it with Docs and a smile."

"Love!" Nicole squealed. "Rare is the outfit that can keep everybody satisfied. Now listen, here's the deal for Saturday: To get you alone, there's a signal. Ethan will suggest a visit to the picnic table out back."

"A signal, you say. I'm intrigued."

~ ~ ~

The night of Ethan's house party, Honey wore the striped top and the boot-cut jeans. She got separated from Nicole and Jimbo early on, and as she wandered through the crowd, Honey realized that she was visitor to a frat house, but for grown-up guys.

Virility and brotherhood were vigorously celebrated within the walls of Ethan's abode. Testosterone was in the air that evening as large, sunburned men with loud voices became louder, determined to be heard over the bellowing of their boozy peers. One group of men in the corner stood pulling up their shirtsleeves in order to literally compare the size of their biceps—a cloth measuring tape was involved. Members of another crew slapped each other's backs, howling with laughter at a video being played, for their eyes only, on a burly bro's phone. A ping-pong game near the sliding doors became blood sport when a mad smash sent a white ball rocketing toward a young man's nostril, and a boisterous crowd had gathered in front of the flat-screen TV, where red-faced viewers screamed at a basketball game in progress. Throughout Machismo Manor, much alcohol sloshed from red Solo cups.

To remove themselves from the fray, the women gathered on the back deck, and that's where Honey ended up.

"Cute top," a redhead said to Honey.

"Thanks, I love your moccasins."

Honey had never wanted fringed moccasins before she saw the ones that rested near her kicks on the boards of Ethan's deck. Several women, understandably attracted by the topic, gathered 'round as the redhead revealed where in the Tampa Bay area such avant garde footwear could be sourced. Their boho discovery session was interrupted by a crash from inside the house. The sliding doors trembled in their frames, and the guttural roar of 30 rageful men emanated from the living room.

"Guess the Celtics won," a blond said, and the women around her nodded knowingly.

~ ~ ~

After the wrong team won, the energy of the party ratcheted up, and not in a good way. Honey decided to venture back inside *Casa de Pecker* in search of Ethan, before the fights broke out. She found the host holding court in the kitchen, where men with broad shoulders and small hips were roughhousing to gain access to the fridge.

They parted for her, though. Any woman bold enough to enter that kitchen alone obviously had a goal in mind. The men assumed that this young woman was looking for Ethan—and they weren't wrong. With gentlemanly ease, they stepped aside, and made a path for her.

"Hey Ethan," one of them called over. "Check this out."

Honey's eyes met Ethan's, and they both smiled.

Ethan said to his crew, "You better excuse me. I believe it's time to make a visit to the picnic table out back."

The assembled men hooted their approval, as if they knew that sex happened on that table—and might again, that night. The guys gave Honey the once-over as she approached Ethan, and she knew they were doing it, but our girl was full chill as she reached out toward him and took his hand.

As Honey led Ethan out of the kitchen, her head held high, with the hint of a smile on her face, the men in the kitchen grew less vocal. All eyes were on the couple as they left the room, and it was quiet enough for everyone to hear the whisper from a man near the door as Ethan passed by.

"Good luck, man."

~ ~ ~

As they approached the picnic table in the shadowy darkness out back, Ethan seemed in fine spirits.

"Yo, yo, yo, my lady," he said. "Watch your feets."

They sat on the top of the table with their feet on the bench, looking back up the hill at his house, where every window was lit and the guests were pretty lit, too. Honey enjoyed his choice of music, his deck full of interesting women, and his modest tastes. *He could've had a mansion, with his money*, Nicole had told her, *but he said he'd rather have the land.*

"Look at the stars," he said, and Honey stopped off to admire him, on the way. It was dark, but she could see how the material of his shirt pulled valiantly against the thick muscles of his shoulders, and she wondered if it was normal for a man to have brawny definition on his neck, like that. But once Honey's gaze was fixed properly skyward, she didn't see any stars—there was too much light pollution. She let it slide. *He's happy, and he's the kind of guy who looks up, and both of those things are good.* She felt quite comfortable with Ethan.

"Where's your drink?" he asked, and when she shrugged, he held out his Solo cup. "Want some of mine?"

"Thanks." Honey hoped that their hands would touch when she took the cup, and they did. *Altogether encouraging.* But when she took a sip of the drink, Honey spewed it out across the lawn in a fan of droplets, each brilliantly illuminated by the house lights beyond.

"Omigod! What IS that?" Coughing and heaving, she hunched over to wipe her burning lips—her flowing saliva hadn't eased the pain—and Ethan put his hand on her back in commiseration.

He said, "Think of it as the bastard child of Everclear and Fireball. My boys call it Memory Wipe."

"I can see that," Honey said. She straightened up, though she was still coughing a little. "Whoo!" Her shocked body produced tears that gushed down her cheeks to join the waiting lake of spittle on her chin.

"We're trying to patent it," Ethan said urgently, like he'd discovered alchemy or quantum fusion. He said, "Imagine this."

When he didn't continue, Honey realized that he wanted her to look at him, because he intended to demonstrate the coming narrative with interpretive arm movements.

"Imagine this: Like, you got the recipe, right? You got a LOT of equipment for distilling." He threw his arms out.

"You got LOT of raw material, ready to cook." His arm-space was even bigger now.

"And to keep everything secret from the tax man's pryin' eyes, you got a BIG ASS warehouse." His arms scaled to infinity.

"Oh, like that warehouse?" Honey pointed South through the trees, where the brightly lit paved lot around a big-ass building hosted an idling semi-truck. Men with dollies loaded identical boxes onto the lift.

She couldn't see his face in the dark, but Ethan's body language did not signal glee. From the house deck uphill, the faint sound of celebration as a porch umbrella went sailing over the rail.

"They said you were smart," he said. "Nicole and Jimbo."

Ethan finished off the remains of his Memory Wipe and set the cup aside. "So, what is it you do, anyway? Like, for a living?"

Honey told him what she did at Touchstone. Ethan nodded as she began to describe it, then he sat up straight when two figures approached. Nicole and Jimbo, making their way forward in the dark.

"Hey, lovebirds," Nicole called out.

Ethan launched himself from the picnic table. In three steps he'd reached the proceeding couple, to whom he yelled, *I feel like I'm on a date with my fuckin' mom!* and then he kept running, up the hill to the house.

~ ~ ~

SUITOR 4: MASON DICKSON

Honey dated Mason Dickson for three months. She liked everything about the guy, and her friends were relieved. Some of them had been afraid that Joe would return to town, wanting Honey back. Some of them didn't want that, because they knew that she could fall right back in. Her friends were determined that Honey be matched with someone more traditionally articulate, and less enamored of progeny. So, they were thrilled with Mr. Dickson.

"He's just what you're looking for," Nicole said. "A smart, tallish guy with a great smile and no interest in kids."

"He's perfect for you," Milana said. "So handsome. So employed."

Mason was all of those things. He was a top residential Realtor for high-net-worth clients, and she'd seen him at the gym. She'd noticed those impressive washboard abs, and those lively green eyes, and that ready laugh. She even liked his haircut, which others deemed too short. He'd approached her at the gym's juice bar, and asked for a date. They met for drinks two nights later at a bar on Beach Drive, and the attraction was instant. Soon, they were seeing each other several times a week.

Honey believed that she was simpatico with Mason. They made a striking couple, a petite blond woman and a big, buff man, both happy with life, looking toward the future, feeling empowered. Honey was at the top of her game professionally, and so was he.

The physical attraction was apparent to them both, and our girl found it difficult to refrain from kissing him, once she'd tasted those lush lips. When he ran his finger across her forearm, Honey felt lit from within. The night they first slept together, there were fireworks.

Literally, there were fireworks, because it was literally New Year's Eve. As orgasm after orgasm rocked her thin frame, Honey watched through his expansive loft windows as explosion after explosion blossomed in the sky, red, blue, gold. The boom of the ordnance was the boom of her heart as Mason did his forceful magic.

That was really quite remarkable, they agreed. *We're really good together.*

~ ~ ~

She was smiling when she stopped by Mason's place one day on a whim. Honey had visited a new bakery that morning, and planned to buzz her crush to see if he wanted something extra sweet at 8:00 a.m.—or if he just wanted a custard tart; our girl was prepared to deliver either, or both, or both simultaneously if her man was in that kind of mood.

As she entered the lobby of his building, Honey looked across to the seating area, and there sat Mason, deep in conversation with three men.

She didn't approach, because his friends looked shady, like the kind of men who were not unfamiliar with danger, prison bars, or habitual steroid use. Honey could clearly see a gun holster under one guy's unzipped hoodie. The vibe was so strong that our girl backed away. She left the way she came and ate the tart herself while she pondered the possible meaning of what she'd witnessed.

The next night at dinner, when the moment seemed right, she said, "Mason, you seem like the kind of guy who has a lot of friends. Am I right?"

"Yeah, I've got a few."

"Who are you closest with?" Honey asked.

He didn't respond, at first. She watched him rotate his wineglass, using his fingertips on the base.

What are you thinking right now? Honey wondered, and then Mason revealed exactly what he was thinking—and everything they were building began to slip.

He didn't meet her gaze. "I saw you in the lobby yesterday. Those guys I was with, they're not friends. They're cops."

Uh-oh. What? Honey didn't want to overreact, but this was not what she expected.

"Well, that explains the firearm, then," she said.

"I'm in a tight spot," he said miserably. Mason lifted his head and looked into her eyes. "They're triple-teaming me because they're trying to convince me to work undercover. If I don't, uh, I'm kinda—looking at doing time, for felony assault."

Everything they'd built was crashing down.

"This is a good time to tell you something," Mason said with the beautiful mouth that she'd kissed with such vigor. "I might have a problem with my temper."

Luckily nothing can be built too high or too strong in three months. Honey was sorry that he faced prison. She was sorry that he was being pressured by the police. She was sorry that their simpatico sex romps had come to an end. But she wasn't sorry to draw the line with Mason Dickson, right then and there. Because if he might have a problem with his temper, then she might have the desire to stay the hell away from him.

There are more fish in the sea, her mom said.

~ ~ ~

Honey began to work out every day, with the goal of perfecting the bait that would lure the big fish. She did spin class on Mondays, Wednesdays, and Fridays. She spent the other days in the gym, with a focus on weight training. Every sleeveless blouse in Honey's closet came into rotation as her body became more toned and cut. The one time she wore yoga pants to Publix, two old men followed her throughout the store, growling their gruff admiration, and then tried to chat her up in the checkout line. She never did that again. *Lesson learned.*

Our girl got more validation that her workout regime was effective when she met her friends one night for drinks.

"I'm scared of your arms," Milana said, regarding Honey over the salted rim of her margarita.

"Me, too," Nicole said, "I mean, I'm envious, but—is it too much?"

"What do you mean?" Honey's voice sounded sharper than she intended. She consciously tempered her tone as she continued, "There's no such thing as too much, really."

"I don't know about that," Nicole said, and she and Milana exchanged a glance.

Our girl couldn't understand their negative attitude. Maybe they'd forgotten what it was like, to be on the dating scene.

"You both have your men," Honey stated, and the bald truth of it made her friends duck their heads. "Time's a-wastin' for me. I think I'm looking supremely datable, these days."

Honey slowly lifted her bare arm. She popped off a bulgy bicep. BOINK.

"Look, Austin," a passing man said, "Her fuckin' arms look better than yours."

His buddy grimaced. "I wouldn't date that."

All three women had heard this exchange. Two of them shrieked with laughter as the remaining one snatched her toned arm back to her side, fast as a flash, and flushed bright pink.

"Ooh, look at her now," Milana howled, "Lil' Ms. Iron Limbs don't like it when the truth comes out."

Nicole was laughing so hard that she had to support herself by hanging onto the bar. "Let me get you a sweater, sweetheart, cover those things up! My God, you are actively driving the men away."

To Honey's everlasting dismay, this moment was captured in Girlfriend History, to be recounted to delighted audiences everywhere, anytime the topic of gyms came up, or the topic of Honey's vanity.

~ ~ ~

SUITOR 5: NOAH BELL

Our girl was excited about her first date with a fresh candidate, Noah Bell. They'd known of each other for years, but were no more than peripheral members of friend groups that overlapped. They'd never had a moment where they shared a smoky glance across a smoky room. They'd rarely interacted one-on-one. He was just another pretty face in the crowd, back then.

She got the word from one of her St. Pete peeps, CeeCee. "Noah Bell wonders if you would agree to an official date."

"Well, sure," Honey said. *Let's find out if he's more than another pretty face.* "What do you know about him?"

"He's a doll. Super upbeat, you know, always thinking big. I think he's working in insurance, somehow, and he's doing pretty well because he lives in Tierra Verde. He's definitely, um, down to earth, I guess you'd say. And you've seen him. So handsome."

Honey remembered a tall and angular man, with cheekbones like a fashion model, always with a gorgeous woman on his arm.

"He likes the ladies," she said.

"That he does," CeeCee laughed. "Hey, and there's something else he likes: blues music. Isn't that something you do? Keisha Tucker told me she heard you singing one night, and playing guitar, and she was blown away."

"I'm learning," Honey said. "That's about all I'll admit to."

~ ~ ~

Noah and Honey met for their date at Tippy's Smokehouse on the river, but he was nearly late, and they didn't have any time to talk. They were there for the biggest show of the season—the king of jazzy Southern blues, Sir Stokes. Fans followed him from gig to gig, she'd heard, like a bluesman's version of a Deadhead crew. The tall, gaunt Black man even sported a Jerry Garcia beard—big, bushy and mostly gray.

The artist had drawn a standing-room-only crowd that night, and by the end of the show, Noah and Honey were hoarse from cheering. She could swear she saw tears in her date's eyes when Stokes played his encore, *Sweet Home Chicago*. As the place began to empty, Noah appeared both energized and surprised when Honey offered to take him backstage.

"No fucking way," he said in a delighted tone, and it was the first thing he'd said all night that Honey could really hear. "You're gonna fucking get me backstage after a fucking show like that? Fuck me! You can get me backstage?"

"Um, fuck yeah," Honey said, because his over-use of the expletive was so much on display. *Is this what CeeCee calls "down to earth"?* Our girl vowed, right then and there, to have a word with CeeCee, once this fuck-filled fete was finished.

The mood backstage was raucous, the energy high. The staff greeted Honey with enthusiasm, and her date seemed impressed by how many people she knew. Our girl was familiar enough with the backstage protocols to know that for the first hour or two, not much would happen. Munchies would be munched, drinks would be drunk, joints would be sucked down to nubbins. But if any interaction with the headliner would occur, it would happen after two in the morning. Honey knew that she had some time to kill, and something in her gut was telling her that she didn't want to spend that time with Noah Bell.

Her date had other ideas. "You are so fucking beautiful," Noah said, pulling her close against him, throwing an arm around her shoulder, like he'd done with every other woman she'd ever seen him with, now that Honey thought about it.

He asked, "Can I get you a drink? Fuck, they have pizza! I'll scavenge these fucking tables to get you the fucking best, sweet thing."

Do not kill Noah, Honey reprimanded herself. *Do. Not.*

"Actually, I'm going to run to the restroom," she said, vaguely indicating a direction. "It's right over there."

At a quick pace, she stepped away from him and began to move toward the deck outside. She could hear him back there, though, shouting into his phone.

"She fucking knows where the fucking restrooms are, backstage at fucking Tippy's! I'm backstage with Sir Fuckin' Stokes, man. This is the best fucking night of my life!"

~ ~ ~

The night did not rate in the Best category for Honey.

At least, not yet.

The night is young! she thought, and for somebody 26 years old, in her situation, this was a completely valid response. By the time Honey came back from hiding in her car, it was two in the morning, and Noah was long gone. As she approached Tippy's, she heard the sound of a particularly plaintive acoustic Gibson, and knew that Sir Stokes was holding court outside on the deck, with the dive-bombing moths and the erratic background rhythm provided by full-throated Florida bullfrogs in the swamp nearby.

Stokes seemed to be relaxed and in charge in front of the group of 20 people. He channeled Mose Alison on *Rollin' Stone*, and Blind Lemon Jefferson on *Matchbox Blues*. It was when she heard the opening riff to *Black Coffee* that Honey was inspired to sing. She did so from the very perimeter of the deck, back in the shadows, providing sotto voce background to his sweet guitar. It worked, somehow, and she was glad that she had the courage to be heard, especially by somebody she respected so much.

It could've gone badly wrong—but it didn't. This was a night she would always remember.

The bluesman approached her later, as Honey was saying her goodbyes.

"That was nice tonight," Stokes said.

"Thanks. It's an honor."

He held up his Gibson. "You play?"

"I'm learning," Honey said. "That's about all I'll admit to."

~ ~ ~

Honey had become a popular speaker at the New York City magazine-production seminars, and was invited to be a panelist at the National Magazine Conference, where she and other industry professionals would address *The Future of Magazine Publishing* in the glitzy ballroom of a storied New York City hotel. She would play the role of Token Woman on the panel, and would share the stage with men who were some of the premier CEOs and publishers in the United States.

She soon found that this type of visibility attracted vendors.

Honey been sought out as a dinner companion by a guy named Dudley Dawson, who was the Vice President of Sales at a printing company that wanted Touchstone's business. She hadn't even considered accepting the invitation until he said the magic words: Le Bernardin.

"Join me and my team for a night like no other," Dudley said, and Honey was down for that. All these years she'd dreamed of that restaurant and what it represented—and now, she would achieve the dream. Our girl took a second to acknowledge her happiness, and to consider all the hard work that had brought her to that moment. *Sometimes, life is sweet.*

~ ~ ~

Once the panel discussion had concluded—with the premier magazine publishers shooting Honey dirty looks for her contention that in the future, mass print was doomed—our girl left the stage and was met by the rotund and red-faced Dudley Dawson, who stood waiting at the foot of the steps.

"Hello, hello!" he bellowed, like she was standing 20 feet away from him, instead of 20 inches. He pumped her hand enthusiastically, and his grip was far too firm.

"Ow," Honey said, attempting to pull away.

But this joker just tightened his hand on hers.

"What's wrong?" he asked, smiling into her eyes. He had the look of a fellow who enjoyed torturing animals, and Honey wasn't amused.

"If you want my business," she said, "let go of my hand."

He did.

"Jesus," he groused. "You know a man's conviction by the strength of his grip, right? That's the prevailing wisdom, as I fucking understand it."

"It's an outdated construct," Honey said mildly. She was wondering whether she should change out of her business suit, before dinner at Le Bernardin.

"We better get moving," Dudley said. "City traffic is a nightmare this time of day." He looked out over the crowd of people who were dispersing from the ballroom at the close of the session, and snapped his fingers at a group who sat together at a table. Two suited men rose and began to hurry toward them.

~   ~   ~

In the taxicab, Honey sat wedged between Dudley and Brent, who was one of the salespeople coming along to dinner. Brent's colleague, a young man named Marcus, was the junior member of the printer's sales team, and thus had to sit crushed up against the far door. Traffic was indeed a nightmare, and progress was measured in feet, not miles, as the time ticked past. Honey kept looking up ahead, to see the awning for the restaurant of her dreams. But their reservations weren't until seven, Dudley's calendar invite had told her. There was probably plenty of time.

Brent and Marcus, Honey saw, let their boss do all the talking—

and Dudley was accustomed to it. He pontificated at length about the number of printing facilities that his company boasted, how many years of experience their collective workforce could claim, and how crucial it was for a vendor's sales team to be close to the customer.

"I wouldn't mind getting a little closer to you," Dudley chuckled. "All my other clients are guys."

We couldn't get much closer. Honey's body met his tightly, from shoulder to knee, there in the back of the cramped car. She wondered what sort of example this guy was setting for his junior trainees. They were watching his every move—and Dudley's next move was to yawn and stretch his arms, so that when his right arm dropped, it rested behind Honey's shoulders.

She immediately leaned forward, and they rode the next 30 minutes like that as he sat back to explain the caring service she should expect, if she moved Touchstone's business to his company. Dudley spent quite a bit of time talking about his own achievements, most of which seemed to center around his financial validation in corporate sales contests. *I've been King's Club for seven years running,* he boasted, as if the whole world knew what King's Club was, or cared. Honey began to suspect that the sales minions were his real audience, not her.

It was cold in the taxi, and Honey might've been getting a cramp in her side from leaning forward like that—but after all, this was the price of dinner at a place she'd been convinced she would never experience. She scanned for the restaurant's sign. The neighborhood looked sketchy, but our Florida girl was learning that a lot of the City looked that way, from her sunshiny perspective. She watched people in puffy coats and hoods battle the fierce wind of a cold front that had swept down from Canada that day. Everyone out there was wearing gloves, scarves and snow boots as they trundled toward their frigid destinations.

Honey wished she'd brought her overcoat, now. But she only had a few feet to traverse, didn't she? Eight feet, between the door of the cab and the door of Le Bernardin, where a doorman would be waiting.

~ ~ ~

The vehicle finally stopped, double-parked, and Brent paid the cabbie while the rest of them extricated themselves from the back seat. Honey looked over at the restaurant door, expecting to see the smiling greeter. Instead, she was greeted by a sign:

CHOPPED CORNED BEEF

"Katz's deli is a New York City landmark," Dudley beamed, extending his arm toward the restaurant. "I hope you're ready for a night like no other."

The icy wind cut through the loose weave of our girl's suit, super-chilling her so completely and so quickly that she lost her breath. Honey's jaw juddered as she squeaked, "I thought we were going to Le Bernardin."

"Nah. They're booked."

For the first time, young Marcus piped up. "Let's go on inside. Honey might be cold out here."

"I'll be the judge of THAT," Dudley snarled, putting his protege in his place.

Nobody moved as Marcus learned his lesson. Brent skidded over to join them on the ice rink that was the sidewalk.

"I—I—actually am cold," Honey whispered through chattering jaws. All feeling was gone from her fingers and toes. Without waiting for a response, she threw her half-frozen body in the direction of Katz's front door. There was no doorman waiting, but by then all Honey wanted was heat.

~ ~ ~

Midway through the meal at Katz's, Honey realized that this evening outing was indeed for the vendor sales team, and not for her. Dudley was showing his boys exactly how to milk the expense account that they might someday inherit. This was a rare trip to the City for the sales crew, she learned. Honey listened as the three of them debated at length the pros and cons of New York City entertainment compared to such client-worthy distractions in Chicago, the western boundary of their shared sales territory.

Honey chewed her corned beef and tried to appreciate its historical value to the City. She was still angry that Dudley had been deceptive about Le Bernardin, but at least her feet were warm. Though she soon had to admit that corned beef wasn't her jam, Honey was delighted to learn that Katz's made a nice egg custard.

The men at her booth were howling with laughter at a story Dudley was telling about a client he'd hoodwinked with a lie about paper-stock quality. He told this bold tale with no fear. It was almost as if Honey wasn't a prospective client with a brain in her head.

"Stupid fool didn't even know I was playing him," Dudley roared. "He still doesn't know it."

Interesting, Honey thought. She happened to be acquainted with Dudley's client—they served on a Magazine Association committee together. *He'll know it now.*

Once they wiped the tears of hilarity from their eyes with Katz's paper napkins, the Sales Threesome moved on to the next topic: where to go for drinks.

"Let's get this party started," Dudley hooted, and his compatriots high-fived.

"I think I'll just head back to the hotel," Honey said, but they wouldn't hear of it. They protested so vehemently that she assumed that if she wasn't present, they couldn't write off their expenses—and these guys wanted to party in the Big Apple. That's why she was invited, our girl realized. To Dudley, she was in no way a prospective client. She was just a flesh ticket to a night out on the town.

"Let's go to Elaine's," Dudley said. "It's right near Central Park, we could do that carriage-ride thing. It's supposed to start snowing later, real pretty."

Honey could see the headlines now: *Woman's frozen corpse recovered from Central Park carriage ride.*

"I'll join you for a drink," Honey said. Carriage rides notwithstanding, she'd heard plenty about Elaine's, where the most-recent issue of *Vanity Fair* revealed that a famous disgraced film director sometimes showed up to play a wind instrument with the house band. Would this be one of those nights?

~ ~ ~

Honey nursed a gimlet in the darkened room while her companions had four rounds each. Dudley spent some time quizzing her about whether her Nikes were for comfort, or if they were a statement of some kind, since she wore them with "such a hot-lookin' suit." Honey didn't tell him that years of standing on concrete press-side had wrecked her feet, and that comfortable footwear was now a necessity in her world.

Elaine's was busy that night, and Honey kept her gaze moving, scanning for the disgraced film director—but he did not appear. She enjoyed the band, though, and she appreciated their considerable talents while Dudley and crew appreciated their considerable expense account. Everybody seemed content until the Sales VP's next suggestion.

"Let's order oysters," Dudley said. "You know about oysters, don't you, Honey?"

"Why, no," she said, though she did. "Tell me."

"Ooh, they'll make you crazy," he murmured, leaning closer. "Oysters get a girl hot, you know?"

"Hot? What do you mean?"

"You know. Charged up, sexually."

She tipped her head. "What do you mean, charged up?"

Honey saw that young Marcus kept his eyes down. *He might be the smartest one.*

"Charged up!" Dudley tended to yell when people didn't understand his point. "Like, hot! Wet! Wanting it! You get my drift?"

All the people at the surrounding tables got Dudley's drift, by then.

"Hm, well then," Honey said, "No oysters for me."

Their faces fell. All three men wanted oysters, obviously.

Ever the salesman, Dudley tried to salvage the chance at a $200 plate of expense-paid seafood by posing a question: "Oh, are you saying you're already hot enough?"

It's official, Honey thought. *He's had too much to drink.*

"Not so you'd notice," she said, smiling placidly.

"Just taste one," Dudley said. "Here, I'll order a platter, and you can just see if you like 'em."

"No oysters for me," she said again.

"Damn it," Dudley exploded, slamming his fist on the table. "Just say you'll try one. What is your problem?"

Honey noticed that Marcus looked over at Dudley, and then looked away. He might be embarrassed of his boss. *We all are, my boy.*

"Oh, DO go ahead and order them," Honey said. "I know you'll all enjoy them."

Dudley leaned across the table, and his elbow bumped a water glass, which tilted precariously before it righted itself. He peered directly into Honey's eyes, to make sure she paid full attention to what he said next.

"Tell. Me. You'll. Try. One."

His aspect was deeply disturbing. On an instinctive level, Honey was glad that other people were around.

"No oysters for me." She smiled when she said it, and it sent him around the moon.

Dudley leaped up from his chair, which fell over backwards onto the floor with a crash. The band's drummer looked over, concerned.

"Damn it," Dudley shrieked, and when he took a step toward Honey, Marcus and Brent both jumped to their feet.

"Yo, man," Brent said to his boss, "it's only oysters."

"It's more than that, and SHE knows it." Dudley pointed the drunken finger of blame at Honey.

The host approached the table. Honey was the only person sitting, and he chose her to address. "Everything okay here, mademoiselle?"

"Absolutely," our mademoiselle said. She stood. "Could you call me a cab?"

As the host nodded, Honey came to stand next to him. "Thanks, guys," she said to the salesmen. "This has been a night like no other."

Only young Marcus smiled.

~ ~ ~

SUITOR 6: SHANE McLANE

Back home in Florida, Honey held high hopes for her next suitor, Shane McLane. He owned a bottling plant for market-leading soft drinks in the fast-growing Central Florida area, and had recently purchased a home on Tampa's most prestigious street, Bayshore Boulevard. He owned a fleet of luxury vehicles. He had box seats for the Tampa Bay Lightning hockey games, and he'd been divorced from his high-school sweetheart for several years. Shane was playing the field, and so was Honey. Curious, she readily agreed to a lunch date.

Unlike the other men, Shane had called her directly. He hadn't gone through her friends, to test the waters. Maybe single billionaires like Shane knew that the only answer they would get was a resounding *Yes*. So, it got to be Honey's delighted honor to deliver the news of this development to her crew.

"You cannot mean Shane McLane," Nicole said. "Swoon City, wow. He's so, um—"

"Handsome?" Honey prompted.

"Wealthy," Nicole laughed. "I think that's the word I was looking for."

Then Honey called Milana, who said, "Ooh now, Shane McLane. There's a name everybody knows. He's—he's so—"

"Handsome? Wealthy?"

"Old," Milana said. "I think that's the word I was looking for."

~ ~ ~

Shane picked her up for their date in an Irish-green Porsche. *Sweet*, Honey thought, but that was before she had to find a way to fold her legs into the passenger side of the tight cockpit. Her date closed the door behind her and passed in front of the car, and she noted that he moved with a spring in his step, like somebody who was looking forward to life. He was a fit, energetic fellow. Shane had the eyes of a curious child and the wardrobe of a CEO. His deep tan showed off his salt-and-pepper hair. He was 39 years old, the oldest man she'd ever dated.

Conversation flowed easily on their ride to lunch, since he was talking about himself, and Honey was delighted to hear that he was a longtime subscriber to *Touchstone Business* magazine.

"How's my buddy Casey Caruthers?" Shane asked.

Oh, you're buddies with my boss? Good to know. Honey said, "He runs a tight ship."

"Ha, yeah, I bet he does. He's pretty damn young, to be running the show."

"Well, he's doing a fine job of it," our girl said. "How do you know him?"

"Yacht Club." Shane downshifted into second gear and accelerated through a turn. "St. Pete, not Tampa. Though of course I'm a member of both."

Of course, Honey thought, although in her estimation it was bad form to belong to both organizations, when they'd been bitter rivals for 80 years. *Pick a team*, she wanted to say.

They stopped at a traffic light in the shopping district, and a woman crossing in front of the Porsche waved at Shane. He waved back.

"Who's that?" Honey asked.

Shane depressed the clutch and threw the car into first gear, waiting for the green light.

"Can't remember," he said. "Somebody I fucked."

Well, well, Honey thought. *The plot thickens, here, with Mr. McLane's social skills.*

~ ~ ~

Most of the men Honey dated never got around to asking about her goals, her passions or her background, and Shane was no different. Once they arrived at the restaurant and were seated outside by the water, he'd launched into a description of the house he'd bought on Bayshore, and then Shane specified at length about how he would improve it. He'd finished recounting the first-floor renovation plan, and was moving on to the scrupulously detailed program for the second floor, when the female server stopped to see if they wanted more wine.

"We might have another glass," Shane said. "What do YOU think, Heather?"

Honey couldn't figure out why he was asking the server what she thought. Then she realized that the young woman's name tag read *Annemarie*.

Omigod, our girl realized. *He just called me 'Heather.'*

"It's Honey, not Heather," she said, looking across at him. *How will he react? That will tell me a lot.*

"Did I say 'Heather'?" He slapped his forehead. "I am so sorry. Please forgive me, I am a dunce."

Good recovery, I guess. "No more wine for me, thanks," Honey said.

"Me either, then," Shane said to Annemarie. He turned back to Honey with an apologetic smile. "Wow. That was a bonehead move on my part, huh?"

The restaurant's host was leading two glamorous women past their table, and both gliding females simultaneously downshifted into second and coasted to a stop.

"Shane!" the brunette exclaimed. "Is it YOU?"

"Well, hello," her platinum-haired friend said to Shane. "Long time no see, stranger."

Let me guess, Honey thought. *Somebody you fucked, times two.*

Shane had a spirited conversation with the two women about the expected weather in St. Tropez, while the host—and Honey— waited patiently in the bright sunshine. There were boats on the bay, and plenty of time to appreciate them, as the three-way discussion continued.

"Where are my manners?" Shane inclined his head toward Honey. "I haven't introduced my date."

Then the three women introduced themselves, and Shane didn't have to recall a single person's name. *Neat trick,* Honey thought. *But I won't be practicing that one.*

As they took their leave, the brunette (Jacqueline) and Ms. Platinum (Charlene) waved to Honey—Jacqueline called back *Have fun* and Charlene said *You'll need it* which didn't make a lot of sense, really, but Honey was just relieved that they'd taken their St. Tropez elsewhere. It was beginning to dawn on her that Shane McLane might be intimately acquainted with every woman in the Tampa Bay area, whether he recollected their names or not.

As if in affirmation, Shane pointed toward the host stand, where a curvaceous blond in an enormous sunhat waited alone.

"Look," he said. "That's the girl from the Neiman Marcus shoe department. I fucked her."

"Don't tell me who you've fucked," Honey said.

He looked across the table, surprised. "Why not?"

"It's rude, that's why."

"No, it's not." Shane's brows were drawn tight in a frown. "It's flattering," he insisted.

On what planet? Honey said, "Flattering? How so?"

Her date looked around blinking, like he was caught in some prank he didn't comprehend. He said, "Because they're gorgeous. That puts you right up there in their league."

This probably makes total sense to him, Honey thought. *Bless his heart.*

She probably shouldn't have done it. She probably should never have asked the question.

"What's my name?"

Shane flushed and looked away. "What kind of fucked-up game is this you're playing?"

The Florida sun was winking off the water in blinding flashes. High, weak clouds did nothing to dim its fury, and a puff of hot breeze carried the scent of brine. A woman in exceptional shoes grabbed the brim of her sunhat.

"I'll give you a hint. It's not Heather."

Shane tilted his head back and closed his eyes. Perhaps he was wishing he could fly away on the breeze, like a winged seed pod or a Marvel action hero.

He opened one eye and asked, "So, what are you trying to prove, here, exactly?"

"I don't know." Honey was already tiring of her own name game. "Nothing, I guess."

"You seem a little on edge." Shane reached to wipe his forehead with his napkin. "I gotta tell you, Holly, this is the weirdest date I've ever been on."

~ ~ ~

Honey thought that she would never see Shane McLane again, but because their first date had gone so monumentally badly, the man seemed intrigued—or maybe he was just stymied by his failure to impress her. Some guys were like that, our girl knew, and Shane proved to be very persistent.

Every Monday for six weeks, flowers arrived at Honey's office. And this wasn't just some forget-me-not bouquet with baby's breath. This was a towering collection of exotic tropical florae that took two men to carry, probably because the crystal container itself weighed 30 pounds. It was flown in via FedEx from Miami, where the florist claimed that it was the same arrangement that was shipped each week to El Chapo.

On Monday mornings at Touchstone Business, junior staff began to gather at the twelfth-floor reception desk, anticipating the mincing procession of that week's over-the-top floral delivery. Promptly at nine, the elevator doors opened, and Honey stood waiting.

She said, "Same place, the office right through there. Just put it on the credenza by the windows, guys, thanks."

Kirk, one of the content writers from the creative side, came walking up the hall. He watched the blossoms bounce as the deliverymen struggled to transport the monstrosity past Reception without spilling water on the floor. Kirk had never spoken to Honey before, even though they'd worked at the same place for eight years.

Now he said, "Somebody's making amends."

"Oh, is that what this means?" Honey asked.

"In my experience. Who messed up?"

"Shane McLane."

"Holy shit, no way." Kirk took a step away from her. "I mean, really?"

He blatantly looked her up and down. "YOU. Are dating Shane McLane."

"Not anymore," Honey said.

"Reassessment time," Kirk said. He smiled. "Tell me about yourself."

~ ~ ~

"I can't forget you," Shane McLane said on the phone.

Honey, of course, heard *I can't forget you, Holly*, so she wasn't real concerned about Shane's distress.

"Let me make it up to you," he said. "Let me fly you to Staniel Cay next weekend, no strings attached. Give me one more chance."

~ ~ ~

The flight to Staniel Cay took a little under two hours on Shane's private jet, including a stopover on Andros Island to get their passports checked on the tarmac by a guy who was also selling guavas. Staniel Cay, Honey had learned, was a small island located in the Exumas archipelago off the southeast coast of Florida. Thunderball Grotto was the big draw on Staniel Cay, it seemed, an underwater cavern with a perfectly circular opening to the sky, made famous by movies like *007 Thunderball* and *Splash*.

She and Shane sat next to each other on the luxurious little Embraer, with Honey closest to the window since he'd seen the view a hundred times, and she had seen it zero times. Our girl could hardly take her eyes off the drama of the scene below. The water sparkled in perfect turquoise, and in the shallows, it was gin-clear, dotted with a sprinkling of desert islands that might offer only a single deep-green coconut palm, surrounded by sand so white it burned her retinas to look at it. Enormous sting rays were visible below the surface, traveling in groups.

"Pretty nice, huh?" Shane asked.

"Amazing," Honey said. She couldn't wipe the grin off her face. "Thanks for inviting me."

He smiled like he was embarrassed, looking like a little kid somehow, and Honey found it charming. Shane had dressed down for their overnight excursion and looked a lot more approachable in a long-sleeved T-shirt and khakis. His Rolex watch caught her eye, which after all is the raison d'être' for that sort of timepiece, and that's when she noticed the inside hem of his shirt sleeve, where Shane had written a word in blue ball-point pen: HONEY.

She wasn't sure if this was endearing because he cared, or disturbing because he couldn't be bothered to remember.

Time will tell, our girl thought. *Let's see what the weekend brings.*

"I'm so glad you agreed to come," Shane said. "I didn't like the way we left it, last time."

"Me, either." As she recalled, she'd given him the silent treatment all the way home, and he hadn't offered to walk her to the door. It felt like they were glad to be rid of each other, that day.

"You didn't have to call me again," Honey said, "or send those flowers. You could've just moved on. Why didn't you?"

He shrugged. "Like I say, I didn't like the way we left it."

She smiled over at him. "We're two adults. We can talk things through, can we not? We can communicate."

"Well, sure," he said. "That's what they'd have us believe, anyway."

~ ~ ~

The most impressive infrastructure on the little island of Staniel Cay was the 3,500-foot pier that had been built for visiting mega-yachts—and since it was high season, most of the slips were filled. Honey was looking down at the pier from a cliff, where a man from the Staniel Cay Yacht Club was driving the golf cart that ferried she and Shane from the strip of sandy concrete that locals called "the airport."

"That's my boat," Shane said, pointing. "The one on the end. The *Carpe This.*"

119

When Honey laughed, he looked over. "You think that's funny?"

"It's great—where did you come up with that?"

A shadow crossed his face then, an expression that he quickly replaced with a smile. "It wasn't my idea. Brandy suggested it."

Honey knew that Brandy was Shane's high-school sweetheart, his ex-wife.

"You miss her, don't you?" Honey asked, and she was surprised when he jerked away from her and nearly fell from the moving cart. She reached out, grabbed two handfuls of his T-shirt, and reeled him back in. Now his cheek was close to hers, so when he spoke, it was a whisper.

"We're not going to talk about her, are we?"

Well, that was quite a reaction, Honey thought. *I believe I struck a nerve, there, fella.*

"Let's talk about Thunderball Grotto," Honey said. "Do you think we'll have time to snorkel, before lunch?"

~ ~ ~

They changed into their swimsuits on what Shane called his "boat," a 62-foot motor yacht whose carbon-fiber superstructure made it look like an attack vehicle from an adolescent boy's Mad Max dream about the android future. To keep herself protected from the brutal tropical sun, Honey wore a mid-length caftan of white linen and a charming bucket hat.

When she got out to the deck, Shane was waiting, looking trim and fit in navy swim trunks, but with old-man saggy skin around his pecs that no amount of time at the gym could reverse. His chest hair was graying, too.

"What you got under that sheet?" he asked, and Honey made a face.

"The stuff of dreams," she said.

"Well, okay, big talker—let's see it. Come on."

If she hadn't been confident of what he'd see, Honey never would have removed her hat and whipped the caftan off by its neck in one motion. But looking good in a bikini was Honey's forte. In one fluid move, she performed the Big Reveal: a tiny bronze bandeau and thong that were exactly the color of her skin. At first glance, she looked naked—and she knew it. Taut-tummied and toned, our girl stood proud in the brilliant light of the Exumian sun.

"Wow, I thought your tits would be bigger," Shane said.

Okay, in the spirit of communication between adults, let me tell you why a comment like that is perceived to be rude, Honey could have said. Instead, she took a more direct approach.

"You fucking jerk!"

Not eloquent, perhaps, but it did get Shane's attention. And then they were able to have the conversation, which mostly consisted of Honey yelling at him at top volume all the way to the Grotto, on the skiff that bore them across the choppy waves. She was louder than the outboard motor, it was true. That day, she had to be.

~ ~ ~

Sometimes you have an experience so otherworldly that later, you're convinced that it was never true—that it was a fiction. A fantasy. The melody of a memory that could never be real. Thunderball Grotto was all of that for Honey. She believed that it might have happened to somebody other than her, somebody who was more qualified, mentally and spiritually, to appreciate the honor.

Noon was the perfect time to enter the Grotto, which required Honey and Shane to take a deep breath on the surface, sink down, and swim through a scary lava-rock tunnel. Popping up into the darkness of the cave, with the cacophony of other swimmers' voices bouncing on the rock, Honey found herself suspended in a chamber under a beam of light. Sunlight sliced through the crystalline water to illuminate pink coral 60 feet below, and she saw little fish of many colors darting through the shaft of sunlight, sparkling in the beam like living jewels.

She watched bold bars of saturated color as they moved around her, flashing bright against the black walls of the cave. Honey thought of her mother, suddenly—*why?*—and then there was Shane, swimming over to her.

They treaded water a foot apart.

"Still mad at me?" he asked.

Supported by warm, transparent water, suspended in a refracting prism of moving color and light, our naked little human looked up at the sun.

She said, "All is forgiven."

~ ~ ~

They probably shouldn't have gone on the guide's boat ride that afternoon, slowly circumnavigating the island while they had lunch, then walking for miles on the pink sand of the pristine beach where he'd dropped them off, talking in general about love and human nature, and talking specifically about the past, the future. Whatever topics they covered that day, Honey shouldn't have been out in the sun that long, because: sun poisoning.

Her symptoms didn't appear right away. She and Shane had returned to the *Carpe This*, showered in their respective suites, and changed for dinner. As she dried her hair and put on makeup, Honey could see in the surrounding mirrors that she'd gotten too much sun. Despite repeated slathering of industrial-strength zinc oxide throughout the day, the tropical sun had broken through such flimsy barriers. The skin on her shoulders was beginning to throb in an uncharacteristic way. Honey saw that her nose was red, and her cheeks were, too.

Don't need blusher now, our upbeat gal said to herself, and she slipped on the little black dress that she'd brought to wear to the Staniel Cay Yacht Club, where dinner would be served. During the long walk up the pier, Shane told her what to expect.

"This Yacht Club is just a big bar room, sitting right on the water for the breeze, 'cause there's no air conditioning. Real tropical, right, with a roof made of palm fronds. There might be spiders in the thatch, so be watchful. They've got a fully-stocked bar, but no bartender—it's an honor-system thing, where you mix your own, and tally 'em to a list, and you settle up before you leave port. There's a smaller room out back for dining, it's like NOT fine cuisine, but somebody else is doing the cooking, which works for me."

Outside the dining-room door, a menu board:

DINNER
Conch ceviche
Fried conch with conch fritters
Conch chowder (hot)

It was as Honey was sipping her chowder that the sun poisoning symptoms appeared, and then began pacing each other in rapid succession: extreme inflammation of the skin, blisters, headache, nausea, dehydration, and fever. Our girl was in for one wild Saturday night.

And guess what? Shane McLane stepped up.

He helped her back down the long, long pier to the yacht, holding her hair when she paused to barf conch back into the waters from which it came. He cleaned her up with a washrag, and then he took off her shoes, laid her onto the bedspread, and found cool compresses. When Honey mewled, *I'm so thirsty*, Shane ran to the galley for Gatorade. When she cried from the pain of her headache, he fetched ibuprofen and made her take three. He stayed by her side, ever watchful.

Finally, just before dawn, Honey had nearly recovered from the chills that often accompany a high fever like hers. She was wrapped up in a blanket, leaning against the headboard and sucking on an ice pop to soothe her raw throat, with Shane watching from the foot of the bed.

"Where'd you find a lemon Popsicle?" Honey asked. "Do you stock them in the freezer, for when your girlfriends get sun sickness?"

"I went next door to Duke's." He meant the mega-yacht moored next to his, which was owned by Duke Devine, the popular preacher at a Texas megachurch. "He has boxes of them. That's his favorite treat."

"I thought his favorite treat was Indonesian boys," Honey said. She read the news.

"Blasphemer," Shane said.

~ ~ ~

"I know I'll always love her. But she won't have me back."

It was sunrise on the *Carpe This*. Shane was laying on the top of the covers, while Honey was buried underneath. The topic had turned to the love of Shane's life: Brandy, his former spouse.

"You just need to give yourself some time," was Honey's counsel. "Stop dating around. Stop fucking everything that walks."

Shane said, "Well I can't do that. How am I supposed to have sex if I'm not dating around?"

"I hear what you're saying. But you can have plenty of sex without dating around. Let me ask you this: Who's your favorite person to have sex with?"

"Susan," he said without hesitation. "And Leigh Ann."

"Well, which is it?"

"Both. I mean, Susan by herself isn't enough, and Leigh Ann by herself isn't, either. But you get the two of 'em together in bed with me, and by God, that's magic, there. That's the best sex in town."

Honey pulled herself up against the pillows, so she could look him in the eye. "So you have your little sex parties with Susan and Leigh Ann. And you leave the rest of the dating pool alone, until you know how you're going to replace Brandy, in your heart."

She could see that it hurt him to hear that. Shane might have been a billionaire, but no amount of money could buy him out of a broken heart. Honey watched as he closed his eyes and took a couple of breaths. He was thinking it through.

"Nobody can replace her," he said.

That's very sad, Honey thought. *Dude loves her.*

She asked, "Did Brandy ever re-marry?"

He shook his head.

"Well, then, do you want to fight for her? Are you willing to fight to get her back?"

He rolled up a pillow and put it underneath his chin, laying on his stomach and looking over at her. Honey met his gaze.

"I AM a formidable adversary," Shane said, and Honey saw a new light in his eye, a focus she hadn't sensed before, in him.

"Yeah, so I hear," Honey said. She did indeed read the news, and knew of Shane's ruthless reputation in business.

The slap of the waves was loud against the hull. Shane smiled over at her.

"You're one smart woman, Holly."

And when she lurched to slap the tar out of him, Shane laughed and rolled away.

"Kidding!" he giggled, "Just kidding! Can't you take a joke?"

~ ~ ~

In the jet the next day, flying back to civilization in her destination T-shirt, a tomato-red Honey said, "I'm thinking I like you way better as a friend."

"Me too," Shane said, and that was that.

~ ~ ~

During her time at Touchstone, Honey learned that revenues can rise when employees have a voice. This approach ran counter to everything that old-school managers believed, of course. Nobody who worked the floor could possibly know more about growing their business than a new MBA grad from Wharton. But Honey had been reading in her industry publications about something new: Six Sigma, a process methodology that required feedback from all levels of an enterprise.

She learned that the leaders at Exceptional Press were on board with the approach, and had held a meeting of their entire workforce, from president to pressman, to introduce the commitment to Six Sigma.

One night when she was on-site for a press check, Honey found herself in the break room with Pat, the big guy who'd been first to greet her on her initial plant visit. Pat loved a practical joke, but he took his job seriously. He oversaw print operations and had accumulated decades of experience with all kinds of presses—and with all kinds of organizations. Honey had been quick to notice that when Pat spoke, everybody around him stopped talking and listened. She'd made it a point to do the same.

Pat was sipping coffee and filling out a form. He seemed intent.

"What are you working on?" Honey asked.

"Six Sigma report," Pat said.

"So, what do you think of it, really? Is Six Sigma just a fad? Some flash in the pan?"

The big man had looked up at her then, through his thick eyeglasses.

"It's the best thing that's come along for quality, in my opinion," he said. "I've been doing this for 30 years, Honey, and every time senior management gets some wild hair and calls another meeting about some new program, I just roll my eyes. I've seen it all, and none of it ever worked. But Six Sigma is different. I've never seen anything with as much potential to improve results."

"Wow," she said. He was completely serious—she could hear it in his voice. "But why? What makes it so different from all the other things management has tried?"

"Because now they listen to me," Pat said. "Now, they have to."

~ ~ ~

SUITOR 7: LUCAS HUGHES

Honey's next prospective suitor was Lucas Hughes, who as she recalled looked good in a T-shirt—and who looked good on paper, too. He held a recently minted PhD in English Literature, and was working at the University of Tampa as a professor for incoming freshers. Lucas had been a fixture on the club scene, back in the day, in those snug T-shirts of his, and Honey had always believed that he was one of the best dancers on the floor. Our girl liked a man with rhythm. That always boded well, in her experience.

So Honey was tickled to learn that Lucas had expressed interest in dating her. She tapped into the Palmetto Express to learn more.

LIZ: I liked him when he was 20. But then he was away all those years, getting that doctoral degree. So, I can't really guide you on this one.

MILANA: He was a ton of fun eight years ago.

NICOLE: That man can dance! But professors don't earn much, Honey. Think it through.

CEECEE: I'm staying out of it. Look what happened last time. So, no comment. But you might try Brittany B.

BRITTANY B: He can be quirky, I won't lie, and sometimes he can come off as a bit effeminate, but I think that's just because he's overeducated. I guess I'd say that he's unconventional, yet somehow adorable.

Based on that input, Honey agreed to meet Lucas Hughes at the Rathskeller, a beery space tucked away beneath the grand building that had been constructed as a hotel by a robber baron in the late 1800s. The green grass of the University of Tampa's manicured landscape still glowed bright, even as autumn leaves rustled beneath Honey's feet. She walked toward her most-recent first date, looking up at the Moorish minarets that sat atop a red-brick structure that stretched for a quarter of a mile. She saw that each minaret was topped with a silver crescent moon. Unconventional, yet somehow adorable.

It's a sign, Honey thought. She quickened her pace for her date with Lucas.

Five steps led down to the little hobbit door of the student bar, where a neon sign had been erected to help buyers navigate more expediently to the brewskis. RAT SKELLER, the sign announced with its dead H. Honey hoped this wasn't another sign of things to come—she didn't like rats.

The ceilings were low, and the lights even lower, when Honey stepped into the room. Sconces on the walls cast a feeble auburn glow. The scent of beer, soaking into the floorboards and wood-paneled walls for 100 years, was overpowering, and Honey realized that she'd have to wash her hair as soon as she got home.

Undeterred, our girl scanned the Rathskeller's darkened interior. She spotted Lucas right away, since he was the only person in the room wearing a knit scarf and tweed. The T-shirts were gone from his wardrobe, it appeared, now that he had attained his terminal degree and was ensconced in a place of authority on the University's academic staff.

Honey learned a lot that night. She learned that young girls like tweed, for example, which was evident from the three coeds who were simpering for his attention as Honey approached. Lucas was good-looking, there was no denying that. With a leonine mane of hair, a closely cropped beard and fierce eyes of greenish gold, young Dr. Hughes drew attention. He possessed the barstool like it was his rightful throne.

"Begone, my ladies!" he said to his entourage, waving his hand. "Yonder Venus, in her glimmering sphere."

Honey thought, *Seriously?* But sure enough, the three young women turned, looked at Honey, and fled in a tartan-skirted herd toward the Rathskeller door.

"I feel like I'm walking into a play," she said. "Lucas, it's good to see you, after all this time."

He didn't stand up from the barstool, so she leaned over and gave him an awkward hug. The tweed jacket was rough and so was the stubble on his cheek. Honey was immediately intrigued by this sensory jolt, but the feeling was fleeting, because of the way he then greeted her.

"You look better!" Lucas exclaimed, as if surprised.

"Better than what?"

Realizing from her tone that he might have stepped in it, Lucas quickly backtracked. "No, no, that's not what I mean. I mean, um, in fresh numbers number all your graces, Honey Malone."

Ugh, it's Shakespeare quote night at the Rat, Honey thought. She wondered if she'd be able to engage with his erudite repartee, or if she possessed sufficient inclination to even try. She couldn't get over that rough stubble, though, and it thrilled her to imagine rubbing up against that tweed again, so our hopeful girl decided to spend a little time appreciating just how handsome he was—there was so much to catalog. She moved to sit on the barstool next to him.

"Oh, let's get a booth," he said. He was looking around the room, almost like he didn't want to be seen with her. But of course, he'd chosen the venue. He had personally selected the redolent Rat as the place for their reacquaintance. Though Honey would have preferred to stay at the bar, where the lighting was better for her planned Handsome Details Catalog, she was amenable. She'd gone into the evening with a positive spirit, and she wanted to keep that going. *Let's see what Lucas has to offer, other than deep knowledge of the Bard.*

Her date walked her to the back, to the booth where the lighting was dimmest and the stench of stale beer strongest, and they sat across from each other in the fragrant gloom. Century-old beer mist cloaked them like a yeasty hug. Lucas made a show of reaching up with both hands and raking great locks of gorgeous hair away from his face, like any woman in a TV commercial for moisturizing conditioner. A votive candle, clothed only in its tiny tin, burned on the scarred wooden table between them, and Honey wondered just how quickly open flames could engulf an 1880s-era structure like the one that rested just a few feet above.

"Can I get you a beer?" Lucas asked.

Honey craved cabernet that evening. "Do they have wine?"

"It's a beer hall," Lucas said, half-smiling and lifting one eyebrow like he was talking to a child. "There's no wine here."

"I'm good, then. Maybe just some water."

He frowned with those expressive eyebrows, which were better groomed than hers, Honey noted. "It's Tampa water, though," he said, and they both made a face. "Let's see if they have bottled."

While the server went off in search of something potable, Lucas turned his attention to his date. He leaned forward and propped his chin against the heel of his hand as he trained his flecked eyes on hers. He nudged the little candle closer to her and heaved a deep, dramatic sigh. "You look beautiful by candlelight."

Did Lucas stage the votive? She wouldn't put it past him.

He reached out and took both of Honey's hands in his, saying, "Stars, hide your fires. Let not light see my black and deep desires."

His animal eyes glowed gold and green. His lashes were thick and long, like a girl's, and his hands were warm against hers. As Honey took in the many handsome details of his lovely face, Lucas batted his girly eyelashes. The movement was unnerving, somehow, but by gosh she was there to get to know the guy, wasn't she? *Let's play along.*

Honey blinked her eyes exactly twice, in super slow motion, showing off the ability of her carefully applied false lashes to cut through beer fog and still appear beguiling. It was the War of the Lashes in the back booth of the Rathskeller, and her date was probably winning.

She whispered, "It appears that the prince of darkness is a gentleman."

His fingers clamped down around hers, and he lurched forward. His nose was inches from hers.

"You can't be sure." He released her hands and sat back, but held her gaze with those gold-speckled eyes.

What I can't be sure of is whether I want to play this Shakespeare game much longer, Honey thought. *I'd forgotten how exhausting academic calisthenics can be.* But what the heck? She could make it through dinner, to see where the evening went. She might yet get the opportunity to put her cheek against his—soft against rough—and then he could write his own poem about that.

"No bottled water," the server reported back. "Y'all want food?"

"The bratwurst is to die for," Lucas said, fingering his scarf fringe.

"Maybe not." Honey scoured the menu for a vegetable of some kind, and came away disappointed. The Rat offered nothing that she cared to drink, and nothing that she cared to eat. As if to remind her of this, Honey's stomach growled.

Lucas ordered the bratwurst and another beer, even though his date ordered nothing. When he smiled across at Honey, she noticed his perfect teeth. There was a lot that was perfect about Lucas, it was true to say—and that didn't mean she wasn't hungry.

"Every time I think of you, I'm reminded of Sonnet 65," the professor announced. "You know it, of course."

He was waiting for Honey to indicate that she did not, in fact, know it. And she'd forgotten more than she remembered from her studies, so she spoke the word.

"May I recite it for you?"

Honey could have said *Oh, how lovely, please do*, but she was peckish, losing patience with the Shakespeare display and fed up with the lash batting, so she just muttered *Sure*.

Lucas placed a limp hand over his heart and looked toward the ceiling, which loomed low above them, low enough for graffiti. *Shannon H = Skank*. Honey watched as he took a breath, squeezed his eyes shut, and spoke the verse in a voice that was a tad too stagey.

O, how shall summer's honey breath hold out
Against the wreckful siege of battering days,
When rocks impregnable are not so stout,
Nor gates of steel so strong, but time decays?

He sat back against the booth. They looked at each other, the same level gaze.

"I thought you said I look better than you expected," Honey said.

His eyes lit up, bright as the flame guttering in its cup. "Time's ticking," he said. "Isn't it, Honey?"

And … final curtain. Honey scooted out of the booth, and Lucas didn't even lift his eyes to watch her go. He was still looking across at the empty spot where she'd sat when he asked, "Have you ever dressed up like a schoolgirl?"

Honey's finely calibrated creep alert sounded at that time.

She wanted to tell him *Nature's fragile vessel doth sustain* or some shit, but he wasn't worth the effort. Honey walked out, leaving him alone with his sad flame and his dreams of schoolgirls.

She'd live to date another day.

~ ~ ~

Her brother Max called her one night at 11:00, far later than he usually called. This made her wonder if something was wrong.

Something was.

Her brother got right to the point. "Mom is leaving Dad."

"What? Oh my God, why?"

Max took in a quick breath. "You know why."

"I really don't." Her mind was spinning. She remembered the phone call, at Christmas. "Is this about that woman who called the house?"

His voice was resigned when Max said, "He's been cheating on her for 30 years, Honey."

Our girl's stomach churned with the sudden nausea that truth can sometimes trigger.

"You don't know that," she said.

"No, Honey, YOU don't know that. Everybody else sure knows. Everybody in town."

Honey tried to process what she'd just heard. She felt a surge of resentment for her brother, who was the bearer of this bad news. But then it occurred to her that because Max and Dad had always been at odds, Honey had been free to claim the role of favorite. A realization rose up: their dad had always referred to her—in public and in private—as "my number one child," with little Max standing right there.

"Where do you think he was, all those nights?" Max said. "When he only came home at dawn, to shower and change for work?"

~ ~ ~

Honey called her dad to talk about the breakup of his marriage and what would come next, but he never picked up. So Honey phoned her mother, who answered every time.

"How are you doing, Mom?" Honey asked. "Are you enjoying your new place?"

Honey knew that Mom had moved to a ratty rental on the wrong side of Tallahassee, because Dad continued to resist the idea of a divorce settlement.

"It's just lovely. I've started a little garden out back. Flowers, mostly, and some vegetables."

"I didn't know you liked gardening."

Honey's Mom could have said *Yeah, I never got much chance, since we moved so often*. Instead, what she said was, "Oh yes, it's fun to have the time to do it, now that I'm on my own."

"I'm just now understanding how badly Dad treated you," Honey said. "I was blind to it."

She heard her mom heave a breath. "You always put him on a pedestal."

"Well, you hoisted him up there," Honey said. She instantly regretted saying it.

But Samantha burst out laughing, which our girl didn't expect.

"I sure did," Mom chuckled. "I sure did."

"I worry about you," Honey said, and even as the words passed her lips, she realized that she'd never expressed concern like this before—not for her mom.

Her mother's voice was choked with emotion when she said, "Thanks, sweetheart. Thanks for saying that." She took a moment to steady herself, and then Mom said, "It is what it is, right?"

~ ~ ~

The second time a man touched her inappropriately in the workplace, Honey wasn't expecting it. And she certainly wasn't expecting it from Leprechaun Skippy, the QC guy at the printing plant.

The two of them were well into their ninth year of doing press checks together, so they'd developed an easy rapport. Communication seemed to be good, though they had an unspoken difference of opinion about drinking on the job. Sometimes Honey thought she smelled liquor on Skippy's breath, but everything else about him seemed unchanged. She'd watch him, to make sure. His eyes were clear, his memory sharp and his gait, if anything, less jumpy as Skippy scurried between Honey in the client booth and the men who ran the press.

After years of close observation, our girl knew the culture of the men on the Exceptional Press work floor. She knew that if Skippy had a substance problem that impacted safety, the rest of the crew wouldn't stand for it. Every man out there had stories of close calls, injuries—or worse. So Honey let them take the lead, when it came to Skippy's nipping.

Had she smelled liquor on his breath the night he ran his hands up the outside of her thighs, from her knees to her hips? She couldn't remember. She'd been sitting on a high stool in the client booth, facing him, as she had a hundred times before, because they were engaged in conversation. But this time as Skippy stood and walked past, he stopped and turned. He reached out and touched her like that.

"No!" Honey jerked away from him so violently that she lost her balance on the stool. She threw out an arm to steady herself on the light board, and proofs cascaded across the floor.

Skippy stood blinking, like he'd just awakened from a dream.

"What the fuck, man?" Honey was already grabbing her jacket as she made a beeline for the door.

Behind her, she heard him say, "Uh-oh."

Honey slammed the door behind her when she left, but the sound was lost in the cacophony of the presses. Nobody noticed.

~ ~ ~

After what happened with Skippy, no one would blame Honey if she became less open. After all, if she couldn't trust her own instincts, what could she trust?

Perspective is a hopeful thing, however, and by the next morning, Honey had accumulated enough of it that she felt confident in how she'd handle Skippy. That afternoon, she called him from her Touchstone office across town. She knew his shift started at three.

137

She also knew that the two of them were scheduled to work together that night, for the next press form that would require quality approvals.

She waited while they paged him, and soon he was on the line.

"It's me, Honey Malone. Here's what's going to happen. Either you go to your boss right now and tell him what you did last night, or I'll tell him. What's it going to be?"

Skippy was considering his options. Honey gave him all the time he needed.

"I'll tell him," Skippy said.

"Good. Have him call me, to let me know next steps. Right now, I don't have any inclination to go out there tonight for form four. Will you tell him to call?"

"Oh, Mother Mary," he whispered, and then he hurried to say, "Okay, okay!"

But Honey should have known that the incident would turn into a big hairy deal. Skippy's boss told his boss, who told his team lead, who told the plant manager, who called Honey's superior, Casey. She suspected this because her boss had closed his office door to take a series of urgent calls, and when it opened, Casey walked straight over to her. All the walls in the place were glass, so she could see him coming. He looked angry. He didn't often look like that.

Casey stopped at the threshold of her open office door, holding a folded sheet of paper in front of him. Maybe the paper contained bullet points on how to have this conversation.

"I heard what happened at the plant last night. I'm so sorry. Are you okay?"

"I'm okay. A little rattled, to be honest."

"This guy, this Skipper guy—" Casey made a face. "He won't be around for a while, if ever. He's made the decision to go into rehab."

Honey nodded. That seemed reasonable.

"Expect a call from the plant manager here in a minute," Casey said, and they both looked at the phone on her desk. Honey felt embarrassed to be having this discussion with her boss. He'd probably spoken with the corporate crisis-management team, or something. *I had this handled*, Honey thought. *Oh, well.*

"He'll apologize on behalf of his team," Casey was saying.

They heard voices from the hallway, and he stepped into the room, then reached back and closed the door.

"You don't have to go out there for press checks," the boss said. "Until you feel totally comfortable with it. Right now, you should go home. Take a few days. There's counseling available, too, if you feel like you want it."

That seemed reasonable, too.

~ ~ ~

One weekend in August, Honey drove up to Tallahassee to spend some time with her mom. As she followed GPS to her mother's rental house 12 miles from town, Honey turned off the main road onto Sycamore Pond Road, and her heart dropped. There were no sycamores. There were no trees at all, and the road soon became rutted gravel and sand. She saw small frame houses on large, untended lots. She saw chain link fencing that held back raging Rottweilers. Across one sunbaked field, she saw a rusted camper trailer that looked like a meth lab, complete with a skull-and-crossbones symbol painted in black on the door.

Three more miles down Sycamore, a curve in the road led Honey to a more serene view. A clear stream ran by the road now, and the vista opened to reveal a carpet of deep green grass, and a pristine lake that was ringed with oaks, maples and sycamore trees. In the leafy shade, Honey saw it: a little blue cabin on the water, with a white picket fence and flowers in the window boxes. Mom's rental place.

Once you get there, it doesn't look half bad.

Honey saw her mother in a floaty dress the color of bluebells, waving from the railing of a deep front porch, smiling that signature Samantha smile. She looked tanned and toned, probably from working in the garden. Honey waved back through the windshield. She pulled in next to Mom's Honda, and had just enough time to cut off the engine before her mother snatched open the driver's door.

They stood in the yard and shared a long embrace. Mom put her hands on Honey's shoulders, and pulled back to look into her daughter's face. Then she came back in for another hug, and whispered *I'm so glad you came.* It had been 10 years since the two of them had been alone together without Max around.

"You look beautiful," Honey said, "That shorter haircut suits you. And your arms! What are these, triceps? Damn." She opened the trunk. "Hey, I brought you something." Out of its nest of bubble wrap she pulled a big glass vase, and handed it to her mother.

"It's so heavy," Mom said. "It must be lead crystal. Thanks, sweetie, I've got the perfect place for it."

Honey got her overnight bag, Mom carried the vase, and they walked up the path toward the front door. Honey heard the hum of bumblebees, and caught the scent of honeysuckle from the hedge. The shade of the front porch felt 20 degrees cooler. Two tempting rocking chairs faced the lake.

"What a sweet house," Honey said.

"I've done my best with it. Come in, come in, we'll get some iced tea."

Honey hadn't expected much from the interior of the cabin, so she was surprised to see shiplap walls, freshly painted white, the ceiling above clear blue. A crystal chandelier hung over a round dining table, which held a bright blue vase of fresh-cut flowers.

"What is this, now?" Honey looked around, blinking. "Am I in the cover shoot for *Home Design* magazine or something? You told me when you moved in that it was dark."

"It was. So something had to be done about it." Mom placed the crystal vase on the round table and transferred the water and flowers from the blue container. She stepped back to admire it.

"Look! Look how nice that vase is, there."

"You think so?" Honey asked. "Well, I've got five more at home just like it. They're yours if you want 'em."

"I do want them! Thanks." Mom walked over to the tidy kitchenette, put the blue vase on the counter, and opened the refrigerator to get the tea.

"Stunning," Honey said, taking in the decor. "Those curtains. This sofa. Just gorge."

"Look around," Mom said, and her daughter visited the pristine black-and-white tiled bath, then peeked into the small bedrooms, which were looking sweet with handmade quilts on the beds and mounds of pillows covered in crisp hemstitched percale. One window provided a wide view of the lake, and looking out, Honey saw a swing suspended beneath the oaks.

"This place is amazing," she said. Her Mom had been standing at the counter, and seemed surprised when Honey ran up to hug her from behind. "Oh Mom, it's a showplace! How did you do it?"

Her mother looked back over her shoulder, green eyes flashing. "I had a plan."

"Ooh, tell me more! Can we take our tea out to the porch?"

Her mother smiled. "You bet. I can sit out there for hours, looking at that lake."

~ ~ ~

Samantha Malone, it seemed, had made the decision five years earlier that she would leave her husband, once her kids were reliably self-sufficient. She'd squirreled away money right up until the day when she'd finally reached the limit of her patience with the man. Samantha's best friend in the neighborhood knew of Samantha's plan—and she knew too how much she admired Samantha's taste. This friend contracted with Honey's mom to oversee renovation of a decrepit cabin on Sycamore Pond, which was to become a vacation place and Airbnb. The friend allowed Honey's mother to live there, rent-free, to ensure that every last detail of the little place was perfect.

"I'm finding that interior design pays pretty well." Mom looked out at the water. "And good thing. Your father cut me off, froze the bank accounts, cancelled my credit cards. I had to use all that money I'd saved to engage an attorney that's as much of a bulldog as his. Your dad's still living in the big house, but all things considered, I've been okay."

"Max says he was cheating on you for years."

Mom's eyes widened at this bold statement from her daughter. A lifetime of beautifully papered walls had been constructed around this mother's emotions, after all. But Honey saw a little smile at the corner of her mother's mouth.

"He said he was working, and I believed him."

"You wanted to believe him," Honey said, but her mom shook her head.

"No, I actually did. Until the day I didn't." Mom reached out and squeezed Honey's hand. "Denial is a powerful thing. It exists for a reason, you know?"

~ ~ ~

The two women took a walk out back, where Honey got a tour of the raised garden beds. Some were for growing vegetables, and some held flowers. Samantha walked down the center aisle, pointing out what grew where. "Broccoli, carrots, beets and collards. Over there, muscadines and strawberries. In that one, I'm trying loquats, and figs."

"I don't even know what a loquat is," Honey said.

"Oh, it's an interesting fruit. Tangy on the outside and sweet on the inside—sweet like mango, with a little floral under-taste that's nice. I use it for chutney, and it makes a nice tart." Mom stopped to show her daughter six small bushes with skinny leaves. "Loquat's great for Florida because it can tolerate full sun."

"I'm not seeing any fruit," Honey said.

Mom laughed. "Yeah, it'll be three or four years before they fruit. They become trees, Honey, really full and big. So I'll have to transplant them further down by the lake, before I move."

"But why are you putting in all this time and energy? For something you won't ever see, full-grown?"

"Sometimes it's not about tasting the fruit," Mom said. "It's more about setting the seed. It's more about the process, sometimes. Making it strong, you know, so it can face whatever's coming." Honey's mother looked out across the water. "Maybe there will always be loquats at Sycamore Pond, from now on."

The breeze off the lake lifted her hair, and Mom sighed.

"I needed this so much, Honey. I'd almost forgotten who I was, you know? I've learned a lot about myself, from all this, from everything that's happened with your Dad. It's been a pretty interesting journey, I guess, for me." She looked over at her daughter, and Honey saw raw confidence in her eyes when Mom said, "And this is just the beginning."

~ ~ ~

Honey felt so happy for her mother. That lasted until the afternoon heat drove them inside into the air conditioning—and when she closed the front door, our girl saw a portable security bar waiting there. A wave of anger swept up as Honey imagined her mother living alone and vulnerable, her nearest neighbor a likely meth lab.

Mom saw her looking at the steel bar. "The security system gets installed in November. My friend will save money if her nephew does the work, but we have to wait until he's free over Thanksgiving."

Well, that's too long, Honey thought.

On her way out of Tallahassee, she stopped by a storefront and ordered a full security system to be installed at her mom's rental. The sales rep balked at her urgent deadline, but when our girl paid extra, they went out to Sycamore Pond that very same day. Within a week, Mom's friend had sent a check for reimbursement.

~ ~ ~

In her tenth year at Touchstone, Honey made the decision to enroll in the five-day Brilliant Autumn photography workshop, which was to be held in early November at a nature center in the Smoky Mountains of Tennessee. This seemed like a promising idea for Honey at the time. *Vacation AND photography education in the field? Ideal.*

Our girl was determined to see if she could learn more about the camera equipment that she'd carried with her for years, and the colorful Brilliant Autumn brochure claimed one instructor for every three students, an encouraging ratio for somebody who had a lot to learn. Honey was comfortable shooting portraits—she'd spent a lot of time learning about lighting, through trial and error—but she had no clue how to capture the beauty of nature. Surely that would be a worthwhile thing to learn.

Honey did not have a close relationship with the outdoors. She'd never been an athlete, a camper or a hiker. She preferred a nice couch and a book, to be honest, or a blues club with good music and cold beer. But her mom was outdoorsy. Her brother, too. Eager to prove that she possessed a genetic predisposition to actually appreciate nature, despite a life of interior-oriented sloth thus far, Honey forged ahead full steam with her plan to discover a more outdoorsy side of herself.

That time of year, the hills would be alive with Brilliant Autumn color. Honey learned that there were two waterfalls within walking distance of the nature center where formal classes would be held, and she learned that vans were available to take the photographers further afield on group expeditions that required little strenuous climbing.

Perfect, Honey thought. This vacation would be the ideal balance of relaxation, nature and education. Well worth the money Honey invested in tuition fees, the Airbnb rental, and the boatload of equipment that she was expected to bring along when she met with the top instructors of landscape photography in the southeastern United States. "All skill levels welcomed," the brochure said. *Excellent.*

~ ~ ~

The night before the first session, Honey laid everything out on the bed in the spare bedroom at her sweet rental cabin in "downtown" Townsend. She went through the checklist, to make sure that she was properly prepared for the next day's early-morning photo shoot.

Camera – DSLR, mirrorless, or point-and-shoot
Memory cards
Interchangeable lenses, including wide, telephoto, and macro
Lens hoods
Camera manual
Tripod
Tripod head with L-bracket
Batteries and charger
Remote shutter release
Polarizing filter
Neutral density filters
Graduated ND filters
Flashlight or headlamp
Lens blower and/or cleaner
Camera bag or belt system
Laptop
Laptop charger
Card reader
USB drive

Honey managed to fit it all in the backpack she'd purchased, but barely, and she'd been forced to hang some of the bulkier equipment off the pack's outside hooks. But now all she had to do was slip it on in the morning and race out the door to catch the mountain sunrise at the Brilliant Autumn field session.

~ ~ ~

The alarm was jarringly loud there at the Airbnb, but it needed to be. Historically, Honey was not an early riser. She set some strong coffee to brew, brushed her teeth and pulled her hair back in a ponytail. She didn't bother with makeup. After all, she wasn't there to impress anyone—she was there to learn, dammit. And who knows? She might get used to the natural look. Maybe she'd discover her inner Earth Mother, out there in the wild. *This is how people learn*, she thought with more than a little self-satisfaction. *It's good to try new things.*

Honey had been told to dress in layers, so she started that morning with long underwear made of tightly woven polyester. *Nothing like trapping your aura right from the start*, she thought, and then she reached for polar-fleece socks and a long-sleeved thermal tee. Her jeans and a sweater came next, then the new hiking boots, the heavy scarf, the knit beanie, the headlamp and the down jacket.

Moving with all the grace of the Michelin Man, Honey lurched down the hallway toward the back bedroom, giant Frankenstein boots booming against the floorboards. At the end of the hall, her backpack waited on the bed, looking for all the world like a dead body in the pre-dawn gloom.

At the outfitter store where she'd bought the pack, the salesman had chatted with her long enough to learn that Honey had never experienced "the outdoors" as anything other than a concept. He strongly encouraged her to practice getting in and out of the gear once it was fully loaded, and that was Honey's intention as she flipped on the bedroom light.

~ ~ ~

First she couldn't lift it, so that was a problem. Honey realized soon enough that if she used both hands and flung her weight backwards, she could drag the dead carcass of the 30-pound backpack to the edge of the bed. Her idea was, since the thing was on the mattress, it was already halfway up to where it needed to be: her shoulders. So if she could just find a way to use her legs to provide some jack-power momentum, she could hoist the backpack up another two feet, swing it around, and get one shoulder strap on. The rest, she figured, would be cake.

Too bad there were no hidden cameras at that particular Airbnb. Viewers of such footage would learn just how many attempts might be made to hoist and swing, hoist and swing, one arm flailing blindly to hook a strap that remained steadfastly elusive. That video would reveal how many times Honey spun around, fighting for balance, cursing the many layers of thick clothing that put the kibosh on any proper bending of arms—a crucial element of success, as it turns out. The footage would document just how valiantly our girl tried to prevent damage to thousands of dollars' worth of delicate equipment as she lost her grip during a turn, and the backpack plummeted to the floor.

Sweating in her thermal layers, dizzy from the spinning and breathless from exertion so early in the day, Honey pulled the headlamp off her nose and moved it back into place on her forehead. This action proved a handy way to keep her bangs, now damp and tangled, from falling into her eyes, now that she'd lost the beanie cap down the back of her jacket. With the ledge of her bangs hovering at the perimeter of her vision like a hairy visor, Honey leaned back against the bedroom wall to catch her breath and reassess. *I can't take much more time with this. I don't want to be late, on the first day of class.*

The backpack was now on the floor next to the bed. Mocking her, like dead bodies will. She'd had some success in getting herself out of tough situations in the past, so maybe that was the reason that Honey felt so confident, right then. She formed a plan to get down onto the floor next to the backpack, slide her arms into its padded straps, and then use the side of the bed as a way to pull up. *I've seen babies do that, pull up on furniture. How hard can it be?*

Our girl dropped down onto the floor next to the backpack, turning it like a pig on a spit, because she knew by then that it was important for the straps to be easily accessible. She hadn't considered the fact that she still could not bend her arms, however, and a moment of disillusioned panic ensued. Pivoting quickly in her strategy, Honey set a new measure of success: one arm in one shoulder strap. Then pull up on the bed.

As Honey was to learn, it's not easy to lift 30 pounds off the floor, even with a strap involved. She stripped all the covers off the bed trying to pull up, frantically grabbing at them with all the dedication of a swimmer about to disappear over the brink of Niagara Falls. At the last second before success, as she got one leg under her and made the attempt to stand, a lock of her hair got trapped in the rubber underbelly of the straining strap—and in that moment of stark decision between physical agony and triumph, Honey chose victory.

She stood—she didn't stand tall, but by God she stood—holding the backpack over her shoulder by one strap. She was heaving for breath, her first three layers of clothing soaked with sweat. A clump of her own hair rested next to her hiking boot. But she had lifted the backpack. Now she could get the blasted thing out to the car, at least, without having to drag it.

~ ~ ~

There was no coffee waiting at the parking lot where the photography students gathered that morning at 5:30, so Honey was glad that she'd brought her own, in an insulated mug. Her headlamp made her look like an underaged miner, and if she looked down, the whole mechanism would slip down onto her nose. She clanked when she walked, from the equipment hanging from her pack that was banging into the tripod, but by golly she'd gotten out of bed at 4:30 in the morning on a vacation day, hadn't she? She'd halfway shouldered the backpack, hadn't she? She was a trooper, obviously.

Maybe that'll become my trail name: Trooper.

It was 28 degrees that morning in the pitch-black parking lot, and up the hill, two vans idled. Honey relied on the light of her head lamp to guide her as she clinked and clanked up a steep path composed of loose gravel, headed for a group of shadowy figures. Their head-lamp beams jerked and swooped in the dark, and she could hear them talking as she approached. They all seemed to be men, and they all seemed to know each other.

"Rich! I haven't seen you since Boulder."

"Jim, glad to see you made it again this year."

"Randy, did you get my email? I tried that Photoshop trick."

"Brian, great to see you. Did I hear you got the cover of *Field and Stream*?"

"Scottie, come meet my buddy Manuel—he's still using Canon, but we don't hold that against him, eh?"

Honey, winded from the treacherous uphill crabwalk with 30 pounds of weight suspended from one shoulder, stood away from the men to catch her breath. In the frigid darkness of that lonely mountainside, under that cold moonless sky, they didn't seem to notice her, which was good. There was no way she could mingle, no way she could join in with conversations like the ones she'd just heard. She certainly didn't have the photographic chops to get any of her images on the cover *of Field and Stream*. Honey was just a newbie, and she knew it.

All the moisture that had accumulated in her soaking-wet layers had flash-frozen, there on the hill in that gusty wind. She'd forgotten her gloves in the car, so Honey clamped her frozen fingers around the metal coffee cup as the rest of the muscles in her body shook violently in an effort to generate heat. She was quite thankful to be cloaked by darkness. The chattering *ching-ding-ding* from her array of trembling metal soon betrayed her presence, however, and somebody said her name.

"Honey Malone? Is that you, over there?"

This must be Bertrand, the organizer of the workshop. The light from his head lamp shone down on a clipboard.

"Right here," she said. Since her feet were made of ice inside the blocky boots, she stumbled as she stepped toward him—but like the gazelle she was, Honey caught herself.

"Careful," Bertrand said. "There's wet rocks under the leaves."

Honey took a second step, slipped on a wet rock under the leaves, and toppled like a tree, planting face-first in the ground. *Bam*. Down she went. Her headlamp smashed against her forehead. Pain ricocheted up her left leg, then back down again to her foot, settling with maximum agony at the point where her fibula met the top of her hiking boot. Her shoulders were pinned to the ground by the weight of the backpack, which meant that her face was mashed six inches deep into the Brilliant Autumn leaves. The brochure had promised that the workshop would bring her closer to nature—and sure enough.

"Uh-oh," a man said, "she fell." He didn't move to help. He was just voicing an observation.

"You okay, there?" Bertrand quickly came closer in the darkness, as if he were managing the rocks and slick evil leaves with the uncanny balance of a mountain goat with night vision.

"Mmff," Honey said into the bed of mulch.

Bertrand had reached her. He leaned down, and his headlamp blinded her as she tried to look up at him. She turned her face back into the leaves, where it was blessedly darker. The pain was intense. *My leg*, she thought. *Wow, wow, ow.*

The instructor leaned closer. "You think you need some help getting up?"

The pain was so bad that tears were leaking from Honey's eyes. "Just give me a minute," she said, voice muffled by the foliage.

The photography pro stood up. "Okay," he said cheerfully, and turned away. "Hey now, is that Barry Fleming I see? How you been, man?" Bertrand skipped away across the boulders to greet his buddy. "How was the drive up from Atlanta?"

The pain was crazy bad, and Honey could barely catch her breath. Her mouth was filled with Brilliant Autumn, and the business end of the headlamp had broken away from its band and rested like a dead bird next to her cheek. She was grateful that the darkness was complete, because that meant the assembled guys couldn't see the blood that ran freely from the deep scratch on her forehead caused by the broken headgear. They couldn't see the tears that dappled the leaves around her, as she made a futile attempt to rise. *Holy shit, I've broken my leg*, she thought. *I haven't even been here five minutes.*

More cars pulled up, and Honey laid still in the frigid dark and listened to old friends calling out to each other. Soon more heavy steps were coming closer through the crunchy leaves, and she heard somebody say, "Hey, Bert, who's that, there on the ground?"

"She's gathering herself," Bertrand said coolly.

"She fell," a deadpan voice explained.

"Huh. She new?"

"First timer," Bertrand confirmed. "But at least she shoots Nikon."

~ ~ ~

She drove herself to the nearest Urgent Care clinic, which was a 40-minute drive away in the bustling metropolis of Toad Bottom, but at that hour of the morning, Honey was the only customer. She'd bruised a rib where the coffee cup had smashed against her chest during the fall, and an X-ray revealed that she had indeed fractured a bone in her leg. Long after sunrise, our girl drove herself back to the rental place in Townsend, with her torso wrapped in an Ace bandage, a supersized Band-Aid pasted to her forehead, and her left leg encased in a Big Black Boot of Shame that extended all the way from her toes to her knee. It looked like something that the survivor of a car accident would wear.

Honey's foot was black and blue, and bruises were beginning to bloom from her ankle to her knee. "That's some impressive swelling," the doctor had said, and Honey was forced to agree. She'd never fractured a bone before. *Surely it'll heal quickly, once the swelling goes down.* According to the doctor, she'd spend six weeks in the boot, two months in an ankle brace, and after three or four months of physical therapy, she'd be good as new. Good as new, in six months to a year.

Having wasted two grand on the photography workshop, 100% percent of which would continue without her, Honey hobbled into her Airbnb and got on the phone. She called her friends in Florida, to see if anybody wanted five days free in a charming Smoky Mountain cabin.

Nicole and Margo arrived the next day. They nursed her, and brought her ice packs and Advil, and helped her inch her way down the steps to the fire pit, where they made s'mores and drank wine and had a wonderful little vacation together, looking up at the stars at night, and sleeping late every morning.

Honey never took a single photo of the Brilliant Autumn sunrise in the Smokies. But she caught some excellent candids of her girls around the fire.

~ ~ ~

"I wanted you to be the second to know," Max said to Honey. "I'm engaged."

No wonder he'd called her at the office. This was big news, though she wasn't surprised. "Bro! That's wonderful. Did you get Peggy a ring, and everything?"

"The whole nine yards," Max confirmed. "Got down on one knee in an alpine meadow when we went hiking on Saturday, and popped the question."

"I couldn't be happier for you. You called Mom first, right?"

"Well, sure."

Honey was somehow heartened that her brother was taking this step. She never thought that Max would be the sort of guy to get tied down. "I thought we were united in our embrace of serial monogamy," she said. "What changed?"

Max chuckled. "Yeah, that's a fine approach until you actually fall in love with somebody. You'll find out."

"Yeah, probably not."

"You just wait," Max said. "Mark my words."

"You're just caught in the bliss of the moment, bud. How about Dad, though? Does he know?"

Max hesitated, and then he said, "He doesn't have to know. Even if I called him, he wouldn't answer."

"Yeah, that's probably true. He doesn't answer MY calls, and—"

"—and you're his favorite," Max said.

The Malone kids could milk a good joke. They both laughed at that one, old as it was.

"Well, I assume he's not invited to the wedding," Honey said. "But maybe he'd want to at least know you're getting married. Could you, I don't know, send him a note or something, in the mail?"

"I could," her brother said, "if I knew where he was living these days."

After Mitchell Malone had been forced to give up half his assets to Samantha in the divorce, he'd left the big house in Tallahassee. Now, nobody knew where he was staying.

~ ~ ~

In January of each year, Touchstone held a day-long event called the Annual Retreat. Let's note that this event was held in the conference room, so the term "retreat" was not used to imply any sort of "getaway" or "respite," but was employed more in the sense of "forced fellowship." Other than this one day of the year, the Touchstone creative staff never interacted with anyone other than themselves. These men ate at their own table in the cafeteria. They'd avoid passing someone from Advertising in the hall, if they could. They never set foot in Operations.

Honey loved the Annual Retreat, and she might have been the only employee who did, including the leaders who'd instituted it. Strong coffee was available throughout the day in an effort to keep attendees alert, and lame icebreakers routinely failed to wipe the dour frowns off the faces of the professionals gathered. Fresh ideas were met with snark and cynicism. But the concept of it—to bring together employees at all levels to learn about customers, spark enthusiasm and build team spirit—was irresistible to our eager businesswoman.

Team spirit was hard to come by in an enterprise that had been intentionally organized to stratify individuals by discipline area. Considering the clearly visible boundaries and secure fencing that surrounded the creatives, shared enthusiasm wasn't an easy ask at Touchstone. *But every little bit helps,* Honey thought. *Let's at least try.* For years, she brought to the event two platters of home-baked cookies, which proved a hit with the creative team. They wouldn't meet her eye in the hallway, but they'd eat her sweets just fine.

Honey's favorite session occurred during the closing hour of the Retreat: the Featured Speaker segment, where an actual outsider would enter the room to offer wisdom, inspiration or counsel. One year, the guest speaker was an organizational behavioral scientist from MIT. Bartholomew Wagner, PhD, agreed to speak to the Touchstone group only if he could observe the entire day's antics—and Casey had agreed.

The good doctor did a great job of staying in the background that day. He himself took full advantage of the strong coffee, Honey noted. If Dr. Wagner made notes about his observations, she never saw it. Our girl watched him, though, and she saw that Dr. Wagner paid close attention during the brainstorming exercise, where the one rule was that "there are no bad ideas." Perhaps the visitor noticed that every time Honey or another woman came up with an idea, some man was quick to shoot it down.

When it was time for the Featured Speaker segment, Dr. Wagner stood before the group, then waited patiently until he had everyone's full attention.

He reached into his pocket and drew out a napkin.

He unwrapped a cookie and held it high.

"Never equate optimism with ignorance. Cynicism, at its heart, is cowardice."

~ ~ ~

Ten years. A long time to work at one place.

For a decade, Casey's bosses had big plans for him. And he had big plans for Honey. Too bad he didn't mention the Touchstone corporate strategy to her, though, because she probably would have said *Print is dead, wake up*. But he never shared his plan, nor did he ask for her views. Honey and her colleagues had to find out slowly, during those final years, that the company couldn't pivot fast enough. Leaders had set a course that was driven by reader appreciation of print, such a core belief that their strategy felt unassailable. Across all of the conglomerate's newspapers and magazines, paid-subscription numbers plummeted. Advertisers bailed for digital in droves.

When it came time to lay somebody off as part of a digital transformation, a well-compensated print-manufacturing director would be the first to go. It was sensible, really. A sound business decision, nothing more.

Honey tried to take it well. Casey had given her six months' notice, so she was prepared financially. She still felt empty inside, though, and then even emptier as the six months passed, as she had to face up to how much of her identity had been tied to the job. She was the President of her state industry association, for God's sake! She had Director in her title!

Ego, Honey thought. *It's probably common among businesspeople.* Now she was looking for another job at the Director level, armed with niche skills that were hardly in demand, and she was 35 years old with no husband, and thus no husband's salary to fall back on. Despite the face she put on it, Honey felt stunned and a little adrift.

Maybe that's why she didn't comprehend the impact of that last meeting with Casey, when he'd told her that her last paycheck would be much larger than usual. Honey figured it was an exit bonus, and she'd appreciated the thought. She'd thanked him, and shook his hand. There was egg salad on his tie.

That was the last time Honey saw Casey. Our girl would be an old lady when she found out that forward-thinking Touchstone had offered an old-fashioned pension plan back then—and since she'd worked there for ten years, Honey had left fully vested. And according to the plan documentation that arrived in her mailbox decades later, the amount of the monthly cash benefit was based on one thing: the final paycheck.

BOSS 4: pretty preston

Honey's title: Director of Print Manufacturing, National Condition Foundation

If any enterprise is set to flourish, it's a national non-profit that's dedicated to managing a health condition that nearly every old person eventually gets. Honey's next employer, the National Condition Foundation, was the kind of place where money gushed in at high momentum, courtesy of a network of well-maintained pipes and tubing.

It was true that the organization had deep pockets. It was also true that their primary demographic, older Americans, still preferred print content over digital. *Condition Today* magazine, chock-full of colorful pharmaceutical advertising, was distributed free to eight million readers every month. Hundreds of millions of printed brochures and pamphlets were sent annually to doctors and medical clinics. The Condition Foundation needed a professional to manage its multi-million-dollar manufacturing budget, to negotiate print contracts, and to attend in-person press checks for the flagship magazine.

There was a great job waiting for Honey Malone—in Atlanta.

~ ~ ~

She sold her little house near the beach, and her friends threw a going-away party. But after Honey had moved to Atlanta and was alone in her sumptuous jewel box of an apartment in Buckhead, one memory of her time in Tampa Bay revealed itself surprisingly often: the face of the guy she'd been dating down there, when she'd told him that she was moving away.

That face tended to pop up in her consciousness at the oddest times, like when she did feel hopeful.

Funny, the things that persistently rise up like that, to make you wonder.

~ ~ ~

Honey's next boss was a pretty boy. So pretty, in fact, that even a seasoned woman like Honey had been taken aback. Preston Hedges was a white guy in his late 30s, tall and trim, with a dark tan that only made his perfect teeth look whiter when he graced another human with his smile. His perfection was so uncanny that a viewer might believe that they beheld a hologram of the definition of male perfection, because from every angle, Preston looked flawless.

She knew going in that her background was exactly what the Condition Foundation was looking for. She hadn't even tailored her resume, because her skills and experience exactly matched the job description they'd posted. Honey remembered little of the Atlanta job interview except that she'd never spent that much time sitting that close to a man who was that physically perfect. It was like being interviewed by a male model who could talk a good publishing game and had eyes like Taylor Swift.

~ ~ ~

Honey called Ashley, a college friend who had once worked at *Condition Today* magazine as a designer, and the person who had alerted Honey about the open Director of Manufacturing position.

"How do you work for somebody that handsome?" Honey asked.

Ashley didn't answer right at first. Then she said, "He doesn't look so pretty, after a while."

"Oh, so I'll get used to it?"

Again, Ashley hesitated. "I don't want to jinx it," she said. Ashley was aware that, as a 10-year veteran of the dying world of print, Honey didn't have many career options. "You'll do just fine with Pretty Preston," Ashley said, and Honey felt heartened to hear it.

In her initial weeks on the job, Honey would find herself holding her breath when she was in the presence of her new boss—a visceral human reaction to the presence of divine perfection, that's how Honey explained it. Up until she met Preston, Honey thought she knew pretty. After all, she'd dated Trevor Bankhead for a while.

~ ~ ~

Business life was very different in Atlanta. Different and better, because in this large Southern city, Black businesspeople existed. And took charge. Sixty percent of the employees of the National Condition Foundation were people of color—and many worked in Research, the most powerful and well-respected division of the nationally-known organization.

The Research building was filled with Black medical doctors and PhDs, and their rule was clear: no member of *Condition Today*'s magazine staff, tainted as they were by advertising dollars, could step foot there. Because confidence comes from power, this line could be clearly drawn, and clearly enforced. From what Honey could see, this cohort seemed to have no time for bullshit. She assumed every businessperson celebrated that attitude—even if they worked for a nonprofit.

~   ~   ~

Honey stood in her new office at Foundation headquarters, hanging her inspiration board. She'd brought it along when she moved, because it made her feel centered to see the familiar collection of quotes, and the photos of musicians and singers who inspired her the most. At that time in her life, Honey was a songwriter who played fingerstyle guitar and sang contralto with good pitch. She was a woman, too, of course, so in her off hours, our girl sang the blues.

The inspiration board was hung at eye level, and it looked fine in its new surroundings. Then suddenly there was her boss in a striking white dress shirt, stopping at her door. "Let's talk about the print contract," Preston said. "It's coming up for renewal this time next year."

"You bet," Honey said. She followed him down the hall to his office, where his door was always closed, whether he was in there or not, the drapes over his windows drawn tight against the adrenaline traffic of I-85 hurtling past just 30 yards away.

Maybe the dim lighting was meant to prevent visitors from staring too raptly at Preston's handsomeness. Honey looked down to take notes on her laptop. There in the casino darkness, the boss told her about the current printer of *Condition Today* magazine, a large vendor with locations across the country called Mainstay Press. Quality was good, Preston told her. There might be a small issue with the way the mailing labels were affixed as copies came off the binding machine, but overall, the printer got top marks.

"You'll be going up to Virginia for press check in two weeks," Preston said. "Get to know the sales rep."

Preston handed her a business card. *Dudley Dawson, Vice President of Sales.*

No way. This joker. Honey got a chill, thinking of the ill-fated evening in New York City, four years earlier—the evening that had not included the promised Le Bernardin.

"Will do," she said, trying to modulate her voice into something that didn't contain a sense of dread. She took a breath. "I'll take a look at that finishing line, too."

"Yeah, I expect you'll be too busy in the client booth. There won't be time to get out on the floor."

"We'll see about that," Honey replied. She thought that the boss would be pleased to hear that she was the kind of person who'd take initiative. But instead, he frowned and looked away.

~ ~ ~

It was Christmastime at the Malone's—sans Dad.

The divorce was history, now, and Samantha was living large, happily ensconced back at casa grande in Tallahassee, and the recipient of a healthy financial settlement, thanks to the bulldog attorney that Max had recommended. There was plenty of room out back for Mom's vegetable garden, and she'd planted day lilies in the raised bed by the pool.

Their mother had opened an interior design business in the state capital—and she was booked in advance for two years, thanks to recommendations from the wide range of friends she'd accumulated so quickly. Samantha had set up her office just off the front door of the house, and the multiple spare bedrooms in back provided ample storage for swatches, samples, and random collections of furniture, light fixtures, and rugs.

Honey had picked up Max and his fiancée Peggy at the airport, and when they pulled up in the driveway, Mom was waiting on the porch, like always. The short little lady stood taller and more elegant somehow, even though her cross-eyed Santa sweater was working at cross-purposes.

"Look at her," Max said. "She's thriving, I believe."

"She does look happy," Honey said.

"Was she unhappy, before?" Peggy asked, and she might have seen the siblings exchange a look.

"We all were," Max said.

Honey turned off the engine, and Mom hurried toward the car, smiling her excellent smile.

~ ~ ~

Gone were the tapestry wall hangings. Gone, the paintings of stern burghers. All this had probably joined the statue of Pan at Goodwill, Honey realized, as Mom led them through a mid-century modern that had been completely overhauled.

"This place is perfection," Peggy said. Max's bride-to-be was adorable, with a pixie haircut and a gleam of humor in her intelligent eyes. She seemed open to the experience of meeting Max's family, and was the first to pitch in when a turkey needed basting, a last-minute gift needed wrapping, or a mood needed lifting. Honey couldn't stop looking at her sparkly engagement ring, which was like something out of a Disney movie, or maybe Hallmark.

That Christmas Eve, the weather was warm. They'd gone out to the pool to have wine as the sun went down, and Honey took a few photos of the group with the riot of crazy Stargazer lilies in the background. Mom, she noticed, was smiling wide for every shot.

As darkness settled, the mood changed. The newest member of the party realized that her three companions were all looking across the deck, toward the house. Conversation had ceased.

"What happened over there?" Peggy asked, and Mom looked away.

"That's where Dad landed when he fell off the roof," Max said.

Peggy said, "That sounds like quite a story." But her companions offered no more information about the event. Max shook his head, looking down at his lap.

"We're writing our own story now," Mom said. She lifted her wineglass toward them, just as the pool lights switched on. A gleaming reflection moved across her face as she said, "Let's toast to new beginnings, what do you say?"

"Oh, I'll drink to that," Peggy, a recently engaged person, said.

"Me, too," Max said, and his eyes were on his woman.

"Absolutely," Honey said. Her first press check was scheduled for just after Christmas, her first big responsibility at her big new job. She raised her glass high. "To new beginnings."

~ ~ ~

Mainstay Press was located in the tiny town of Ruby, on the banks of a rushing river in the mountains of western Virginia, and was the area's largest employer by far. Once a month, Honey would fly to Washington D.C., rent a car, and drive three hours to the only hotel in Ruby: a lovely bed-and-breakfast that boasted an attached restaurant—the only place within 40 miles that could offer a cocktail or a steak.

The second time she met salesman Dudley Dawson, it was in the restaurant's bar. She'd finished her 72-hour quality inspection for that month's issue of *Condition Today* magazine, which had occurred in a luxurious skybox high above the plant floor. Press checks were a young person's game, since sleep came secondary to approval signoffs. Honey was tired, and ready for some sleep before her drive back to the airport the next morning. She was perched on a barstool, nursing a glass of what was billed as cabernet, when she felt a hand on her shoulder. She turned to see a very round man with a very red nose.

"I'm looking for the prettiest girl in the room," Dudley said.

"Well, goodness, you better keep looking," Honey said, and he belched out a laugh *har-har-har*. From what she could tell, he didn't recognize her as the woman who refused to order oysters at Elaine's. *Guess I'm not that memorable. Just as well.*

"Your reputation precedes you, sweetie," he said, sticking his hand out. "Dudley Dawson." That opening pretty much set the tone for the rest of the evening, which was scheduled to include dinner. Honey was tempted for a moment to feign illness, but her goal was to get to know the guy. Her boss had been clear.

Off we go, Honey thought. She shook his hand. He hadn't learned his lesson about over-gripping, but she grimaced through the pain and said nothing.

Dudley winked at her, like he was in a movie from 1943.

"Mary Ann!" he called to the hostess, snapping his fingers. "Two for dinner."

"I got us the best table," he whispered to Honey. "Wait until you see."

The restaurant had nine tables. It wasn't hard to see.

The gallant Mary Ann picked up two menus and led them the ten steps to their destination, with Dudley greeting every diner.

"You know a lot of people," Honey said as they sat.

"Yeah. Comes with the territory. Those two over there, they're clients like you. Their press check for *Sports Illustrated* starts tomorrow. And those four in the corner? Mainstay execs, visiting from corporate." Dudley smiled and sat up straighter. "And here I am, sitting with you. The prettiest woman in town."

"You gotta stop with the comments on my appearance," Honey said. She could be honest—she was the client, after all. This guy needed to know the ground rules.

"But you're a babe!" he exclaimed. "Own it, har-har."

"Just quit it, okay?"

"I'll try," the salesman said with an unctuous smile. "But it won't be easy. Let's get us a cocktail, what do you say?"

Honey felt queasy. She had flashbacks of Sugar Man as she watched Dudley knocking back glasses of vodka on ice. He had two drinks before the meal even arrived, another two during dinner, and a fifth glass while they waited for the flaming dessert he'd ordered.

Dudley Dawson was totally toasted. And Dudley liked to talk.

"My nose isn't usually this red," he volunteered at one point. He touched his beak, and winced. "Sunburn. I spent the last three days in the Florida Keys with a client. Mainstay keeps the corporate yacht down there. Great guy, known him for years. We had us some charming company on our little voyage, I can tell you that, but none of 'em would hold a candle to YOU, har-har-har."

Dudley liked to be The Man in the Know. "Mainstay is having its best year ever. A banner year, that's what they call it. And between you and me, the Condition Foundation work plays a huge part in that. Good thing we got a lock on the contract, huh? Good thing that evergreen money will keep coming in. Speaking of which, did you hear I was named Top Earner in King's Club this year?"

The VP of Sales was full of random information. But Dudley didn't seem to want to answer questions about the Mainstay plant in Ruby. When Honey brought up the bindery, he reached for his vodka.

"That finishing line needs work," Honey said, and his glass stopped on its way to his mouth.

"You don't know that," he said.

"Actually, I do. I walked the whole line. You've got ancient equipment that can't keep up with the press output. Why? It seems an easy fix. You just told me how well the plant is doing. I know you've got steady revenue coming in."

Dudley sat blinking, looking down into his glass. He took a sip. "Don't worry about it."

"There are subscriber mailing labels flying off the bindery line," Honey said. "They're all over the floor back there. It's not good, Dudley."

"Don't worry about it," he said again. This time, his tone was sharper.

Honey employed her sweetest voice. "It's my job to worry."

He busted out a belly laugh. "Har-har! Good one!"

"I'm serious. Contract renewal is coming up, and I've just expressed concern about the finishing line. That should be good information for you."

"Yeah, yeah," he said, waving a dismissive hand. "You're just new. You're only trying to prove to our buddy Preston how smart you are. That's normal. It's kinda cute, actually, when you do it like that."

I will roast your nuts for supper, Honey thought.

"Looky here!" Dudley exclaimed as the gallant Mary Ann brought dessert. "Cherries Jubilee!" He clapped his hands up in front of his face, like a child.

Mary Ann's eyes met Honey's.

"Mr. Dawson," the server said, "your glass is empty. Let's get you another drink."

~ ~ ~

Back in Atlanta the next day, our girl was called into Preston's cave-like office to give him a recap of her visit to the printing plant. She described what she'd seen on the finishing line.

"We've been using Mainstay for years," the boss said. "I can't really see that the bindery's a big problem."

"Preston, there were mailing labels piling up like snow drifts at the end of the line."

His pretty face was impassive. Displayed behind him, a photograph of his equally pretty wife.

"There are other vendors who've invested in a decent bindery line," Honey said.

"I don't know why you've got such a hard-on about this." Preston rolled his eyes. "I don't have time for negotiations. Ugh."

"You don't have to do a thing," Honey said. "Let me handle it."

"Are you kidding? You think you can do this yourself?"

"Well, sure," Honey said. *What am I, twelve years old? This is squarely in my job description.*

"Ha," he said. "Okay, Miss Negotiator. Tell you what. You get Mainstay to commit to new bindery equipment, and I'll sweeten your bonus at the end of the year."

When Honey didn't respond, the boss said, "Twenty grand in your pocket on December thirty-first."

"Okay," Honey said, "that's generous." *If I can make it happen.* She dreaded interaction with Dudley Dawson, which would be required to gain such a concession. Honey gritted her teeth, imagining it. But she was willing to try. It was her job, after all, if the provided job description was to be believed.

"You need to spend time with the rep," Preston said. "It's in your interest to get to know Dudley." He stood. The meeting was over. Preston walked with her to the door of his office, and when he opened it, light flowed in, illuminating his beautiful sun-tanned face. And his bright red nose.

"Looks like you got a little sunburn going on there," Honey said.

"Yeah," the boss said, "I spent some time in the Keys this week."

~ ~ ~

"Oh my God, Honey," Max said. Her brother's voice was shaky—and that didn't happen often. He was calling from Fort Collins, where he was climbing the tenured ladder of the Accounting School at Colorado State. Max usually sounded pretty upbeat. Tonight, he sounded like he'd been crying.

"What's wrong?" Honey asked breathlessly. "Is Mom okay?"

"She's good, she's good. It's nothing like that."

"Oh, thank God. What is it, then?"

"I went on Ancestry," Max sniffled.

"The genealogy site?"

"The genealogy site," Max confirmed. He took a ragged breath. "Honey, I don't know how to soften this, so I'll just tell you. We have three half-siblings."

This revelation struck Honey dumb. Her mind raced to re-shape her father's history, and their family's, yet again.

"Fucking Dad," she said.

Max barked out a bitter laugh. "Yeah, that's the truth. Seems like he was fucking his way across the United States. We've got a half-brother in Virginia, and a half-sister and half-brother here in Colorado. And that's just the ones we know about."

In that moment, Honey's dwindling appreciation of her father curdled into something dark. Max had seen through Dad's bullshit since he was a small child. Max had Dad's number. He'd known him, all along. No wonder their father never liked Max.

And no wonder he DID like me, Honey thought. *I never questioned him.* Her heart sank with this realization, and more implications joined the race in her head.

"Does Mom know?" she asked.

"Why don't you ask her?"

"No way. Ignorance is bliss, in this situation."

"I suppose," Max said. His voice was sad.

Maybe the discovery of three half-siblings is a happy revelation in some families, but for the Malone kids, this news felt like bad news. From Honey's perspective, there was an element of sorrow to the whole situation. Those three children never knew their dad. And those who did know him, like Honey, did not exult in hearing the news of the man's latest hurtful actions. Small wonder she felt shook.

From Max's perspective: "He could've worn a condom, jeez."

~ ~ ~

Honey's goal that year was to get Dudley Dawson to agree to install upgraded bindery equipment at the Mainstay printing plant in Ruby. So she did what she had to do to make this happen: spend time with him. The sales VP often stopped by the client suite during her press checks, to look through the open door with that leering smile of his, so the next time he did, Honey called over, "Come on in for a second, Dudley. Let's talk."

"Happy to do so!" He moved fluidly for such a big man. Dudley stepped inside and clicked the door shut behind him.

The client suite at Mainstay was quite dramatic, compared to the little room at Exceptional Press down in Tampa. In this large, darkened space, sound-dampened by thick carpeting and tufted-fabric walls, the focus of the show was the brilliant scene that beckoned from the twenty-foot-wide observation window. It overlooked the three-acre plant floor and offered an astonishingly well-lit view of 24/7 manufacturing and American commerce. Seven complex web presses whirred, forklifts scurried, and workers in jumpsuits and hard hats zipped through the vast space on Segways, using special lanes marked on the concrete in bright pink. Beyond the banks of presses, vast stacks of paper rolls extended all the way to the back wall, a quarter of a mile away. Any businessperson would be inspired by the sight, unless that person happened to care about sustainability to any extent.

Honey stepped away from the neutral-gray bank of light tables and indicated to Dudley that she'd meet him in the lounge area that was arranged between them. Our girl stopped at the kitchenette and poured coffee into two Mainstay-branded cups.

As they sat in armchairs in front of a coffee table the size of Spain, Dudley nudged his chair closer to hers. He reached out for his coffee, which rested on a large sheet of paper that held 16 pages of colorful magazine images, from the prior client's press run. Dudley moved his cup and lifted the top sheet. He held it out for Honey to see.

"Nice," he said, low in his throat. "I love it when a beautiful woman wants to be alone with me, and THIS is what she's got waiting."

Honey's stomach flipped as she looked at what he held. The last client in the suite had represented the *Sports Illustrated* production team, and had been performing quality checks on the annual swimsuit issue. A sea of bulbous breasts greeted Honey's gaze, and more perky butts than she'd ever seen collected in one place.

"Look-a here at this blond," Dudley said, holding the sheet closer, his index finger resting on a nipple. "She looks just like you!"

Honey reached out and ripped the sheet from his hands. She stood, grabbed the other papers off the table, and crammed them in the trash.

"Maybe you should have wine, not coffee," Dudley said. "You seem a little stressed."

Give me strength, Honey thought. She sat down and took a breath. The fact was, she wasn't at Exceptional Press anymore. This client suite smelled like old money, not hot plastic. The coffee in her cup was fragrant, brewed from fresh-ground beans, and she took a sip.

Honey didn't need to formulate conversation at this point, because she knew that Dudley couldn't stay silent for more than 10 seconds at a time.

Right on cue, he said, "Let me guess. You want to talk about the finishing line."

"That's right. That's the topic for tonight."

"You seem pretty, um, fixated on that." Dudley pulled a flask from his jacket pocket and poured liquor into his cup. "Want some?"

"No thanks."

"You're such an effin' Girl Scout," he said, smiling over at her. He was probably somebody's husband, somebody's father. She tried to humanize him, but Honey's patience was thinner than newsprint at that point.

She said, "That's the rumor."

His eyebrows twitched up and he snorted, "Har-har! You're a sweetie, aren't you? I bet you're pretty sweet, away from work."

Honey didn't even know how to respond to that, so she didn't. She crossed her arms over her chest and sulked at how much time she was spending on this man. There were no surprises here, with Dudley. Nothing thus far was unexpected, because she'd learned the man's pacing by then. She knew she had to tolerate complete crap for twenty minutes before he'd wound himself down enough to even begin to communicate about business.

Meanwhile, at the next 10-second mark, Dudley piped up with another bit of news. "The pressmen are still talking about those tight jeans you wore last month."

"Ew." Honey made a mental note to leave the jeans at home next time. "But I wasn't on the floor last issue. So, I don't believe that."

"Word travels," Dudley said. His eyes drifted to her cleavage. "That's a nice blouse."

Lord have mercy, make it stop.

"Let's imagine—" she began.

"—Oh, I'm imagining—" he chuckled.

"—how a new bindery machine might improve Mainstay's final product."

He sat back in his chair and looked at Honey like he might burst out laughing. His eyes were bright as Dudley said, "Let's imagine what you'd look like if you took your hair out of that bun."

"Jesus, Dudley." Honey's patience was gone. "Are you trying to get a rise out of me?"

He shifted his weight in the chair, adjusting one leg of his pants, saying, "I'm the one—"

"Don't say it," Honey snapped. "Let's stay on fucking topic, here."

He seemed delighted to have provoked her. "Har-har-har," he hooted, "You're a piece of work, girlie," and Honey began to wonder if any $20,000 bonus was worth this bullshit.

"The bindery, Dudley," she insisted. "The bindery. Think about a new machine, and how much value it could bring, for the plant. You could personalize by zip code. Publishers like that."

The VP of Sales stood up from his chair. "You're all business, aren't you? Maybe it's in your best interest to lighten up."

Dudley stepped across to the light switch by the door. He twisted the knob on the rheostat, and lights dimmed throughout the suite.

When he turned back, all Honey could see was the bulky shadow of a man whose dark eyes flashed with anger, and whose balance was off.

"That's better," Dudley said, and he took a step toward her.

~ ~ ~

One night in early May, Honey got a call from Shane McLane. They'd become fast friends after their trip to Staniel Cay, and our girl had spent time encouraging him to step up the pace on his courtship of Brandy, his delectable former spouse.

"How are you liking the ATL?" Shane asked.

"I like it. It's so much more diverse than Tampa, and there's a lot going on."

"Great music. Great clubs. Great food."

"Exactly!" Honey said.

"I knew you'd like it. Is the job going any better?"

"It's going."

"You sound down. And I've got a proposition that might cheer you up."

"Oh yeah?" Honey never knew what Shane had up his sleeve. "Spill."

"How'd you like to have dinner at the White House on the Fourth of July?"

Okay, didn't expect that, even from you, Honey thought. She said, "Tell me more."

"I know this talent agent out in L.A.," he explained. "Mario Estevez. And he reps an entertainer who's been booked to perform at a picnic on the South Lawn, for the Fourth of July. It's an annual shindig for senior military people and their spouses, so that could make for an interesting crowd. Seems the President specifically asked for this performer, even though he and the First Lady aren't going to actually be there on the Fourth. Mario has a couple of extra passes and wanted to know if we'd join him."

"You bet."

"I knew you'd be down for this."

Giddy with excitement at this unexpected opportunity, Honey tried to remain calm. Her mind was filled with questions.

"Why don't you invite Brandy, though? She'd love a visit to the White House, right?"

"She's already got plans," he groused. "She'll be in Prague."

"Well, I'd love to join you, then. Thanks for thinking of me."

Shane said, "Yeah, I couldn't really bring Susan or Leigh Ann. They're crass bitches."

Honey shifted the phone to her other ear. Her voice was patient when she reprimanded him. "Now Shane. What have we said about calling women bitches?"

"Oh, right, right. I should've said, 'They're crass ladies.'"

"Or you could've said, 'They might feel out of their depth, socially.'"

"Hang on," Shane said. "I'm gonna write that down. I've got all these little notes and napkins where I try to capture your phrasing on stuff like this."

"I don't even know if you're being serious right now."

"That's one of my endearing qualities," Shane explained. "I'm a man of mystery."

"Uh-huh, keep telling yourself that. But honestly, I'm so excited! What should I wear? It's picnic, you say?"

"Yeah, there's a dress code or something. Let me check."

She didn't much care for the sitting President, truth be told. But that didn't mean she'd turn down an invitation like this one, especially since POTUS wasn't going to be there, so she wouldn't be put into the position where she had to shake his hand, or thank him, or anything.

Honey Malone at the White House, our girl thought. *How about that.*

~ ~ ~

Honey learned that the Military Picnic event was informal, with the women encouraged to wear jeans (no capris) or lawn dresses, and flats. She also learned that she'd be required to call a special number at the Secret Service, to provide her social security number, address, phone number, employer contact information, and three personal references.

What does one wear to the White House? Just asking that question felt surreal. Honey decided that she could see herself on the White House lawn under the fireworks in a sleeveless cinched-waisted dress of pastel linen, with a full skirt that fell just below the knee. Altogether flattering with flats—and altogether on-point with the provided dress code.

Our girl had a little trouble finding the right dress, however. You'd think with all the stores in Atlanta that sold women's wear, she'd have an easier time finding what she wanted. But at store after store, she ended up having the same conversation.

SALESPERSON: How can I help you today?

HONEY: I've been invited to the White House, and I'd like to try on some lawn dresses.

SALESPERSON: How exciting for you! Here, you wait in the dressing room, and I'll bring you some options.

HONEY, looking at the proffered options: But these are all long dresses.

SALESPERSON: You said you wanted to try on some long dresses.

HONEY: Lawn dresses, yes.

SALESPERSON: Yes, exactly, and here are ten great options!

HONEY: But they're all long.

SALESPERSON: You asked for long.

HONEY: Yes, I asked for lawn.

SALESPERSON: Yes! And that's what I brought. What am I not understanding?

HONEY: Let me go look around myself.

SALESPERSON, as Honey returns with several dresses: But you said you wanted a long dress.

HONEY, holding one up: This is what I consider a lawn dress.

SALESPERSON, gauging its length: Really?

~ ~ ~

No thanks to the linguistic skills of the sales staff at Atlanta clothing boutiques (or no thanks to her own Southern drawl), Honey did find the perfect dress. She bought a new pair of flats. She got all her ducks in a row with the Secret Service, whose representative reminded her several times to bring her driver's license.

Shane had booked two rooms at the Hay-Adams hotel, and the afternoon of the White House picnic, a large, unmarked van arrived to pick them up. This was the Secret Service vehicle, Shane told her. The driver sat behind bulletproof glass. Shane posited that they were being X-rayed and surreptitiously sniffed for explosives as they rode in silence with a dozen other attendees the few short miles to the White House gate.

There, each person in the van held their ID pressed against the closest window, so that a guard outside could examine their credentials through the glass. The uniformed man briefly shone a high-powered spotlight into each face, and then he waved the van through. Honey wondered if this lackluster show of security precautions was normal, but then she realized that most everybody in the van was a senior military official. Maybe this was standard procedure, for people the government felt that it could trust. Everybody probably knew that if trouble arose at the picnic, the trained military officers present would follow their training and instantly, instinctively pounce.

Once they departed the van inside the White House gate, Shane found his buddy Mario, whose nostrils were ringed with white dust, and introductions were made. Mario revealed that unlike the other guests, the three of them had special access to the Green Room, where the entertainer and his family waited in what was known as the least-formal White House parlor.

The Green Room looked plenty formal to Honey. The grass-colored moiré wallpaper was hung with many paintings in gilded frames, covering the walls from the ceiling down to the wainscoting, and the draperies were green, too, made of gorgeous silk, and edged in red-orange tasseled ribbon. A chandelier, covered in crystals, hung from the ceiling. The period furniture was antique, spindly, and looked supremely uncomfortable.

Our girl met the entertainer, a young Country singer who'd had a smash cross-over hit about the joy of being an American man. The artist seemed distracted and bored, and so did his wife, a pale waif-like being of similar demeanor who sat squirming on a settee. Honey met the two little girls they'd adopted from China, who even at the age of four looked bored, too. They'd no doubt seen a lot, traveling with the band. One green room probably looked like every other, to a kid.

"Look, there's the Rose Garden," Mario said. They'd left the Green Room to explore the festivities outdoors, and now the three of them took a detour toward the fabled garden. But they didn't get far. Fifteen feet from their goal, an armed guard stepped out of the hedge to block their path. *Off limits*, he said, and his tone was dead serious. A helmet with a blackout visor covered his head. He held a rifle across his chest, at the ready, and stood with his feet apart. Honey saw that he was slightly crouched, so that he could spring toward any one of them with ease, if his hot bullets proved insufficient. She noticed that the Rose Garden was ringed with metal grating. Probably there were nuclear warheads down there, ready to blast out their lethal load at the slightest provocation. She was happy to turn away.

The White House lawn was quite a sight. A thick carpet of green turf covered the expansive space that led past a forceful spouting fountain, which was ringed with perfectly uniform red flowers— Mr. Meloso would've loved it. The Washington Monument loomed its phallic presence off to the left, and straight ahead across the Olmsted-created landscape, guests had an unobstructed view of the Jefferson Memorial.

The crowd of 200 people had plenty of room to spread out, since picnic tables had been set up on the grass, and the smell of barbecue from the four grill stations made Honey's mouth water. She was delighted to see that various photo ops had been orchestrated, with professional photographers standing ready to snap instant Polaroid pictures of Shane and Honey sitting atop hay bales, or perched on the seat of a horse-drawn wagon that was filled with flats of fragrant strawberries.

"Look at these old-school Polaroids," Shane said, fanning one to help it develop.

Honey stopped his hand and peered down at the image. "It's even got an antique tinge around the edges. Very folksy."

"More folksy than these folks." Shane looked around at their fellow revelers. The high-and-tight haircut on every male head was a jarring sight, and even the women were straight and narrow, with perfect posture and an eye to the sky. Because the guys at the party wore the prescribed denim and plaid, instead of their everyday chestful of medals, the party vibe felt very Halloween, somehow. Every military person was masquerading, in a way, at this catered hoedown, which might explain why everybody wore reflective sunglasses whose lenses flashed orange—another unsettling sight. Nobody in this particular crowd had a desire to chat with strangers, so Shane and Honey stayed to themselves.

The talent agent Mario had spent most of the afternoon in the Green Room with his client, no doubt sniffing coke from the counter of a White House bathroom while NSA PsyOps staff watched via hidden cameras. Mario did join Honey and Shane for dinner, at a gingham-covered picnic table on the perimeter of the crowd, closer to the vigorous fountain. There were no paper plates at this posh picnic—and there was no alcohol, either. Iced tea was the drink of choice at that Independence Day soirée, served in sugar-rimmed Mason jars, which were stuffed with mint and lemon wedges. The barbecue was deliciously smoky and sweet, served on fine china, and there were ice-cold watermelon slices, somehow seed-free. The grilled corn on the cob tasted of salted maple.

A team of servers cleared the tables as the sun went down, leaving behind a clever basket that held bottled water, chocolate-chip cookies and sparklers that could be lit with a special abrasive scratcher pad, since lighters weren't allowed. Now, in the dusk, each table held an arrangement of pretty battery-powered candles that sprouted White House-branded patriotic pinwheel toys in red, white and blue. There was a nice breeze that night off the Tidal Basin, and pinwheels spun gaily across the green as roadies prepared a raised platform for the evening's headline entertainment. In the meantime, there were speeches.

~ ~ ~

Honey could feel the percussion of each explosion in her chest. Our girl had never seen Fourth of July fireworks from that particular viewpoint, as if the whole display was created just for her, laid out above the Jefferson Memorial like that, with the Washington Monument thrusting itself up with flair into the rockets' red glare. It was a night made for fireworks—there was no moon, and the air was warm but clear.

KA-BOOM

BOOM BOOM

"I'm in a dream," Honey said to Shane.

"Me, too."

SSSSHHHHHH

A fusillade of tiny explosions sizzled in the sky. Honey said, "I bet you wish you were here with Brandy."

He drew in a deep breath.

KA-BOOM

AAH from the crowd.

Shane cut a look at her. "I always said you were a fucking mind-reader." They smiled together, and the sky was bursting blue behind him as he said, "I wish you could be here with your whoever, too."

~ ~ ~

Mainstay Press had held the Condition Foundation contract for the better part of a decade, and other than the bindery, Honey could find little fault with reproduction or manufacturing. But the price was high—too high, in her opinion. She remembered the little sign that hung in the client booth back at Exceptional:

PRICE. QUALITY. TURNAROUND.
Choose any two.

Our girl was convinced that it was time to entertain competitive bids for the manufacturing of *Condition Today* magazine and the other web-press work, and she was quite sure that the Foundation could get similar quality—and acceptable turnaround—at a lower price. Any money saved would be that much more money for medical research, that's how Honey saw it.

She knew that Preston was in pretty tight with Dudley, so she wasn't surprised when her boss balked at her suggestion that the Foundation open up the contract for bids. But Honey was persistent, and finally earned his lukewarm permission.

"Sure, go ahead," Preston said, "if it makes you feel better."

~ ~ ~

One by one, the vendor reps flew in to meet with her.

The first print salesman arrived at her office while Honey was finishing up a call. His company was a direct competitor of Mainstay, so the rep was motivated to impress her. She waved and indicated that she was almost done, so the man waited near the door, looking at her inspiration board.

When Honey closed out the call and stood to greet him, the man jerked his thumb toward the collection of images that was anchored by a large black-and-white photo of Bessie Smith, with images of Robert Johnson, Etta James and Billie Holiday tacked up around it.

He said, "Relatives of yours?"

You racist fuck, Honey thought. *Why would you say something like that to the person whose recommendation you need for a ten-million-dollar contract?*

"I wish," she said. And then she told him that their meeting was over.

His eyes blazed. "Sweetheart, I made a special trip down here for this."

"I know you did, sweetheart. Goodbye."

~ ~ ~

Honey had a group chat going with her Tampa Bay friends, and one day the conversation went like this:

Nicole > bumpersticker today
Madness takes its toll. Please have exact change.

Milana > I saw one
That's not a haircut, it's a cry for help

Honey > Were these on same green car - 53 Pontiac Chieftain?

Milana > Yes what

Nicole > YES WHAT

Honey > I know that guy - CeeCee saw one
National Sarcasm Society. Like we need your support.

CeeCee > I so want T shirt of that!!! My bday is coming size M :)
blue OK? pontiac guy is supr cute btw

~ ~ ~

Honey was driving back to Atlanta from seeing Mom in
Tallahassee. On that Sunday morning in late February, a cold front
had just moved through, and purple clouds scudded low on gusty
winds. There are no other cars on the road. She set her GPS and
began her lonesome journey on US Highway 27, a two-lane road
through southern Georgia.

She hadn't wanted to leave Mom's. The day before, her mother
had revealed that she'd been called back into the doctor's office
for a breast biopsy. There was an anomaly on her X-ray, Mom told
Honey. Nothing to be concerned about. The biopsy was just an
extra step to make sure that all was well.

Our girl was processing this, motoring along on cruise control at
exactly 60 mph, remembering Nicole at her own mom's funeral.
Then suddenly on both sides of the road, acres and acres of
symmetrically planted pecan trees. This time of year, no leaves.
Each perfect row of trees contained a vanishing point, and as she
registered this, Honey got the sense that her car was standing still.
Somehow, she'd lost the ability to track forward motion. Time had
stopped.

It was such a powerful illusion that Honey had to shake her head
to clear it. The bare branches of the trees jerked in the wind,
skeletal, desperate, and the sky was leaden gray beyond the fast-
moving clouds. She imagined her mother's death, how the services

would be structured. The rows of thrashing trees clicked past, row by row, mile by mile.

She saw it then in her rearview mirror, a vehicle that came out of nowhere and passed her, fast. When she looked over, she saw a big white Cadillac hearse, circa 1974, with curlicue insets of glinting chrome.

They were the only two cars on the road. The hearse pulled in, in front of Honey's car, and the two vehicles drove in tandem through the flat, regimented landscape.

By this point, Honey was chuckling and chastising God for his heavy-handedness.

And then the question became: *Do I follow that hurtling hearse—and if so, how closely?*

This tickled her even more. Our girl let the hearse pull away.

"You go ahead on," Honey said to the Cadillac, and it raced off past line after line of lashing trees.

She'd been highly amused at the irony of the experience, but at some point, Honey realized that her car's cruise control was switched off. Her foot rested on the gas pedal. And that's when our girl understood that she'd been keeping the hearse as far away as humanly possible—but still in sight.

~ ~ ~

Honey read an article in *Rotman* that piqued her interest, and she immediately wanted to tell her brother. She called Max at ten o'clock at night, and he answered right away.

"What's up, sis?"

"I'm reading this story about the one way that leaders can predict which employees will become standout stars. Seems like two universities got their researchers together, and they did a global survey of 30,000 knowledge workers."

"So?"

"So, the research shows that there's only one identifiable indicator of top talent. It has nothing to do with a person's education, economic background, race, sex, IQ, skill set, or years of experience. The only thing that top talent has in common around the world is this: these individuals were raised in an environment where they received little attention, or inconsistent attention, from an authority figure."

Honey waited while Max digested this information. Sure enough, she soon heard that long, one-note whistle.

"Oh my God," the very successful brother said to his very successful sister, "this explains so much."

~ ~ ~

"I think I have good news," Shane McLane said. He sounded excited—and scared.

"You THINK it's good news?"

"It's good, it's good," Shane hurried to say. "Brandy agreed to let me take her out on her birthday."

"Fabulous! I knew you could do it. Great job, my friend."

"I guess," he said. "But now the pressure's on. I gotta really impress her, you know? This night has to be extra special. That's why I called you."

"Sure. How can I help?"

"Help me with ideas. Help me come up with something SO special, she'll change the way she looks at me."

"That's a pretty big ask, buddy. Is it a dinner date?"

"Yeah. I already know her favorite restaurant, so that's a lock. But she wants to see my house on Bayshore. I've been talking so much about the renovations, she's curious now."

"Well, that's a good thing," Honey said. "When is her birthday?"

"Month after next, the twenty-first."

"Okay, then. You've got some time, so here's the plan: you concentrate on creating a room in your house just for her."

Shane was silent, but Honey knew that he was quick on the uptake.

"That's actually a great idea," he said, "But realistically, I can't make something, like, just for her, if I don't know what she likes."

"Shane, Shane, Shane. You know what she likes, you just haven't accessed that information in a while."

"Or ever," he muttered.

"That's appropriate," Honey said. "So let's investigate a little. What is it you love about Brandy?"

"The way she smiles," he said straight away. "It's pretty incredible, actually. Her face, I don't know, it just kind of lights up. There's this look in her eyes, you know?"

"I know," Honey said, and then she was thinking about the guy she'd left behind in Tampa. He'd smiled like that. "So, tell me about a time when she smiled that way."

"Aw, man. I didn't call you up to start crying."

Shane really was a sweetheart, deep down. Too bad about all the inadvertent ways he offended people—too bad, because sometimes it was hurtful, and there's no excuse for that. Honey was determined to wring every last bit of self-importance out of him, because he was her friend. He deserved the attention.

"Crying might actually be the point, here, though," Honey said. "We're talking about emotions. Think back, to when she smiled like that."

Honey waited while her friend investigated something new for him: memories of the past that involved someone other than himself. Shane was a powerhouse of business. He was sharp, professional and successful. But he hadn't spent a lot of time considering emotions—his or anyone else's. Our girl knew that she might be waiting awhile, but she also knew that Shane could do it. He could reach back and find what he needed. She was sure of it.

"Okay, here's one," Shane said. "When we were first dating, I took her to this place for what they called High Tea, at some little house in Hyde Park that had been turned into a tearoom. It was like a British place, you know, with the doilies and the teapots and the fussy little cups and shit. There was a lot of shiny fabric with big flowers on it."

"Chintz," Honey said.

"I guess. Anyway, she flipped out when she walked in there. She was looking all around, and she had this look on her face—" He choked up and had to stop.

"I know," Honey said. "But really, this is exactly what we need. Think about it, Shane. You have that breakfast room downstairs, off the kitchen, right? Turn it into an English tearoom, just for her."

"You've never been in my house. How do you know about the

breakfast room?"

"Oh, sweetie, you told me ALL about it on our first date."

He laughed then. "Yeah, that sounds like me."

"Do you like my idea?"

"It's a stellar idea. I can only imagine what she'd think of that. But how can I get it done in time for her birthday? My interior design people do minimalist, not chintz."

Honey said, "Oh, I might know somebody who can help."

And that's how Shane McLane got introduced to Samantha Malone, who sourced every curtain, tablecloth, tiered cake stand and Wedgwood cup, and who visited the mansion on Bayshore Boulevard to put together a proper British tea room that would make any Anglophile's heart skip a beat. That's how a billionaire bottling-company executive took the first step toward reconciliation with the spouse who'd spurned him, with good reason, all those years before.

"You should've seen her smile," Shane said.

~ ~ ~

It was springtime in Atlanta, and every parked car was heavily flocked with yellow pollen. Across the metro area, thousands of musicians of every stripe were prepping for the influx of spring breakers—the bars would be packed, and the bars that offered live music would be mobbed.

One Sunday afternoon before the Blues Station music venue opened its doors, Honey sat on a barstool picking her Sigma dreadnought, trying to find the right pitch for a song that she was attempting to conquer. It was written by one of her favorite songwriters, and she was determined to get it right. She noodled with chords, and with the frequencies in her voice, that might get her where she had to go.

Used to be a girl, then a woman, then nothing
Quilt is in the corner by the oak console
The phone rings once a day
Just like a daughter
Waiting for Marty
Waiting for Marty to get home

"Who's that, singin' Kelly Joe Phelps?" somebody demanded, and Honey turned to see a tall Black man approaching—the headliner, Sir Stokes, the artist she'd be opening for that night. She hadn't seen him since she'd sung from the shadows backstage at Tippy's, all those years ago.

Stokes didn't look much different. His beard was certainly just as grand. They said he was 60, but to Honey, he looked 85. Probably gigging across the South for the last 40 years hadn't been a spa-like experience. She wondered what those sharp old eyes had seen.

He joined her at the bar.

"Can I buy you a beer?" she asked. "My name's Honey Malone. I'm opening for you tonight."

"Huh," he said, raising two fingers to the bartender, "Well, don't be too good."

Smiling, Honey said, "Can't make that promise."

He smiled, too, and cut a look at her. Ice-cold beer appeared, and they both lifted their bottles to their lips.

"I heard you singing," he said. "We met before."

"Yes! At Tippy's Smokehouse down in Tampa one night, backstage. You played *Black Coffee.*"

The bluesman nodded toward the ceiling, remembering. "There

192

was frogs."

They sipped their beer. Honey thought about all the time that had passed since that night at Tippy's, and all the decisions that she'd had to make, personally and professionally. Decisions that had seemed so right, when she made them.

"You're struggling a little bit," Stokes said. "With the pitch on that verse."

Honey frowned. "Yeah, that high note—I can't find a way to it."

He reached out for her guitar, and she was quick to hand it to him. She was conscious that a group of servers at a table across the room were watching them, transfixed to have blues royalty so close. Stokes did a test strum, adjusted the E string that tended to go sharp, and then played out the melody perfectly—all without taking his eyes from hers.

"Don't go looking for that note," he said. "It's not some mountain you gotta climb."

He played the song, picking it sweetly and with purpose, stretching the B-minor so fast and sure that Honey was surprised to see it happen. Her instrument seemed to love the B a little more, like that. She'd have to practice.

Stokes sat across from her, and she watched his foot tapping against the boards of the scarred oak floor. The sun through the skylight was a spotlight on his moving fingers, and if Kelly Joe Phelps had been in the room, he'd be proud.

"Now sing it." Stokes started back at the top of the verse, and Honey sang along. Then he suddenly stopped playing.

"Don't go looking up ahead," he said irritably.

He played it again, right up to the troublesome note, seemingly satisfied with her progress, but when she arrived there, Honey faltered again.

The bluesman's fingers stayed poised over the strings. Stokes looked at her closely. "You got a momma?"

She nodded.

"Then look back, not forward," he said, and that made total sense to her. The next time they tried the verse, just like magic Honey was able to produce the high note, for the first time. No effort was required.

He handed her the guitar. "See there?"

"Thanks," Honey said. "Really."

She slung the Sigma around her back and touched her camera that sat waiting on the bar. "Can I take a couple of pictures? I'll send you the prints." Stokes fluffed his beard while Honey attached the flash. She used the back of a barstool to steady the Nikon, and took six quick shots before somebody called his name—and then Sir Stokes looked up and lifted his chin to acknowledge them. Under the skylight like that, he looked like a hero. Her seventh shot, the best.

"Who booked you?" he asked as he stood to leave.

"Here tonight? Maximillian." Honey meant the local talent agency who'd scheduled her for the gig.

He turned to leave. "Don't show me up, now," Stokes said, and both of them knew that there was no chance of that. "Thanks for the beer."

~ ~ ~

Max and Peggy were to marry against the dramatic backdrop of

Cheyenne Mountain in western Colorado. Honey and her mom had arranged to room together at the wedding venue's hotel, excited beyond measure that "our little Max" would be a married man.

The night before the ceremony, the two women had catalogued their ensembles, laid out their selected jewelry, and deemed themselves ready for the coming festivities. They took hot chocolate out to the balcony and sat looking up at stars that seemed close enough to touch. This was not the sky of a heat-saturated, humid Florida, where even the moon was often blurred.

"So, you got a clean bill of health on that breast thing?" Honey asked.

"Thank God." They sipped their chocolate, happy to have the time alone together, before the crush of the crowd the next day. Happy that this conversation, which could have turned dark with a different diagnosis, could still carry on as hopeful.

"Does it bother you that Max is younger, but he's getting married first?" Mom asked.

"Not at all."

"Good," Mom said. "Just checking."

It seemed like a good time to ask, so Honey said, "How about you? Do you think you'll ever get married again?"

"Done with that," Samantha stated.

"Really? Are you sure?"

"I'm so over it," Mom said. "I mean, there are a couple of men who've expressed interest, but I just can't see myself going there. I'm still exhausted from the last one, honestly. Why would I sign up for more?"

Okay, Mom sounds bitter, Honey thought. *That's not like her.*

"I'm led to believe that not all men are like Dad," Honey said.

Her mother snorted. "Not ready to test that premise."

Honey looked over at Samantha, who looked more savvy than bitter, actually, now that our girl examined her more closely.

Her mother said, "I can't tell you how many nights I stayed up, just praying he'd pull into the drive."

Look back. Until that moment, Honey hadn't recollected the image of her mom sitting on the porch steps at midnight, looking down the road. Now it came rushing back in full color, so familiar. She'd seen it happen often enough, she realized, now that she was able to remember.

"That's so sad," Honey said.

Mom warmed her hands on her cup, turning her eyes to the stars. "What I've learned is that there are all kinds of people in this world. And they're not all like me. We like to think that we're all the same, basically, right? But I've come to understand that some people care about pleasure in the moment, more than anything else. They might have great plans, you know, to be a better person and all, but if the chance for pleasure pops up, they'll take it every time. They crave it, you know? It's like an itch they have to scratch, or something."

Honey remembered Joe Stecher, pulling up her skirt that morning before the job interview that would set her whole life on a new trajectory, and how she'd participated with gusto in what Joe had to offer. She shifted in her chair. *Maybe it's in the genes, or something.*

A gust of wind made Samantha pull her sweater tighter. "I tried so hard to make it easy for you and Max, you know? I thought I was living my denial quite well, and I wanted the two of you to follow my lead. But then guess what? You both grew up, and you both were smart and observant. You had questions—and that made me want to ask them, too."

Mom looked up at a blanket of stars made evident by the crystalline air. "There was one thing I would never do for Mitchell, though. I don't know why I chose this one place to take a stand, but I did. Right from the start, once I saw how he behaved, I decided that I would never smile in a family picture. That was my lame idea of rebellion, I guess." She took a sip of cocoa. "Kind of pathetic, isn't it?"

"I wouldn't call it pathetic," Samantha's daughter said. "I'd call it understandable."

~ ~ ~

One afternoon while she was in her Condition Foundation office, Honey got a call on her cell. Jasmine, from the Maximillian talent agency.

"I have great news. Sir Stokes wants you to open for him, on his road tour. He liked what he saw last month at Blues Station."

Honey was delighted to have impressed Stokes. But of course, she couldn't leave her job to go on the road—not for Stokes, not for anybody. Music was her side gig, and nothing more.

"I'm sorry, Jazz, I can't do it. I'm working, you know."

"But Honey," Jasmine urged, "This is the chance of a lifetime. You should be flattered."

"Oh, I'm super flattered, for sure. I just—you know, I have a career, and it's important to me. I've got a day job."

"And you're going to put all your eggs in that basket?"

"You better believe it," our businessperson said.

~ ~ ~

By mid-December, Honey had compared all the printing bids. She'd also spent many hours sitting knee-to-knee with flippin' Dudley Dawson in the hush of the dim client suite, and had managed to convince him to commit to installation of an upgraded bindery line at Mainstay, if the Foundation renewed its three-year commitment. The stipulation made its way into the new contract, and Honey felt like she'd finished a marathon footrace. When she walked away from Dudley that month, she felt triumph—and relief. There was something deeply unsettling about the man, and she hoped to be rid of him.

Back in Atlanta, she arrived at her year-end meeting with Preston feeling confident that there were several good print-vendor options on the table. The boss's desk held a tabletop Christmas tree, and its twinkle lights were strangely comforting to her as Honey began her spiel in the gloaming.

She made her case for the vendor she preferred, the second-lowest bid, from a printing company that produced fine work, that could reduce turnaround by four days each month, and whose plant machinery was state-of-the-art. Their bindery line could customize advertising by target audience, according to zip code—a function that could bring more dollars into Condition Foundation research, as advertisers swooned to take part in such digital magic. It was easy for Honey to make the argument for change—but the final decision, she knew, would be in the hands of Pretty Preston.

Beyond the blackout drapes, she heard the sound of semi-trucks blasting past on I-85.

"We'll be going with Mainstay again," the boss said.

No big surprise.

"Can I ask why?"

Preston smiled in her direction, and Honey could see the muted gleam of his perfect teeth, flashing in time with the Christmas lights. He didn't answer. But Honey wasn't shocked to hear his decision, considering his obvious bond with Dudley. *Maybe money changes hands on that babe-infested yacht in the Keys, who knows?*

So now, ever the optimist, our girl looked on the bright side.

"Okay then," Honey said, "I guess I'll look forward to that big bonus at the end of the month."

Preston was silent.

"The extra money you promised me," she said. "If I could convince Mainstay to install a new bindery line. It's in the contract, so I've delivered."

Preston said nothing.

"It wasn't easy to get that commitment," Honey said, remembering Dudley's vodka aura, his nasty insinuations and lingering handshakes. "So, thanks for the incentive."

"I never promised you an incentive," the boss said.

Honey felt the dark office grow dimmer. Good thing, because a flush was rising in her cheeks.

"Yes, you did. You said if I was able to accomplish this, you'd sweeten my bonus. You said I could expect twenty grand in my pocket on December thirty-first."

Preston stood up, to end their meeting.

He said, "I must've mis-spoken."

~ ~ ~

There's nothing pretty about a bald-faced liar. Honey resigned on the spot, and he didn't try to stop her.

BOSS 5: EMMA

Honey's title: Senior Content Manager, The Emma Brandt Agency

The PR person, Helen, was watching from the top of the stairs. "Pete, look out!" she called down. "You have to turn it."

She meant the desk that was being shoved up the stairwell, the desk that would sit in Honey's new office on the second floor of the boutique advertising agency.

Pete, the IT guy, was responsible for the high end of the desk. He called down, "Ready to turn it, Honey?"

"You gotta be shitting me," Helen said. "You've got Honey Malone carrying her own desk?"

Pete grunted as he struggled to gain purchase. "Ronnie's out today. Or he could've helped."

"Don't you know who she is?" Helen asked.

Pete frowned up at her. "This was Emma's idea."

"Honey?" Helen called out. "Honey? You okay down there?"

"Ugh," our girl huffed. The muscles in her arms burned, and deep red welts were forming on her hands as she manhandled her end of the desk, which was filthy from being in storage. Her silk jacket was crusted with stripes of crud and cobwebs. "Uff, omigod."

"Push it, push!" Pete yelled. "It's tipping!"

"Help me," Honey bleated.

"Oh, no," Helen shouted from above, "It's gonna fall, it's—"

Like a whale in full breach, the desk slowly exposed its pale underbelly, then slammed down into the banister, which tilted precariously, bowing out a good six inches. A nail that now protruded from a riser had embedded itself in the side of Honey's shoe.

"Ack," she said. "Ow."

"Maybe if I take the back stairs," Helen called down, "I could run around and help Honey push."

Ow, ow, ow was Honey's contribution. Sweat stung her eyes, but she couldn't brush it away. In that sweltering stairwell in the middle of August, her hair clung to the side of her face like a wet veil.

"No, we almost got it," Pete said between clenched teeth. "We got this."

"I think it's wedged," Helen said. "I mean, from up here it looks wedged."

Pete growled low in his throat, like that might summon strength, and pulled again. He looked up at Helen, stricken. "It's wedged!"

Helen ran to the end of the landing above, and peered down into the stairwell, elbows akimbo. "Oh, my goodness, oh my God. Honey? You okay?"

"There's blood in my shoe."

"What? There's what in your where?"

Honey just moaned.

"I'm so sorry this is happening," Helen called down. "Like, welcome to Emma Brandt, right?"

It was Honey's first day on the job—back in Tampa.

~ ~ ~

Before she joined The Emma Brandt Agency, Honey's four years in Atlanta had been tough.

After her rapid retreat from the National Condition Foundation, she couldn't honestly drum up any enthusiasm for print manufacturing—which was just as well, because there were few positions available anywhere in the United States that would require her level of expertise. Print really was dead, by then. *It's time for a change.*

Honey had seen how successful her mom had been with the design business, and decided that it might be fun to explore her own creative side. She'd already been gigging at blues clubs around Atlanta, and regularly opened for headliners when they booked small venues in town. Our girl had an ear for melody, a foot for the backbeat, and a heart for storytelling; she'd sold some original songs to blues artists in Chattanooga and country singers in Nashville, but the tantalizing tunes had never been released. *What if I could be an actual full-time creative?* she wondered. *They're just like you and me, after all.*

~ ~ ~

Honey's life in Atlanta got a little complicated after she made that decision, and a lot less structured. It was indeed fun to explore her creativity—but it was hardly lucrative. Honey had been renting the jewel box apartment in Buckhead, but it was super expensive, and she was no longer earning top dollar at the Foundation. It wouldn't be long before she had to dip into savings, if she wanted to stay.

But the phrase *dip into savings* didn't sit well with her. *How else can I siphon off some of the money that's hurtling overhead?* She thought about starting a business, but quickly abandoned that idea. When a businessperson becomes an entrepreneur, Honey knew, things can get risky.

She redoubled her efforts to examine her creative choices. Honey liked to dance, but she was too old and too short for creativity that strenuous. She enjoyed photography, but she was no pro. She liked to sing, and was successful at making money that way. *What other ways can I use my voice?* She could market herself as voice talent, Honey theorized. Commercials, and voice-overs. During those initial weeks after her final meeting with Pretty Preston, as she assessed her desires for her future, our girl came to realize that she might also use her voice another way: through writing.

Everybody loves a story, after all. Honey thought about all the Blues folks she'd gigged with, and she thought about the stories they'd had to tell, and why they'd told them. She had written and arranged two songs for Sir Stokes, and his offer still stood: Honey was encouraged to accompany the band on the road, as the opening act, as a pinch hitter when the backup guitarist went rogue, and as documentarian, laptop and camera welcomed. *I can market myself as a music writer*, Honey thought. *I'd love doing that.*

~ ~ ~

Honey had been calling her mom every Saturday, just to check in, and one day our girl finally broached the topic of half-siblings. It had never been easy to get Samantha to share her feelings, Honey knew—but it was getting easier.

She learned that her mom had long been suspicious about her husband siring other children, but she'd never confronted him. And now, all these years later, the former Mrs. Malone had no interest in learning about any other kids that Mitchell might have conceived on all those long nights he'd spent away from his family.

Mom said, "Let sleeping dogs lie."

Honey said, "He is a dog."

"A hound dog," was her mom's response, and then they were laughing together. During Honey's entire childhood, her mother had never said one bad word about her father. Quite the contrary. Mom had praised him as a good provider, a powerful man. A leader in business. For the first few years after the divorce, when Dad's litany of ills came up in conversation, the worst thing that Mom would say about him was *Mitchell is somewhat limited*. But now she and Honey could laugh about the narcissist who had put himself first, for all those years, who cared nothing about anyone except himself and how his fellow men perceived him.

He never read me a book. He never engaged me in conversation. He missed every birthday party, vocal recital and graduation. He subcontracted gift-giving. He'd make lovely promises, but he'd never act on them. He never seemed to care.

Mom finally reached the point that she could reveal the truth to her children: that although he'd provided his family with a fine lifestyle, Mitchell had spent every extra cent on other women.

"He had a condo on St. Bart's, all those years," Mom said. "It came out in the financial discovery. I never got invited to St. Bart's. The closest I got was Jacksonville Beach."

Honey came to understand that her dad had never cared whether she succeeded in business. He didn't care if she became a leader like him. Her father just wanted her gone, so that he could spend her share of his money on the women who interested him more.

~ ~ ~

About the time she left the Condition Foundation, Joe Stecher had started to call her on occasion. Things in Knoxville weren't working out. But Honey didn't lead him on. She'd talk with him, sure, and they could share stories about his mom, now deceased. But Honey knew she'd never trust him again, as a partner, and that they wanted different things out of life—and she told him that. He kept calling, though, and Honey discovered that it was much easier to write down Joe-isms when he wasn't present in the room.

"IT WAS A FIRST-CLASS HOTEL. IT HAD ALL THE ANEMONES."

"SOME HORSES ARE SPECIALLY BRED FOR HIGH-STEPPING IN THE RING. SURELY YOU'VE HEARD OF THE ROYAL POMERANIANS?"

"THEY'LL FEEL LIKE THE RAFT OF GOD IS COMING DOWN ON THEIR HEADS."

She missed him sometimes. That was probably natural.

Sometimes, she missed her dad, too. He had never called her, not once, since she left for college.

~ ~ ~

After she quit the National Condition Foundation, Honey really was on her own. The ensuing years in Atlanta were a whirlwind of deadlines, Interstate highways and late nights as Honey travelled with the Sir Stokes entourage during the summer season and patched together income from a variety of sources. She worked hard, she made sure to back up her creative promises, and she kept a meticulous calendar. There was a river of money blasting overhead, and Honey scrambled to find the proper straws for sluicing.

Those four years were not fun—but there were fun moments. She was alone—but she wasn't lonely.

~ ~ ~

Our girl had signed up with an Atlanta temp agency, swearing that she'd consider any gig that paid a minimum of $50 an hour. She soon got a call: one of the nation's top two candy manufacturers needed a two-week replacement for an executive's vacationing assistant.

I like candy, Honey thought. *Maybe there's free samples.* She showed up for the assignment early on a Monday morning in a building that smelled downright delicious. She knew that the executive was willing to pay top dollar for a temp, because he wanted somebody who'd undergone a full background check—and Honey had done so, years ago, when she worked at Deal Hipper. She didn't have to wonder why candy manufacturing was such a state secret. She'd just read an article in *Business Week* that described that cut-throat world, with a sidebar about corporate spies. The article was titled *Candy Wars*.

She met her temporary boss just briefly. He came to introduce himself on his way to a Monday morning meeting. Let's call him Dick. He was a man who had enjoyed a fair amount of candy himself, apparently, and Honey saw an awkward comb-over, and a sad suit the color of rancid chocolate with a light dusting of dandruff. When he'd stepped into the office where Honey was stationed, she'd risen to greet him. And it was obvious that he was surprised at what he saw.

"Well, well," Dick said, giving her the once-over. "We usually get younger people in here, to cover for vacations."

Honey didn't know whether to respond—or what she'd say if she did—so she just looked at him.

"Not a problem, though," Dick said quickly. "Just an observation. So, listen, I'll be in the war room for at least a couple of hours. Take messages if anybody calls, and whatever you do, don't go into my office."

Honey gave him the thumbs up, and off he went, carrying a large stack of papers in a folder marked CONFIDENTIAL in red.

With no real work to do, Honey busied herself on the Internet, trying to figure out where her next gig was coming from. After an hour, the phone rang.

"It's me, Dick. Listen, I'm up here in the main building, and I forgot my glasses. They're on my desk, can you bring them to me?"

"No, sorry. You told me to stay out of your office."

"Well, now I'm telling you to go in there," Dick said.

"I don't know about this. I'm getting conflicting messages, here."

"Do it," he said. "Just bring me my glasses, okay? I'm giving you permission."

She stepped into his office, picked his eyeglasses up off the desk, and beat feet out of there. It took a while to find the conference room in the main building, but Honey kept asking people, and finally she walked down a darkened hallway and spotted a big sign that read WAR ROOM.

Nothing subtle about these guys. There was a side light on the door, and Honey could see a dozen men sitting around a conference table. Behind them was a wall of closed-circuit TV monitors that showed various scenes—including what appeared to be a shot of Dick's desk from above. She recognized the Corvette model cars.

Honey knocked, was waved in, and placed the eyeglasses on the table next to Dick. Every man in the room was looking at her. *They're probably looking at how old the temp is*, Honey thought.

"Thanks," Dick said.

"You're welcome."

At that was the end of it—or so Honey thought. Twenty minutes later, she'd found her way back to her temporary office, and a woman stood waiting there. The badge on her lanyard read "HR."

"Dick has a new assignment for you now." The woman from human resources turned toward the stairwell. "Come with me."

Down into the bowels of the building they went. A rabbit warren of stairs and hallways finally revealed their destination: a gleaming, well-lit area on the main floor of the plant. Chutes of wrapped candy fed a rapidly moving conveyer belt, where a line of men and women in gloves, hair nets and booties were packing cardboard boxes for shipment. Honey was reminded of an old Lucille Ball skit. *I love Lucy*, she thought. *But I don't want to BE Lucy.* Our girl was uncomfortable with what appeared to be taking place.

The woman handed Honey some latex gloves and a hair net, and pointed to the packing line.

"That's your spot," she said. "Put on the hair net, before you start filling boxes."

The workers on the line were stealing glances at Honey. One of them, a garrulous guy with no front teeth, waved at her. "Come on down here by me, good-lookin'! What did YOU do wrong, missy?"

"We're still paying you fifty an hour," the HR woman said. "That part hasn't changed."

Honey looked down at the hair net that she held in her tightened fist.

"You know what?" she said, "No."

She walked off that job. But Honey kept the hairnet—just to remind her of that unusually low point in her professional life. Shane McLane wasn't the only person who needed help with self-importance, it appeared.

~ ~ ~

One sweltering August night, Honey sat with Sir Stokes at a venue in Birmingham. Burkes McGee, a well-known Country singer, had attended Stokes' show, and came backstage to speak with the headliner.

McGee's star was fading as he grew older, and he complained to Stokes that his elderly audience was uninvolved. The two performers discussed ways to get 60-year-old men on their feet, to spark engagement. A song would do it, they agreed. Just one more hit that hit the mark with that specific demographic.

"I need something redneck," the Country artist said. "I might be old, right, but I still want some kind of boot-stompin' tune, to get these lazy boys up on their feet and energized. Think honky-tonk. Think call-and-response."

Stokes nodded in Honey's direction. "She writes Country music."

"I'm not sure I can do full-on redneck," Honey said. "But what the heck? I'll give it a try. Let me get your number, Mr. McGee."

Who knew that the rollicking song with the call-and-response chorus would become a hit on the Country charts?

Grandma in a Tight T-Shirt

I was new to the bar
I didn't know no one thar
But it was the night for me
Somebody name of Sheila
Bought a round of good tequila
And turned off the karaoke

Seems Sheila's daughter Pearlie
Had birthed a baby girlie
I went to thank the ol' girl for the drink
And then I saw her standin'
Lookin' cute as sugar candy:
A grandma in a tight T-shirt

[chorus]

Tight T-shirt (Tight T-shirt)
Tight T-shirt (Tight T-shirt)
This little bit of heaven
Is only fifty-seven
She's a grandma in a tight T-shirt

Well, I had my share of women
And it ended badly with 'em
When they treated me like dirt
I used to be a hater
Now I want to date her
That grandma in the tight T-shirt

[repeat chorus]

~ ~ ~

The temp agency called again, and this time they'd pay Honey $170 an hour for three weeks of full-time office work at a snack-cake factory near Chattanooga. Since our girl had scored a singing gig in that town, it was the perfect solution. She could work during the day making exceptional money, and still have nights free to sing and play at Rumbles, a bar overlooking the Tennessee River.

She drove out to the snack-cake facility. The grounds at Little Rebel were impressive. A long driveway, overhung by canopy oaks, took her past the facade of a large white-columned building to the employee parking lot, where hundreds of cars were already baking in the sun. Along this journey, multiple signs were displayed, each professionally created in the company colors of red, white and blue, and each presenting the sweet-cheeked portrait of the little girl with yellow pigtails that adorned every box of Little Rebels.

Little Rebel says
"Smile! You're on camera!"

Little Rebel says
"Say YES to honesty!"

Little Rebel says
"Every day is No Slacker day!"

Little Rebel says
"Cleanliness is next to God!"

Little Rebel says
"Be sweet! Don't steal treats!"

Sounds like they've got some pilferage going on, Honey thought. *And some dirty hands.* She parked as instructed in a guest spot, and the air was thick with the scent of peanuts and vanilla as she entered the plant through the employee entrance.

A midsized, unassuming man in a trim gray suit was waiting there. His hair was gray, and so was his shirt, his tie, and the rectangular frames of his eyeglasses. He didn't smile, but he did extend his hand.

"Biff Bangle," he said.

That's a spiffy name for a guy who's dressed in monotone. Biff stood tall, at attention with his chin pulled back, like he might be called to join a military parade at any moment. She shook his hand, and he helped her through the security process, which involved an armed guard, a sign-in sheet, a metal detector and a search of her purse. She tried to remember if she'd read any articles about Snack Cake Wars, but she was pretty sure she hadn't. *If they're so afraid that somebody's going to steal their cupcakes, they ought to move this operation to the exit door.*

Honey could see that Biff was watching her out of the corner of his eye. Probably wondering why an older babe like her would be doing administrative work. She was used to that attitude, by then. Biff led her down a dark, echoing corridor to a door at the far, far end of the building.

When he threw the door open, Honey was blinded by the brightness of the sun. Now they were outside again, on the other side of a soaring chain-link fence that separated the factory's back lot from employee parking—a fence whose top was ornamented with glistening razor wire. Biff marched with purpose across the asphalt toward a tiny, windowless concrete-block building that sat by itself at the far perimeter of the lot. It looked like a place where equipment might be kept, or prisoners.

This is where they put you if you steal too many Little Rebels, Honey thought. She couldn't imagine that she'd be doing office work in an outbuilding, but hey: $170 an hour. As they approached the place on the heat-shimmered tarmac, Honey searched the building's exterior for signs of air conditioning. She was relieved to see what looked like a window unit, sticking out of one wall. *A window unit, but no windows. Weird.*

"Here we go," Biff said, stopping in front of a door made of metal, and unlocking the jumbo padlock that secured it. He reached inside the door and flicked a switch.

"After you," he said.

Honey was in a cool, white-tiled space, about 8 x 8, perfect for torture or coroner dissection. Biff's light switch had activated a single bare bulb that hung from the ceiling—the preferred lighting for any interrogation scene she'd ever seen in movies, or on TV. Our girl saw a small desk with an electric typewriter on it. A straight chair waited behind the desk, and an old-style upright metal file cabinet sat in the corner.

Biff was close behind her. Because the space was so tight with both of them in it, Honey moved toward the desk, and sat in the chair like she owned it, just to get out of his way.

"Very nice," he said.

He closed the door, and suddenly the bare bulb felt more creepy, now that it was the sole light source in the room, and the slamming of the heavy door had caused the bulb to sway, casting menacing shadows. Honey could see that Biff's hair was thinning on top, since the bulb was directly above his head. Shadows from his angular eyeglasses looked like square tattoos on his cheeks—tats that moved in time with the sway of the bulb.

What the hell have I gotten myself into?

She wasn't sure what would happen next, but one thing Honey knew is that Biff would be leaving. After all, there was no other chair in the tiny room. This eased her mind a bit. He looked plenty comfortable standing there, though, and didn't seem in a rush to leave. He'd be giving her instructions next, no doubt. It was time for him to reveal what sort of work Honey would be doing, there in Cellblock C.

"Look in the second drawer of that file cabinet," Biff said. "There's a phone book."

Honey stood, opened the squeaky drawer, and retrieved a phone book six inches thick, a dusty relic of a bygone past. *Chattanooga, Tennessee,* the cover read. *White pages.* This book was tattered and dogeared, with coffee rings on the cover—and it was so heavy that Honey had to use both hands when she handed it to him. Then she sat back down in the chair. Waiting, for what would come next.

The man in gray stood leafing through the pages with enthusiasm, like he might be researching a lover's phone exchange. As he did this, Biff said, "In the desk drawer is some typing paper. You can start with a fresh sheet."

Honey cranked a sheet of blank white paper into the typewriter and fumbled around until she found the button to turn the machine on. *Why are there are no computers in Little Rebel world? Why the typewriter? Why the phone book?* She hoped that all would be revealed, because the whole thing felt fundamentally strange. She was confined behind a closed door with a strange man, far out of earshot of the snack factory. *No one will hear me scream*, Honey thought. Perhaps her demise would spark investigative research, much-needed and long-delayed. There would be a podcast: *Over the span of fourteen years, eleven female temps checked in through Security—but they'd never check out.*

Biff seemed to have found the right spot in the phone book, because he laid the tome on the desk beside Honey, open to the C's. He didn't use this as an excuse to get closer to her, though he could've. Honey saw that Biff pointed to a phone-book entry by leaning way over, and using a pen to put a blue dot next to a name, from maximum distance. *Clover, Matthew B., Delores …. 717 Maplewood Dr. …. 889-6452.*

"Start there," he said, "and type every line until I tell you to stop."

"Why?"

He didn't like it that she'd asked the question, Honey could tell. His eyes narrowed behind the boxy frames of his specs.

"Does it matter why? You're getting paid one-seventy an hour, if I'm not mistaken."

"Good point," Honey said.

She typed and typed and typed, and he watched her. The guy stood there on the bare tiled floor in shoes that could not have been comfortable, and watched a woman type. *Is this some kind of kink?* Honey wondered, as she mindlessly worked her way down the page of tiny words and numbers. *Is he some pervert, getting his jollies off the sight of a woman's fingers on the keys of a typewriter? Yuck.*

Honey finally decided that this situation was no more than a typing test. Biff just wanted to see if she had the requisite skills to earn top dollar. After all, nobody in their right mind paid $170 an hour for a typist, so she was no doubt being prepared for the real work to come. Our girl slowed her pace a bit, so that she'd have fewer typing errors. *Nobody else in the Southeastern United States wants to pay me an hourly wage this high.* Honey was in it for the long haul.

When she had filled an entire sheet of typing paper, she pulled it out of the roller mechanism and turned to look at Mr. Biff.

"Did I tell you to stop?" he asked.

Our girl reached one hand behind her neck and massaged her vertebrae. She moved her shoulders, limbering up to ready herself, and then she cranked another sheet into the machine. She typed and typed and typed. Honey didn't mind the act of typing, really. Her Mom had taught her, when she was just a kid. If you were careful to employ the right posture and kept your feet flat on the floor, you could do it for hours without hurting yourself. You just had to know how to approach it. You only had to concentrate on the Zen of the moment, didn't you, and then you could let your cares about being held captive in a concrete Nazi bunker just flow away, flow away, on every exhalation.

Sheet after sheet was cranked into the mechanism. Page after page of names, addresses and numbers were transcribed. The gray man stood there for all of it.

She lost track of time, there in the fog of her self-induced hypnosis, and Biff seemed to lose track, as well. When she ran out of typing paper, it took him a minute to focus his gaze, to register that the staccato rhythm of the keys had stopped.

"Out of paper," Honey said pleasantly. *Sweetheart, I'll sit here all day and type for a hundred and seventy bucks an hour*, that was her attitude. She'd done some soul-searching, after her hair-net experience three months before.

"Out of paper," she said again.

Biff, shaken out of whatever reverie had gripped him, looked down at his watch.

"Okay," he said. "I'll go get more."

"Where's the restroom?" Honey asked. "I'll do that while you're gone."

Biff looked at her sharply. He might've suspected that the temp worker who sat before him would try to make a break for it, to go over the wall, like all the others who'd tried and failed. He might suspect that Honey would attempt to scale that fence, slap the binding of the phone book over the top of that razor wire, and then climb over to drop down like a cat into the employee parking lot. It would be an easy sprint to her car from there—and he knew it.

"We'll make good use of our time, that way." Honey hadn't had much practice cajoling prison guards, and sought for practicality in her tone.

"I guess," he said. "It IS almost lunchtime."

I've been typing for three hours? Honey was astonished. This was some sort of a record, she was sure. Maybe Biff was from a ratings publisher, and this accomplishment would go down in the Book of Greats. She ached to stretch her arms, her back—but she didn't want to give Herr Bangle the satisfaction. She wondered what kind of job the guy had, that he could be in an outbuilding with a temp for three hours and nobody cared or came looking for him. *Maybe he's an executive, or something.*

Biff motioned for Honey to follow him. He closed the metal door behind them, but didn't padlock it. They began their long walk to the factory's back door. As they approached, that door flew open and a man in a blue suit came bolting toward them, waving his arms like he was on a desert island and was signaling a spotter plane.

As the distance between the parties lessened, Honey could hear the man yelling, "Biff! Biff! There's a call!"

Next to Honey, Biff's steps slowed. When he stopped in the parking lot, Honey did, too. The running man came to a halt in front of them.

"Headquarters is calling," the man huffed, putting a hand on his knee to catch his breath. It was hot on the asphalt that day, and he didn't look like much of a runner.

"They never call," Biff said. His voice sounded hollow, and a little scared.

"Well, they're calling now."

Biff looked less like a Reichstag member and more like a frightened child when he turned to Honey.

"Do you think you can carry on without me?" he asked.

"I believe I could carry on fine." Honey tried for a level tenor, squeezing all joyful connotation from her words.

The two men hurried away to the back door of the factory, leaving our girl to find the restroom on her own. Luckily, she got into conversation with a young Black woman in there, whose name badge read:

Little Rebel says
My name is
MELANIE!

They looked at each other in the mirror as they were washing their hands.

"You doing temp work for Bangle?" Melanie asked.

"Yeah. It's pretty strange."

Honey's compatriot grinned. "Ha, I bet. He got you out in the pump house typing from the phone book?"

"Yes!" Honey said, eyes wide. "I've been typing for hours."

"Let me guess, he's just standing there, the whole time."

"Yes, yes! Omigod, I'm not sure I want to spend three weeks doing that."

"That's why you're making the big bucks," Melanie observed, drying her hands. "Not many temps can hack it. He just keeps jacking up the hourly rate, until somebody bites."

Honey, eager for information about her weird assignment, asked, "Do you know why he does it?"

They tossed their paper towels in the bin. Melanie said, "I quit trying to figure out white guys a long time ago."

Honey held the door for her, and they walked out into the roar of manufacturing machinery, steeping in the cloying scent of vanilla peanuts. Two women in white smocks rushed up.

"Did you hear? Bangle got canned."

The four of them retreated into the restroom, where the excited gossip was easier to hear. Biff Bangle had been axed by headquarters—he had indeed been a Little Rebel executive, an operational vice president. After much dramatic speculation about possible replacements for this fallen leader, and a wager whose payoff was based on sick-day tradeoffs, the three plant workers turned to Honey's dilemma. They were able to offer guidance to the clueless temp worker among them.

"Go up to the third floor and find the HR department," Melanie advised. "They'll tell you what to do." Her colleague said, "Ask for Marlene."

When Marlene in HR advised Honey to continue her scheduled duties for the three weeks, our girl asked who would be reviewing the work she produced. Honey wanted to get paid, after all, so clear knowledge of the approval process was key, as she made her decision about whether or not to bail on the spot.

The harried HR manager said, "You know what, just do your best at it, whatever it is he's got you doing. I'll make sure you get paid, either way. I know you're earning a high rate, so obviously it's important work. Little Rebel just appreciates your willingness to stay and finish what you've started."

Knowing that she'd get paid either way, Honey spent the next three weeks making the pump house her vacation home. Melanie loaned her a little coffee maker, and our girl brought in a cooler to hold drinks and some snacks. She put paperback books in her backpack, and though the guard eyed her suspiciously at security check-in, he let her bring them in.

Honey had three lovely weeks out in her tiny concrete-block kingdom, reading books and practicing her dance moves under the glow of the bare bulb. She spent hours talking with her friends on her cell phone, wrote two new songs, and sorted her digital photo library. Honey left the original typed pages on the desk on her last day on the job, and padlocked the metal door behind her.

Little Rebel says
Take that final paycheck and run for the hills!

~ ~ ~

In Atlanta, Honey became known for many credible accomplishments, but by the end of the fourth year most of her income came from the writing. Her bylines had appeared in *Rolling Stone* and *Billboard*, and when the copy she ghostwrote for a young female blues singer became insanely popular on Instagram, Honey's star rose further. She enjoyed her work as a freelancer for an Atlanta ad agency, where she wrote marketing copy for a software company. The folks at the ad agency seemed to value Honey because she took the time to learn the products before she wrote about them—a pretty low bar, some businesspeople would say.

She had no male companionship during that time. Making the rent was more important than having sex with somebody even halfway safe, and life on the road with Sir Stokes made long-term relationships impossible. For four years, she'd been able to retain her sweet apartment in Buckhead, but it came at a cost. She was exhausted. Honey was frazzled, she was fried, and she was forty. And then came the email: her rent would nearly double.

Our girl found herself with a dilemma: she could either sell the *mola*, now beautifully framed under UV glass and now worth $70,000, or she could move somewhere less expensive.

Honey did both.

~ ~ ~

Our girl returned to Florida, the place she knew best, and the place that held her closest friends. To confirm her commitment to Tampa Bay, Honey sold the *mola* and used the money to put a

221

down payment on a loft in downtown St. Petersburg. Then she started looking for her next job. Her next writing job, that is.

She re-entered her community as an experienced content creative. A whole new Honey.

The girl who loved a challenge now created messages that could compel human beings to change their behavior, in the moment, based upon words that they read or heard. For writers in a digital world who literally have just two seconds to succeed, creating this relevant connection is maddening. It's exhilarating. It's fulfilling. Honey was told, "Go change behavior with words—and PS, you only get five."

What's not to love?

She'd been referred to The Emma Brandt Agency because the local advertising firm wanted an in-house creative to manage its writing staff. A word-of-mouth recommendation was worth a lot in South Tampa at that time, and Honey assumed that she'd scored the introduction because the person doing the recommending was Trevor Bankhead. His five-year marriage had dissolved, and he and Honey were having a grand time getting reacquainted.

~ ~ ~

She'd never forgotten the look on Trevor's face when she'd announced that she was moving to Atlanta for the Condition Foundation job. It was only their third date, at that point, so she hadn't expected that look, not at all. But this was the image that had popped up to surprise her, after she moved away. The persistence of that vision meant something, if a girl knew how to listen.

And Honey had been practicing at that.

~ ~ ~

Now she stood trembling in the Emma Brandt Agency's two-stall bathroom with one shoe off, gripping the counter with a quaking hand as Helen frantically swiped at her jacket with a damp paper towel. Down the hall, Honey's desk was finally in place.

"I think I'm making it worse." Helen stopped wiping, stepped back, and looked into Honey's eyes. "I am so sorry about all this."

"Not your fault," Honey said. "Word on the street is, it was Emma's idea."

"It's good that you can be funny when you're standing in a pool of your own blood and we wrecked your outfit." Helen's face lit with a smile. "You'll do fine here."

It turned out that Helen had been with The Emma Brandt Agency since the beginning—six years. "Boutique" meant "small" back then, but Emma seemed to make a good living with a staff of eight or ten. She had some solid, longstanding contracts with a range of mid-sized businesses. Honey had enjoyed meeting Emma, a tall, brash brunette whose accent carried a dash of eastern European. She spoke in grand terms about how much value Honey could add—not only as a content creator, but as a manager of the sole writer on staff, a young woman who'd been there eight months.

"I hear she's bringing you in to help with Mikey," Helen said. "Here, put your foot on this."

Honey lifted her bare foot, and Helen slipped a stack of wet paper towels under it.

"Oh, that's better. Thanks." Honey raked her damp hair away from her face. "Yeah, I get the impression that managing Mikey is my main goal here, right at first. You work with her. What's your take on the situation?"

Helen looked at the restroom door. "You didn't hear this from me."

"Of course."

"Well, Mikey is the problem employee around here, because she won't meet her deadlines. Like, they make sure she has plenty of time, and they check in on her progress, and she's always saying *No problem, don't worry*. But then she doesn't deliver. She has nothing."

Honey said, "And she's been here eight months?"

"Yeah. She's slowing everybody down, the schedules are just fiction now. It's a mess."

Honey looked up at her reflection in the mirror, and she had to laugh. She looked like she'd been wrestling in the mud, and she'd been the loser of the match. She began to rub grime from her cheek. She thought about an employee who never met a deadline in eight months.

"Why doesn't Emma just fire her?" Honey asked.

Helen had found a First Aid kit in a drawer and was rummaging through it. "Maybe that's your job. Ooh, look, gauze."

The bathroom door flew open, and Emma Brandt held it back with her arm. "There you are. I guess you two are getting to know each other. That's nice."

If Emma saw that her new content manager was disheveled, she didn't acknowledge it.

"Honey, can we meet? I want to talk about next steps. Come with me."

"Sorry," Honey said. "Maybe a little later this afternoon, okay? Right now, I need to go get a tetanus shot."

~ ~ ~

Honey's new boss was on board with the plan to improve Mikey's performance.

"You make it clear to her that meeting deadlines is core to her job," Emma said. "You put her on final notice. So then she knows that if she misses a deadline, she puts her job at risk."

"Yes," Honey said. "A new boss means new rules, sometimes, right?"

"Precisely! I love this idea. I'm sure she'll come around."

Honey wasn't so sure. She'd spent some time in Mikey in those first few days, including a one-hour lunch that proved revealing.

Mikey, it seemed, had recently left a four-year stint in the military, and claimed to miss the discipline that came with it. *It was great to be able to look across a big crowd of people and know exactly who the leaders were*, Mikey said, gazing out at the restaurant full of diners in business suits and dark blazers.

When Honey said *I'm your leader now*, Mikey had laughed out loud. *Yeah, not seeing your campaign ribbons*, Mikey had said. *Not seeing your stars and bars. So, I guess you'll have to prove that to me*. And Honey had said, *Fair enough*.

~ ~ ~

"I'll give her a simple project, with the goal of delivery next Thursday," Honey said to Emma. "I'll check in with her, of course, to see if she's having trouble, or has any questions. I'll reiterate that she's on notice, and that she must meet her deadline. Then it will be a simple matter of seeing whether she delivers. We can address quality later."

"Oh, she'll deliver," Emma said, eyes shining. "I have faith in her."

"Why?" Honey asked, and she saw Emma tilt her head, like she was confused by the question.

The boss said, "Maybe what I mean is, I have faith in you."

~ ~ ~

The following Monday, her second Monday on the job, Honey approached Mikey's cubicle and asked how the project was coming along.

"Just great!" Mikey chirped.

"Let me see what you've got so far."

Mikey sat back in her chair. "Oh, no. It's not ready for review yet. All I have now are notes."

"It's 600 words," Honey said. "Not a heavy lift."

The young woman reached for headphones and put them on.

"Sorry, can't hear you," Mikey said.

~ ~ ~

On Tuesday, Honey appeared again in Mikey's cubicle.

"Your deadline for that copy is Thursday," Honey said. "Two days."

Mikey shrugged. Honey saw that she was playing a game on her computer.

"Need any help with that copy draft?"

Mikey jerked back as if she was insulted, but she left the game live on her screen. She leveled her gaze at Honey. "You don't know my creative process," she said. "You don't know how I work."

"True," Honey said. "But let me know if you want me to review your copy, before you officially submit it to the tracking system."

"Are you telling me I have to?"

"No," Honey said. "It's just an offer."

"Yeah, I'll pass on that."

Our girl stepped a little closer. "I'm on your side, here, you know. I want you to succeed. How can I help?"

Her direct report smiled up at Honey. "Here's something I'm sure of," Mikey said. "You can't help me."

~ ~ ~

On Wednesday morning, Mikey was nowhere to be found. That afternoon, though, Honey saw her slipping through the back entrance to the building with her backpack. Our girl was waiting in Mikey's cubicle when the young woman arrived.

"Are you okay?" Honey asked. "I've been looking for you."

"Oh, I've been here all day."

"Really."

Mikey placed her backpack on the floor and eased herself into her chair. She stretched her arms up over her head, yawned, and smiled.

"How are you coming with that copyset? Will it be ready tomorrow?"

"Stop stressing," Mikey said. "Jesus Christ."

"I ask about it because your job is on the line here," Honey said. "I want you to succeed, not fail. All you have to do is meet your deadline tomorrow. That's all I ask."

"You're full of demands, aren't you?" Mikey's eyes were alight. It was almost like she was having fun.

"Ours is a demanding business," Honey said. "Send me your copy by end of day tomorrow."

"And that's an order?" Mikey gave Honey a snappy salute, then turned her chair away, laughing.

~ ~ ~

Friday morning, Honey and her boss met again to discuss Mikey. No copy had been received.

"I'm just so disappointed," Emma sighed.

"Well, it's good information though," Honey replied. "Now we can get a real writer in here."

Emma sat back in her chair. "But what do you mean?"

"I mean, we gave Mikey one last chance, and she failed to deliver. She knew the consequences. I'll meet with her this afternoon, to give her the news."

"The news?"

"That she's dismissed," Honey said. "Fired."

"Well, you can't do that!" Emma leaped up from her chair and began pacing back and forth. "You can't just fire her," she exclaimed, waving her hands.

What the hell is happening? Honey said, "Emma, I thought we were on the same page here. We talked about this. Final notice is just what it sounds like: final. Failure to deliver means loss of employment."

"But I was sure she'd meet her deadline," Emma said. "I thought she'd surprise us."

Honey looked out the window. "No surprises here."

"Well, we can't fire her." Emma stopped in front of Honey's chair and gazed down with wet eyes. "That wouldn't be fair."

Honey tried to understand what was going on. "It's fair to the business."

"Is it, though? We're a family business."

No, you're not, Honey thought. *None of your family members work here.* She decided to say, "Tell me more about that."

"Oh, Honey," Emma cried out, throwing herself down on the couch. She looked deep into Honey's eyes. "I want to help her. I know I can."

"Who? Mikey?"

"Yes," Emma sobbed. She rubbed her eyes and took a shaky breath. "She just needs somebody who believes in her."

"Ohh-kay," Honey said.

"I've tried so hard to help her." Emma's pleading tone got Honey's attention. "She told me this morning at home that she intends to be the best marketing writer in Florida."

"At home?"

"Well, yes. Mikey lives in my spare bedroom."

Honey sat nodding, taking in this new information.

Emma clasped her hands together. "When she first came to work here, she had nothing. Not even a car! So, I took her in, and she's just lovely. Just a lovely young woman, really. She's overcome so much, Honey, you don't even know. I've been paying for her therapy, of course, and to me, it looks like she's turning the corner."

"That's wonderful," Honey said. "I'm glad she has someone who believes in her. But I have to be honest, Emma. If I'd known this was a family business, I wouldn't have taken the job."

"Oh, really?"

"Yes. So now that I know, I'll tell you that today is my last day at your agency."

"Oh no." Emma put her hands to her cheeks. "But you've only been here two weeks."

"The situation is untenable," Honey said. "I'll go clean out my desk. You can mail my check."

Emma looked confused and flustered. Honey stood, and they shook hands. Emma's face was streaked with tears—and not because Honey was leaving.

~ ~ ~

On her way to her office to box up her belongings, Honey ran into Helen.

"Hey hey," Helen said. "I wanted to see if you're free for lunch. I can't wait to learn more about you."

"Oh, I'm sorry. I just resigned." Honey held up the empty box.

Helen just looked at her.

"I'm not a good fit for this agency," Honey said.

"Damn," Helen said, eyes wide. "You figured that out fast enough."

Honey shrugged. *It is what it is.*

"You're actually my hero now," Helen said. "Wow. I've never seen anybody size up a situation like you have, so fast. But I'm upset, honestly. I was looking forward to working with you. I got the feeling that I'd found a new friend."

"Me, too," Honey said, and they smiled together. "Want to grab lunch next Wednesday? I could drive over and meet you somewhere."

"That would be great."

And that's how Honey and Helen became fast friends forever.

~ ~ ~

Honey's Mom called one night, and our girl could tell that something was up. Mom's voice sounded different, and contained a timbre that was reserved for only the best of news.

"I just talked with your brother," Mom said.

"What's up with him?"

"Peggy's pregnant!"

Honey squealed, as Southern women are prone to do when they

hear such news. She and her mom celebrated over the phone at the momentous impact of what would occur in just six months.

"She's so excited," Mom said. "And Max is over the moon."

"I bet. This is wonderful, Mom, what awesome news."

Her mother hesitated, then asked, "So you're not upset?"

"Why would I be upset?" Honey didn't understand this line of questioning.

"Well, you know … you didn't have children."

"Yeah," Honey said, "And now it's too late. But that's cool. Totally okay. No biggie."

Honey realized that she'd never had a conversation with her mother about children, pro or con. She said, "I never wanted them, you know."

She could hear her mother sigh.

"There's plenty of kids in this world," Honey said. "I never felt the urge to add more."

But still, her mother said nothing.

"Mom," Honey said, "Seriously. It's too late for me now, and I know it. I have no regrets."

The distance between them sounded like static on the line.

Her mother said, "Well, for what it's worth, I think you would've made a great mom."

"Thanks," Honey said. "We'll never know."

~ ~ ~

"I noticed you right from the start," Trevor told Honey. They were at his place, a loft space with windows that faced Tampa Bay, naked under the covers of his bed, listening to the faint *tink tink* of the ceiling fan in the quiet of early morning. "At the clubs, right, you were always the brightest light. Even if you couldn't dance."

"What? I'm a great dancer."

He looked over at her. "You're an enthusiastic dancer. There's a difference."

"Hmph. Well, at least you noticed me."

"Oh, I sure did. I'm a sucker for enthusiasm. But then I went in for that interview with Meloso, remember? And I couldn't believe it was YOU, sitting there at the reception desk. Then I really wanted the job."

Honey leaned over and kissed him, full on the mouth. He tasted delicious, like apples and pears.

"I still can't figure out why he didn't hire me," Trevor said. "Like, I was perfect for that job."

So Honey told him why Mr. Meloso had taken a pass. Trevor closed his eyes and pinched the bridge of his nose as she explained the boss's rationale.

"Just because I moved the chair? That's some weird shit there," Trevor said.

"Yes, sir, it is."

"How long did you work for him?"

"Eight months," Honey said. "It felt like forever."

"Yeah, what felt like forever was my ill-fated marriage to Janine. Looking back on it, I might have been in some kind of rebound situation. You know, after you left for Atlanta."

Honey wondered if he'd ever bring that up—and now he had.

"Let's talk about that," she said. "I guess I can tell you, for years after I moved, this image of you kept popping up in my head, the expression on your face when I told you I'd be moving away."

"Really? Well, that's something, isn't it?" Trevor brushed Honey's hair away from her face and traced a lingering finger across her cheek. "I just knew I didn't have the power to stop you. You've always been so focused on your career."

"You're right about that. Nothing could have stopped me, back then. I guess I felt like I had a lot to prove, maybe. I thought I had to do it on my own."

Trevor moved closer. He wrapped her in his arms. "I know. I was the same way, when I was starting out. But even capable people don't have to do everything on their own. You know that, right?"

She nodded, and felt his bare chest, warm against her cheek.

"I'm here, Honey. I'm right here, and this time, I want to keep you close, if I can."

Honey snuggled against him, and she could feel the beat of his heart exactly matching hers.

Trevor said, "This feels right, doesn't it?"

Above her, *tink tink*, like the *yes yes* sign from an angel, and Honey said, "It sure does."

~ ~ ~

Trevor and Honey arrived in style for the wedding on Bayshore Boulevard, appropriately dressed and ready to celebrate. It was the hottest ticket in town: the re-marriage of Shane and Brandy McLane.

Trevor pulled in past the bougainvillea hedge to the half-moon portico of the two-story, 15,000-square-foot stucco mansion, underneath the stately line of Queen palms. Trevor was tickled when his 1953 Pontiac Chieftain was parked in one of the few display spots near the door. The other cars there were a Maserati Levante, a Porsche 911, and a Rolls Royce Ghost, and none of them had a bumper sticker that read:

If you're happy and you know it see a shrink.

The doors of the renovated mansion stood open, but of course were flanked by hired security. You never knew when the press might try to crash a billionaire's party, or a jilted blond shoe salesperson with a grudge. Nobody wanted that. Trevor and Honey showed their IDs, signed the guestbook, and then our girl took a quick detour to the British Tea Room, to show Trevor her mom's design work. It had, after all, sparked the reconciliation between bride and groom.

"That's a lot of freakin' chintz," Trevor said, looking around.

"It takes a lot of chintz to seal a deal like this one."

The McLane manse had a ballroom, of course—it wouldn't be a proper mansion without one—and 200 hand-selected guests filed in to take their seats under an intricately carved ceiling. Light streamed in through windows two stories tall, and a beautiful woman created beautiful music on a Yamaha Grand stage left. Surrounded by the thick perfumes and colognes of the assembled guests, Trevor had a sneezing fit. It happened, sometimes—and knowing that, Honey had brought tissues and Claritin meltaways.

A minister in a white collar already stood up front, and Honey could see someone peeking out of a paneled door, behind which groomsmen waited. While guests anticipated the upbeat chords of the wedding march, Honey saw that Trevor was looking around the room with wonder.

He said, "I know you've been friends with Shane forever. How did you two meet?"

Honey thought about lying, but she wasn't very good at that. She knew that Trevor wouldn't be surprised to learn that she'd dated around. It was no secret.

"He asked me out," she said. "We had a couple of dates."

Trevor pulled back and stared at her. "YOU. Dated Shane McLane."

Why is this so hard for people to believe? Honey wondered.

"Yes, I did," she said. Our girl saw that Trevor was frowning, not a good look at a wedding. It worried her.

"We were never intimate," she whispered. "If that's what's bothering you."

"Nah, it's not that." Trevor leaned closer to her and rested his hand on her knee. "I'm just wondering, why didn't you hang onto him? Make him YOUR husband, you know, instead of helping him marry somebody else." He looked around the room. "All this could be yours."

"I might have gone that route, if all I cared about was money."

"He's got plenty of it," Trevor said, looking up at the high ceiling, where a thousand tiny globe lights had been meticulously suspended from the beams above on strings of silver. He sat back in his chair, shaking his head. "Man oh man."

It occurred to Honey that Trevor might be feeling the tiniest bit insecure.

"Yeah, but I was looking for something else," Honey whispered. "Turns out, I was looking for you."

Trevor shot a glance her way. "You're so smarmy." He smiled. "I love you for that."

~ ~ ~

One night, Honey and Trevor made the drive from St. Petersburg to Tippy's Smokehouse on the Hillsborough River. The sign at the entrance was freshly painted, but otherwise the ramshackle property looked much the same. Our girl was excited to introduce Trevor to Sir Stokes that night. Stokes had always told her that she'd end up with somebody special—and he'd been right.

She thought back to the night when the bluesman had talked about love.

~ ~ ~

She and Stokes had been sitting at a bar, of course, a blues venue in Clarksdale, Mississippi, just 12 miles from the infamous Devil's Crossroads of lore. The night had been a successful one, the audience engaged and joyful, and band members were in high spirits, having a beer after closing time. Floors mopped, glasses were stacked, and the beer in front of them was super-chilled. Honey and Stokes sat on barstools, and the bassist, Eugene, stood close by.

"How come you never got married?" Honey asked Stokes. She'd never seen him with a long-term lady, though he claimed in his songs to enjoy the female form, particularly its Southern hemispheres.

Stokes looked over at her with a grimace. "The road doesn't mix too good with that."

Eugene said, "He does have a plan for later, though. Don't you, Chief?"

A smile came to Stokes' face, and he shrugged like he was embarrassed. He looked over at Honey and said, "I always wanted to move somewhere cold, you know? I spent my whole life in this heat. I been looking at Oslo."

"Norway? That's a long way from home."

Stokes turned his empty beer bottle in his hand, watching it intently, like he held a crystal ball. Honey noticed the wistfulness in his voice when he said, "Sometimes I think, what if I had a woman? Somebody to sit on the porch with me to keep me company when the weather's nice—and to keep me warm, when it ain't."

"That's every man's dream, right there," Eugene said.

~ ~ ~

Now Honey and Trevor wormed their way forward through the crowd at Tippy's, and when Honey recognized a former busboy who was now head of Security, they were able to climb up three steps and could view the Sir Stokes show from stage right. It was a joy-filled homecoming, and as Honey looked out, many of the faces in the crowd looked familiar, though wrinkles and weight gain made it difficult to be sure. *They probably think the same of me*, Honey thought. She was no longer that fresh-faced young girl who sang from the shadows backstage—and she didn't weigh 90 pounds anymore, either. There was much that was different about this Honey Malone, and much that remained unchanged.

At 2:30 in the morning, after Stokes had put away his Gibson and the backstage interlude had ended, Honey approached to introduce Trevor. As the men got to talking, Stokes found out that Trevor knew a little something about antique cars, and Honey found herself left out of the conversation. *Just as well.* She wanted two of her favorite men to like each other, and it was apparent that they did.

She walked over to the table where pizza had been laid out for general consumption and began to fill a trash bag with paper plates, cups and empty boxes. That's just what you did, backstage. Anybody who was sober enough to clean up was encouraged to do so. Honey carried the bag through the kitchen to the back alley, where the garbage bins waited.

The sound of bullfrogs was louder, this close to the swamp. Two women were snuffing out their cigarettes, turning back toward the steps at the kitchen door. They were both beautiful, Black and middle-aged, dressed in the tan slacks and burgundy tops of Tippy's security, such as it was, and Honey heard a snippet of conversation as they walked past.

"—always wanted to move somewhere cold, you know? I spent my whole life in this heat. All I want is a nice front porch and a nice old man—"

The trash bag landed hard next to Honey's foot. She spun around and saw the two women disappearing into the crowded kitchen. Our girl raced to catch up, yanking the door open, then jumping on her tiptoes to scan across the room. She spotted them, and dodged bodies as she pursued the retreating figures. The tall woman who had spoken looked mighty fine in those tight khakis, Honey couldn't help but notice.

"Wait," our girl called out. The women turned and eyed her warily, like maybe she was trouble. They were Security, after all.

Honey reached them and said, "Listen, y'all, I wondered if you'd like to meet the headliner."

The woman who liked cold weather broke into a grin.

"Well, I sure would," she said. "Sir Stokes is a fox."

~ ~ ~

On the ride home from Tippy's that night, Trevor asked, "Who is this Tisha that you brought over? I believe my buddy Stokes was smitten."

"I thought so, too!"

"Here I was, talking to the great man about F100 pickup trucks and the advantages of manual transmissions, when BOOM his attention gets focused elsewhere. Once he got a look at Tisha, he never looked away. Did you see them when we left? They were cuddled up on that bench out back like they'd known each other forever."

"It sure seemed that way," Honey said, and she couldn't stop smiling.

BOSS 6: WINSTON

Honey's title: Creative Director, Jameson Ross Financial

"Winston Sellers wants me for CD at Jameson Ross," Honey said. It was a cool morning, and she and Trevor were spooned up under a blanket on her couch, going through their Saturday emails.

"Ugh," Trevor said. "Jameson Ross."

"I know," she sighed. It was common knowledge in the Tampa Bay area that the privately held financial services firm had a reputation for being backward. Internecine. An old boys' club. The company had recently been in the news for yet another sexual harassment lawsuit.

"But they pay well," Honey said. "They'd love to hire a woman for such a visible position."

"I bet they would." Trevor brushed her hair away from her face.

"It would look good on your resume, though."

"Right?" *My two-week stint at The Emma Brandt Agency sure didn't make the cut.* "What do you know about Sellers?"

"Not much. We're on a committee together at the club, but I haven't spent a lot of time with him. He's been at Jameson Ross for a long time, like, ten years maybe. I get the impression that he's a little hard to read."

Honey scrolled through the message on her screen. "He wonders if I'd take a phone call."

"No harm in that," Trevor said. He moved his body to spoon her tighter, just the way she liked it. "Go ahead and listen to his pitch. But before you agree to meet him in person, tell him straight out that he can't afford you. Tell him you don't want to waste his time."

"Because that means that I don't want *him* to waste *my* time." She turned her head so she could see his eyes. "Trevor Bankhead, you're one smart guy."

He smiled and pulled the blanket higher.

"Back at ya," he said.

~ ~ ~

It took nearly an hour to drive from downtown St. Petersburg to the far north end of Tampa, and our girl made note of that. When she arrived for her job interview at the glass headquarters building on the 200-acre Jameson Ross campus, Honey found herself in a vast sun-drenched lobby whose marble floors showcased low-slung couches covered in jewel-toned velvet. Every man in sight was wearing a pricey suit, and every woman present wore a skirt and heels. When Honey approached the reception desk, the large painting that hung on the wall proved to be a genuine Jackson

Pollack.

Too bad she had to walk past a Black shoeshine man to get there. *What kind of throwback shit is this? It's the twenty-first century, last time I checked.*

Honey felt a little self-conscious in her black pants suit and Nikes, now that she saw that everyone in the Jameson Ross building appeared to be over-dressed in their Sunday best. Maybe they were dressed for church because they worked at a financial company, and everybody worshipped money. *There's so much to learn about this place*, Honey thought. *But I won't be wearing heels.*

Winston Sellers met her in reception, and they rode together in the elevator to the eighth floor. Honey stole a look at him, and he was doing the same with her. They smiled. The Vice President of Marketing was a good-looking fellow about her age, a blond with a fetching surfer-boy haircut, wearing a bespoke suit of charcoal silk.

"You've got an impressive resume," Winston said.

"So do you."

He cut another look at her, maybe surprised that she'd looked him up.

"This interview is just a formality," he said. "Everybody wants you here."

Who's everybody? Honey wondered, but the elevator doors opened then, and Winston led her through a bustling space to his office. Many eyes turned their way, and Honey remembered that she'd have eight direct reports, if she took this job: five copywriters, an editor, one video director, and the man they called "the podcast guy," but whose name was Jamal.

They settled into Winston's spacious office. Honey learned that

Jameson Ross had 200 financial advisory offices across the US and Canada, and many of those offices would be using Honey's team to help create their own unique branded materials.

"It'll be a big part of your job," Winston told her. "Lots and lots of branding work."

"I love that kind of thing," Honey said, and his eyes widened. It seemed a good time to bring it up, so she said, "Let's talk about my predecessor. Is that person still on staff?"

Winston didn't answer right away. Honey got the sense that he was the consummate cool character—somebody who monitored his emotions carefully, and maybe his agendas, too. But Winston seemed to live his cool in an uncannily natural way, so she couldn't be sure about any underlying intentions. Beneath that adorable haircut might lie the gears of machination, meshed and churning, never stopping, burning oil. Or maybe he truly was a surfer boy at heart—he'd ended up in marketing in Florida, after all. Time would tell, with somebody like Winston.

He sat back in his chair. "Actually, you'll be the first creative director we've ever had who focuses on the words. Before now, we've only just had a design director. Jake Franklin."

"Oh, he's talented," Honey said. *You've never had a CD who focuses on the words? What kind of bush league game is this?*

Winston said, "I'm glad you think so. You two will be working closely together, right from the start. I mean, if you take the position."

They sat looking at each other.

"You think you want this job?" Winston sounded so earnest. He seemed so concerned that she might say No.

"I think I'd be great at this job."

Again, they sat in silence.

"But you're not sure you want it," Winston said.

"I gotta be honest. I don't want to work at a place that has a Black shoeshine man in the lobby."

His aspect did not change. Winston was extremely good at cloaking his emotions. *Maybe he teaches a Master Class in inscrutability.*

"Couldn't agree more—and there's good news on that," he said smoothly. "Milton is retiring at the end of the month, and he won't be replaced. But I still sense something's holding you back. Are you concerned about compensation?"

"The money is important," Honey said. "Because the words are important. Every bit as important as the design, actually. But I'm also concerned that Jameson Ross has a tainted reputation in the community."

Winston sighed and looked at the ceiling. "The lawsuit thing."

"It's not just the lawsuit. It's the fact that it's the latest lawsuit."

"I hear what you're saying." Winston ran his hand through his hair, and Honey watched in admiration as it fell beautifully back into place, lock by lock. "But that sort of thing doesn't happen in our department, I can assure you. That's more of a problem for the advisory group, you know?"

They sat in silence. Beyond the windows, she could see a fleet of riding mowers, moving in syncopated rhythm across the lush turf that surrounded the complex.

"Give us a chance, Honey," Winston said. "We really need a talent like yours, and I swear we've never had anyone complain about harassment in Marketing."

They sat looking at each other. Then Winston sealed the deal with one sentence. He said, "I'd never be anything but honest with you."

Well, that's nice to hear.

He must have noted Honey's positive response to his statement, because Winston pulled a pad closer and wrote a figure on it. That's how some hiring managers did it, she'd learned. They'd write down the monetary offer, so they didn't have to sully the civility of the conversation with crude dollar figures spoken out loud. Winston slid the note across the desk to her, and she picked up the slip and looked at it. It was 20% more than she'd hoped for.

"Is that close to the salary you'd need?" Winston asked.

Honey smiled. She crossed out what he'd written and added another 15% to the figure. Then she slid the note back to him.

Winston looked down at the number she'd proposed. He was indeed hard to read, but when he spoke, it was good news. "I think this would work. Look for an offer letter within 48 hours."

When they parted in the lobby, Winston shook her hand so enthusiastically that Honey felt hopeful. Maybe she'd judged Winston too harshly. *Maybe he'll be a good boss. At least I know he won't lie to me like Pretty Preston, so I'm already ahead of the game.*

~ ~ ~

Honey returned to the world of finance—and it was nothing like Deal Hipper. Her favorite thing about the new job: the people who reported to her. Honey made an effort to get to know each of them, and they seemed starved for that. The videographer said, "I've never had a one-on-one meeting with a manager to talk about my goals, and I've been here ten years." Our girl was disturbed to learn that before she'd arrived, he'd reported to Winston. All of them had worked directly for Winston—and none sang his praises. None of them wanted to say anything at all about Winston Sellers, pro or con. This was a group that kept their heads down. But they were all whip-smart, energetic, and dedicated to the firm's success. That's a fine start, no matter what kind of manager you are.

As Honey learned about each team member's dreams, bandwidth and talents, it was easier to give them what they needed. She had the ability to determine what they'd be working on, and when, so Honey balanced the mundane with the exciting. When they failed in a new assignment, she'd talk privately with them about why. When they succeeded, she praised them in front of their peers.

She encouraged them to correct her when she was wrong. They weren't comfortable with this, at first—it seemed to go against the Jameson Ross way of working. But Honey explained, "You're helping me here. I don't want to fall on my face by making some rookie mistake. Help me understand." And they did. She became a better employee because of the team's open input. But it took a while for Honey to understand just how much they were all holding back. She hadn't grasped the full power of the golden handcuffs that trapped each of them so tightly at one of Tampa Bay's premier employers.

~ ~ ~

Honey was back in town with her girlfriends again: Nicole, CeeCee, Milana, Margo—and now Helen from Emma Brandt, who had slipped into the circle with no effort, because of her acerbic approach to life and her upbeat approach to business. The crew made a standing date for lunch every month, and often the restaurant where they met was Mango's, an outdoor-dining establishment with a shaded deck that overlooked Tampa Bay.

Momentous revelations can arrive innocuously, in the most routine of situations, as was proven this particular Thursday. As always, the six of them arrived early, to grab the big table near the water. Once they'd ordered and had their glasses of iced tea at the ready, Nicole tapped her glass with a spoon.

"I've got news," she announced. The table chatter died down, and five sets of eyes turned Nicole's way. "Joe Stecher got married."

Four sets of eyes then moved to focus on Honey, so Helen looked at her, too.

"Honey lived with Joe, there for a while," Milana told Helen, who didn't know the backstory.

"What was your favorite part about him, Honey?" Helen asked, and then sat back in surprise as her companions exploded with laughter.

"He was a good lover," was what Honey said.

"Nice," Helen said. "I see that you had your priorities straight, even as a young woman."

"And now she's seeing Trevor Bankhead," CeeCee said.

"Omigod so cute," Milana said.

"Most eligible bachelor!" Margo gushed.

"Super hot," Nicole volunteered.

"Oh, I've seen him, haven't I?" Helen asked. "In the press? Nice hair, chiseled jaw, advises politicians?"

"That's the guy," CeeCee said.

"Oh, Honey," Helen said, "maybe you should make Trevor Bankhead your priority, now."

"It's not hard duty," our girl said. Just four words, but something about her tone, and the smile in her eyes, caught the attention of every woman there. That's when they knew it: Honey Malone was in love.

~ ~ ~

"Your people seem to like their stretch projects," Winston said to Honey one day, about a month into her tenure. He'd even stepped into her office, an unusual move on his part. "Where'd you get an idea like that?"

"I had a boss at Touchpoint, Casey Caruthers. He's the one who introduced me to stretch assignments."

"Well, maybe you'd like one," her boss said.

"Getting to know Jameson Ross is stretch enough," Honey laughed. "There's a lot to be accomplished, and I'm still learning my way through it."

"Yeah, well, some stretch projects can't be rejected," he said.

That wiped the smile off Honey's face.

Winston said, "We're starting a quarterly print magazine for high-net-worth investors, and you'll be heading it up, editorially."

Aha, Honey thought. *This is why "everybody" wanted me here: because I know magazines.*

"It's a high-profile project for senior management," Winston explained. "You're crucial to success, because we want to give readers editorial substance. I'll send you the PowerPoint deck, that'll tell you more."

"Okay," she said, because what else could she say?

Winston said, "First issue goes out in two months."

"Two months? That's, um, an awfully short ramp-up."

"Rally the troops," he responded. "Seems like your people would follow you into a burning building."

It was the second time he'd used the phrase *your people,* and it bugged her. They didn't belong to her. They weren't her possessions. But Honey held her tongue. She was still incredulous that the firm wanted to create a national magazine—from scratch—in such a short timeframe. She stood blinking, thinking, already mapping out a compressed Gantt chart timeline in her head. She couldn't help it. It was second nature, by then. Our girl loved a challenge, but this was a big one.

"You see to it that we have two issues published by the end of the year," Winston said, "and there's a financial reward waiting for you."

"Oh?" As a businessperson, Honey wanted to learn more about that aspect of the ask. And once burned by Preston, she waited for the trigger word *bonus* to be spoken.

"A twenty percent raise," Winston said.

"Nice."

"Yep," he said, smiling. "Think that's enough to get your wheels turning?"

"They're turning already," she said, because it was a core tenet of Honey's personal brand to be upbeat. But in reality, she was wondering how an already-overburdened staff of writers and designers could ever meet such an aggressive goal. Resonant content depended on one thing, after all: knowledge of the audience. *And I don't have that. Not yet.*

"Good deal. I knew you'd be on board." Without another word, Winston turned and left her standing there, alone with her fears of failure.

Head spinning from the herculean task before her, Honey went straight to the art director's office, bypassing a designer's birthday celebration that was starting up. Jake was at his desk, and when he looked up and saw her face, he walked over and closed the door behind her.

~ ~ ~

Honey's second-favorite thing about her job was the art director, Jake Franklin. The truth was, Jake saw things that she couldn't. That's the kind of person you want around, when the audience matters. An experienced designer, Jake did more listening than talking, and as time passed it became obvious to all that Jake and Honey were creatively simpatico. The creative staff joked that the two of them went into Mind Meld Mode whenever they brainstormed a new project, and everyone noticed the improvement in quality that resulted from their collaboration. Honey knew she'd need every bit of the Jake's intellect, talent, and support if she was to fulfill their boss's marching orders for the new magazine.

Now Jake shut the door, faced her, and said, "So I guess Winston told you about the magazine."

Stunned, Honey fell into the nearest chair.

"Oh, so it's been a secret?" Her voice was hot. "How long have you known?"

"He told me six months ago."

She and Jake sat across from each other. He didn't look worried, he just looked … resigned. Maybe Jake had been part of this behavior in the past.

Honey sighed and said, "Well, that's kinda good, though. At least you've had some time to prepare."

He was watching her closely. "More time than you."

Beyond the office door, *Happy birthday, dear Chelsea—*

"What the fuck, Jake?"

He smiled and shrugged. Both of them were in their forties. Both of them had been around the block, by then.

Honey said, "It is what it is, am I correct?"

"Good way to put it," he said.

She groaned and threw her head back.

"Listen," he said. "It's nothing personal, really. It's just the way things are done around here. These guys, sometimes they gotta stand up and swing their dicks around. You know, for show."

Honey nodded. She was aware of that behavior.

He said, "They told me to keep it a secret. I'm sorry."

Their eyes met, and she nodded her forgiveness. Her mind raced with all that must be done, to create a magazine from nothing. It was a supremely difficult task, and she'd been kept in the dark. Her anger boiled up inside her.

"How do you put up with this shit?" Honey asked.

"I'm a hired gun." His voice was flat. "The minute somebody else comes along with a better offer, I'm gone."

Honey liked the way that sounded. *Hired gun.* She'd have to practice saying it.

"Here's the good news," Jake said. He pulled his laptop closer and tapped at the keys. "The whole first issue is pretty much designed. We've got approvals on the color palette and the cover concept, and we created some standalone page templates for shorter content. The only thing we're missing—" he turned the laptop screen toward her—"is the words."

Honey found herself looking at a magazine cover, with a gorgeous photo of a gray-haired couple on a deserted beach, laughing together in the orangey mist of their sunset years. But instead of the masthead, the name of the magazine, Honey saw bold type that proclaimed TO COME. Instead of the cover blurbs meant to entice readers: TO COME, TO COME, TO COME. So much for Winston's commitment to editorial substance.

"Those pesky words," Honey said.

She looked up at Jake then and they smiled together, but it was a smile of lost opportunities. They'd been around the block, all right—they could both instantly mourn the lost potential, and then move on.

It's just business, after all.

~ ~ ~

The first thing Honey did after she left Jake's office was to send off an email to her boss. *Just confirming today's conversation that if two issues of our new magazine are published before the end of this year, I'll be rewarded with a pay raise of 20%. Thanks for your faith in me.*

Winston never responded to her email, but Honey wasn't worried. Now, it was in writing. She'd learned her lesson well, with Pretty Preston. In a business setting, spoken promises are worthless. Once it's in writing, you're home free.

~ ~ ~

There was one senior VP in marketing at Jameson Ross that nobody liked. His name was Harry, and it was in a meeting with Harry that Honey saw the most incredible April Fool's joke of her career.

Harry's monthly review meeting happened to fall on the first of April that year. As a director, Honey was aware that most of the employees in her department had issues with this SVP, a dyed-in-the-wool micromanager and serial bully. She wasn't real fond of him, herself. But as a Director, she had to play nice.

As staffers filed into the meeting room that day, Honey noticed a distinct change in the team's collective attitude. She sensed a strange electricity. Instead of settling into their chairs, sighing and staring down at the table, every person on the team was sitting up straight. Holding back smiles. Cutting glances at each other. *Something's up*, Honey thought.

As always, Harry came late to the meeting. They'd all been sitting silently for fifteen minutes before he finally entered the room. Harry took his place at the head of the table and looked out at his underlings. "Let's get down to business. The first item on the agenda is staff tardiness."

"Ironic," the ballsy web guy Jim said. "But actually, the first item on the agenda is: we quit."

Honey looked around the table. Everybody was smiling wide, except she and Harry.

Jim continued, "We got together and decided that we can't take you one minute longer, Harry. When we leave this room, you'll have to go out and find replacements for every single one of us."

Honey would never forget the long silence that followed. She'd never forget Harry's reddening face as his emotions came to the fore—first stunned, then angry.

"You pathetic little motherfuckers," he said. "You can't quit."

And then the boss launched into the rant of a lifetime. Honey watched the employees as Harry's hurtful words washed over them—and saw nothing but pure delight. When the boss said *I'll bury you*, people began to smile. When he said *I'll make it my life's work to destroy you*, they began to laugh.

And when the rowdy laughter overwhelmed the sound of his voice, Harry stopped talking.

"April Fool's," Jim said.

~ ~ ~

Wealth Strategies magazine was a hit. Advisors around the country reported that their high-net-worth clients were calling in to ask about the Kahneman brain-twister riddle that had been the lede on Honey's story about investor behavior.

Many magazine readers wanted to get their friends and neighbors added to the subscriber list—exactly what Jameson Ross leadership had hoped would happen. Surveys showed that the firm's Net Promoter Score had risen by 10 points after the second issue was published, and a corporate press release trumpeted the fact that *Wealth Strategies* had been nominated for a national magazine award. Jameson Ross had scored a win.

Honey didn't know whether to be amused or angry when Winston marched into her office one day with a magazine opened to an editorial page, which presented the same description of investor behavior, with the same Kahneman brain-twister riddle, that she'd written for *Wealth Strategies* three months before. They'd even stolen the graphic. Honey flipped to the cover, to see who'd ripped her off so blatantly. *Quick Company.*

A catered party was thrown to celebrate the success of *Wealth Strategies*. Jameson Ross loved a catered party, and leadership encouraged the ample imbibing of alcohol during such festivities, which were held in the communal space outside Winston's office door. There were even free Uber rides home from the office, that day. Everyone seemed happy, drunk, and relieved. It had been a hard road. The staff was ready to cut loose.

Our girl found herself standing next to Winston, watching as the mostly Caucasian staff attempted to dance along to a Black DJ's jazzed-up hip-hop tracks. She and the boss were smiling as they tapped their plastic cups together in a silent toast, and Winston inclined his head toward his office door. Once they were inside, he closed the door and extended his hand. She shook it.

"Congratulations," he said, smiling wide. "I never thought that you could do it, but you did."

Okay, that's a lefthanded compliment, Honey thought. *But what of it? Probably just a figure of speech.*

"Happy to help," she said. "I'm actually pretty proud of the result."

"Oh, me too," Winston said, nodding vigorously. His face was flushed. "Great job."

They sat in his office until the music stopped at five o'clock— quitting time—talking about upcoming issues of the publication, and ideas for editorial improvement. Honey felt comfortable there with the boss, with a cup of rum punch in her hand, discussing the future. It was the first time she'd felt included in the planning, the first time she felt like her voice was heard, and both of those things felt really good. *Progress,* Honey thought. *Finally.* When she went downstairs to get in her Uber, buzzed from alcohol and buoyed by her hopeful nature, Honey felt like she might be able to overcome Jameson Ross' shortcomings and Winston's lack of transparency. Maybe she had a future with the firm, after all.

~ ~ ~

On her birthday, the staff presented Honey with a custom T-shirt. Emblazoned on the front:

SANGUINE TO THE MAX

~ ~ ~

At Honey's first editorial meeting of the new year, execution was in full force for the third issue of *Wealth Strategies* magazine. The people who reported to her were in good spirits. They said that they felt rejuvenated by the holiday break, grateful for the lavish Christmas party that Jameson Ross had hosted at Disney World, and stoked by the success of the publication they'd worked so hard to create. This gang was ready to rock and roll.

Our girl was smiling when she left that meeting. In the elevator, on her way to her ten o'clock with Compliance, Honey used her phone to check her bank balance—her royalty payment for *Grandma in a Tight T-Shirt* was due that day—and her smile disappeared. Her first Jameson Ross paycheck of the year had also been deposited, and the amount was the same as last year. The 20% raise, it seemed, had not materialized.

A wave of déjà vu washed over her as she remembered that dark day in that dark office in Atlanta with Preston. But she soon calmed herself. *An oversight*, she realized. *An accounting error*. She'd get her raise, retroactive to January first, and she and Winston would laugh about it later.

~ ~ ~

After her meeting with Compliance, Honey stopped by Winston's office, but the door was shut. He was probably in a meeting. She checked several times that afternoon, but the door remained closed. *Unusual*, she thought. *I'll catch up with him tomorrow.*

That night at his loft, Trevor told her that she was concerned about nothing. "You sent a confirmation of the conversation when it happened, right? On email?"

"I sure did."

"Well then, no worries."

A few minutes later, when they were cleaning up after dinner, Trevor asked, "Did Winston ever reply to that email you sent?"

The hairs bristled at the back of Honey's neck. She looked over at him. "No."

Trevor just nodded and kept loading the dishwasher. "I'm sure it will be fine."

"You asked that question for a reason, though," Honey said, and he sighed.

"It'll be okay," Trevor said. "Stay positive."

"Look who you're talking to," she muttered, and then they were smiling together. He often called her *Ms. Positive*. Having met Honey's mother, Trevor claimed to be sure that it was in the genes.

~ ~ ~

The next day, same thing. Winston's door remained securely shut. She knew he was in there, so Honey sent a meeting invitation. Just 15 minutes, a small slice of time out of a busy man's day. He didn't accept. *Is he avoiding me?* Honey couldn't be sure. She figured she'd run into him in the hallway, on the way to the elevator or the restroom. But all day, he remained locked away behind his closed door. *Is he peeing into a bottle in there? What's up?*

Members of the marketing staff knew that something was amiss. Every person on the team had to walk past Winston's office several times a day, because of its central location. Everybody noticed the closed door. But strangely, Honey heard no gossip. Nobody was talking about this aberration in the office zeitgeist. She found herself wondering if they'd seen this before. Her direct reports were uncannily subdued.

And then, that afternoon, nobody she passed would meet Honey's eye.

What don't I know?

She remembered how she'd felt when she learned about the secret plan to start the magazine. Honey walked straight to Jake's office. *He'll know what's going on.*

But Jake's door was closed tight, too, and the lights were off. *Did Jake leave early?* That seldom happened, in Honey's experience. Something was definitely up.

It was nearly five o'clock when our girl walked back to her office. Jamal was waiting outside her door.

The podcast guy was looking at the floor when he said, "Winston wants to see you."

For a second, it looked like Jamal's eyes were glossed with tears. But she couldn't be sure, because he turned and walked away.

~ ~ ~

Winston looked calm as pie when she entered his office. His hair looked particularly nice that day—but then, so did hers.

"Shut the door," he said.

Oh no. Is this happening again?

He motioned to a client chair, and she sat across from him.

The timbre of his voice was modulated with pinpoint accuracy to

259

the Friendly setting when Winston said, "You wanted to talk to me about something."

Honey wasn't nervous. She felt strangely calm, actually. Time seemed to slow down as she took a breath, and when she spoke, her voice sounded steady in her ears.

"Yes. I got my paycheck, and the raise wasn't reflected."

Winston was wearing the suit she liked the most, the charcoal-colored silk he'd worn the day she met him. What the boss said next would tell her everything she needed to know.

He effortlessly switched his aspect to Clueless and said, "What raise?"

~ ~ ~

"So let me get this straight," Trevor said. "He said *What raise?* and you just walked out?"

"Yep." She stripped off the fucking blazer that she'd bought for that fucking job, and threw it across the kitchen.

"Wow. Okay." Trevor didn't often look surprised, but now his eyebrows shot skyward. "That was, um, probably smart."

He drew Honey close into a hug. A fine place to cry tears of frustration.

"I feel like some kind of dupe," she wailed. "Why does this keep happening to me?"

She could feel him smiling, even though she couldn't see his face.

"It's happened twice, Honey. Twice in a long career."

"That's two times too many." Her voice shook with fury.

"True," he said. "But it's just proof that people lie, right? That's no reflection on you."

Honey pulled back and looked him in the eye. "But why? Why do they lie?"

He cupped her face in his hands and used his thumbs to sluice the tears from her cheeks.

"Because they can," he said.

~ ~ ~

Honey never went back to Jameson Ross. Her attorney handled everything, and our girl ended up signing an agreement with the firm: she wouldn't sue them, and in return they would report to any interested parties that she'd resigned, and her personnel file would be officially marked as "would re-hire." Plus, solely because there was an email trail, Honey received a large cash settlement.

Initially she harbored illicit thoughts of espionage when she thought about Winston's lies and betrayal, but Honey's anger soon waned. *It's all over, now, and there's no going back.* Trevor, on the other hand, displayed more longstanding irritation than Honey expected. He talked about Jameson Ross much more than she did, often returning to concepts that she'd already examined as a younger woman in business, concepts like *honesty* and *decency* and *leadership.*

Trevor postulated that Winston knew all along that he'd only need Honey for ten months. Winston just needed somebody to provide content strategy for the new magazine, and to train the team who'd do the work. Once this was successfully accomplished, Jameson Ross had no more use for her.

Trevor told her, "Your days were numbered, right from the start."

Not much solace in that, Honey thought. She secretly hoped that the next time Trevor saw Winston at their club committee meeting, he'd punch him out. But that was unlikely to happen. Trevor Bankhead was way too smooth for that.

~ ~ ~

Honey's loss of the job—and his strong response—sparked some interesting conversations with Trevor as the days passed. One February morning they climbed into the old Pontiac and rode to the beach together. The plan was to have a picnic lunch and maybe take a walk, if it wasn't too chilly.

By the time they drove over the Skyway bridge and arrived at Siesta Key, the cold wind had picked up. They decided to eat lunch in the car, which was parked in a lot facing the roiling Gulf of Mexico. Honey ran around to the trunk to get the picnic basket.

There was a new bumpersticker:

The last thing I want to do is hurt you.
But it's still on the list.

This brought a smile to her face for the first time in weeks. With the wind whipping her hair across her face, Honey hurried to bring the basket into the front seat. Trevor had pulled bottles of root beer out of the cooler, and the couple set about creating their picnic on the expansive bench seat of the old automobile. It was sunny beyond the windshield, but whitecaps leaped on the surface of the Gulf, and the sand blew sideways. In the warm cab of the car they felt safe and snug, protected from the gale.

While they ate their lunch, Trevor talked about the future, and Honey featured prominently in it.

"I'd really like for us to take more vacations. Maybe we could buy a condo at the beach or something, and rent it out when we're not there. And it's not too soon to be thinking about retirement, right?

Will we travel? To South America? Japan? I think I'd like to see Norway, one day."

A blast of wind shook the car as Honey blinked back the tears that had welled up in her eyes.

"What's wrong?" Trevor asked. "You don't like Norway?"

She smiled then, and her voice was gruff when she said, "You think we'll still be together when we're retired? When we're old people?"

"Well, sure. Don't you?"

A thousand nights of wondering condensed into that moment as Honey considered how to respond. She loved him, and he loved her. That's a simple equation—even if it's an elusive one. When a life's dream like this one is right there for the taking, Honey had learned, you don't question. You don't hesitate. You grab it and growl.

"A hundred percent," she said, and then Trevor leaned over and kissed her, despite the sesame seeds on her lips from the bun.

~ ~ ~

Honey had made a meal for Trevor in the kitchen at his loft, which was a big deal because our girl didn't cook. But now that he was working full-time and she wasn't, Honey felt like she'd try to make an effort. She certainly had the time. She certainly knew how to follow a damn recipe. Roasted garlic chicken with rosemary and cherry tomatoes. What could go wrong?

"What are these?" Trevor poked a crisp globe with his fork.

"Tomatoes."

"Are they supposed to be black and ashy?"

"The recipe wanted charred," Honey said, watching him across the table.

"Then you have succeeded," Trevor said. He took a bite. "Hey, it's pretty good. I didn't even know you cooked."

Honey couldn't really say, *It's the first full meal I've ever made*, because after all she was a grown-ass woman, so that would seem strange.

Then Trevor said, "I've never cooked a whole meal myself."

"Really?" She was delighted. "Me either! Until tonight."

"Very cool," he said. "I think you've got promise, in this arena."

"Thanks. I think you're going to like the dessert. My mother sent me the recipe."

"Yeah? What is it?"

"Loquat tart," Honey said. She explained that she'd found the fruit at the Asian market, where long, leafy branches were sold with the fruit still attached. "The minute you pull a loquat from the branch, it starts deteriorating. So it's important that they're fresh."

"You are full of surprises," Trevor said.

~ ~ ~

But Trevor had surprises in store, too, it seemed. That night, after the yummy loquat tart and Cuban coffee, he and Honey took their wineglasses out to the balcony to people-watch. Downtown St. Pete was a festival on weekends. Crowds of folks moved between the bar on the corner and the two bars mid-block, across the street. The sounds of laughter rose up to balcony level, and Honey heard people calling out for each other, and the warring vibes of rap music and Patsy Cline karaoke.

"Here's to St. Pete, the mellow man's New Orleans," Trevor said, lifting his glass.

Honey raised her glass, too, but with her other hand she pointed down. "Look, is that guy pissing in a planter?"

"Let me take your mind off that," Trevor said. He put his glass on the table, pulled her close, and kissed her until long after the man by the planter had finished his business. Then they stood looking out at the gaiety, at the swarm of club kids below. *Club kids, like we used to be.* That's where Honey had first noticed him, all those years ago in Ybor City. That's where he'd noticed her.

"I'd like to tell you about my financial situation," he said. "Is that okay?"

Honey stiffened, and he felt it.

"Just for your information," Trevor assured her. "You don't have to reciprocate, if you're not comfortable."

"Okay, then," she said carefully, wondering why he was broaching the one topic that had been forbidden, until that moment. Maybe his financial situation was not good, she realized, and he'd chosen this moment to reveal trouble. She asked, "Is everything okay?"

He laughed. "Everything's fine. I just think you should know how I'm situated, you know? We've been talking about the future."

"That's true." She thought about the picnic conversation, in the Pontiac. It was clear that they had a future together. *This is just the next step.*

Honey's lover revealed himself financially, right there on the balcony—something he'd never done before. Our girl learned that he was far wealthier than she was, but really that was to be expected. He was an accomplished businessman, and it wasn't a contest, anyway. Trevor talked about his income, his assets, his bank balances, his investments, and his retirement fund. He laid it all out for her.

"So even when I quit working, there should be enough to keep us going," he said. "We'll have to be prudent, of course, because we'll both probably live to be 100."

"I know that's my plan," Honey said, and she rested her head against his shoulder. She was glad that she'd hooked up with a man who could prepare for the future. She tried not to feel inadequate as she said, "Want to hear about my situation?"

"Only if you want to."

So, she told him. For the first time outside her advisor's office, Honey bared her financial soul.

"Thanks for telling me," Trevor said. "I know it's not easy. But we're in a good place, don't you think? For going forward together?"

"It sure feels that way to me."

"Then here's the thing, Honey. We've got the same dreams, the same aspirations. We want to grow old together, and that's not nothing in this day and age. So, I want you to do something for me."

"What's that?"

"I want you to think of us as a team, now," Trevor said.

"A team." She tried it out on her tongue, and it felt good. Really good.

"What I'm saying is, don't ever feel required to seek traditional employment. I've got your back."

I've got your back. These were golden words for Honey. These were the words that her dad had never said to her, after all. Even though she never would have admitted it until that moment, she'd been waiting a long time to hear an admirable man say that.

Trevor placed a black-velvet ring box on the table.

"Move in with me," he said. "Marry me."

And that's what happened.

~ ~ ~

One by one, in different ways, her former Jameson Ross team members reached out. Honey got a sweet email from Jamal and attended a group Zoom call with the editors and writers. They were all happy to talk about their past shared experiences, and would chat endlessly about their families, but every last one of them stayed quiet about what had happened to make her leave. Honey never brought it up, and they didn't, either. They all reported to Winston again, now.

Nearly a year had passed when the video director, a man of few words who was ten years her senior, reached out with a DM: *I never had a good boss before, until you.* Honey didn't need to pin that message to her inspiration board—she held that one in her heart.

BOSS 7: HONEY

Brand content creative lead (contractor), Behemoth Tech
CEO, Leader's Friend, Inc.
CEO, Affluent Advisor Outreach, Inc.
Author, *The Visceral Voice of the Southern Blues | A photographic memoir*

The bayside wedding was beautiful. All of Honey's and Trevor's friends and family gathered to celebrate, and Honey didn't have to worry about finding a white dress since that ship had sailed. She danced with her elderly father—she hadn't seen him in decades, and had been surprised when he accepted the invitation. When the old man leaned down to whisper, *I'm proud of you, Honey,* his daughter's eyes were just as dry as his.

Honey did perform the requisite father-daughter dance, but her gaze sought out her mom, who was sitting next to a scowling Max, watching the show. Behind her dad's back, Honey gave Mom a thumb's up, and saw a smile break across her mother's face. Guests partied poolside until dawn at the 1940s home that Trevor and Honey had renovated in St. Pete's Old Northeast. Dad left early.

It was true that she'd dreaded seeing her father, because it was also true that part of her wanted to show him the woman that she'd become—a ridiculous desire, on its face, because it came with assumption that he would care. Nevertheless, Honey wanted to prove to him that she was worthy of love from a worthy man— and that man's name was Trevor.

That's why Mitchell Malone got invited to the wedding.

~   ~   ~

A month earlier, when renovation had been completed and she and Trevor were just moving into the house in the Old Northeast, Honey came across the two big cardboard cartons that she'd been hauling around every time she changed residences. When you grow up moving every two or three years, you know how to pack a box—and you know how to pay to ship it. Honey knew that these two dusty cartons were full of letters and cards, and she knew that, for some reason, she'd held onto them. Since college. *Maybe I should look through this stuff, then toss it. I haven't opened these boxes in years.*

Trevor found her in tears, sitting on the floor surrounded by paper, holding a hair net. But when she looked up at him, she was smiling.

"What's all this?" he asked.

"Mostly it's cards and letters, from friends and co-workers."

Trevor looked around the room. "That's a lot of correspondence."

"Twenty-five years' worth. It's weird, though, Trevor. Some of these people are thanking me from the bottom of their heart for something I did, but I can't remember what it was. I can't remember what they're thanking me for."

Trevor held up a T-shirt that read SANGUINE TO THE MAX.

"Not important," he said. "All that matters is how you made them feel."

~ ~ ~

Handwritten notes found in Honey's boxes

"UH-OH, I CAN SEE SOME CONFLICTION COMING UP."

"WE DON'T WANT TO BE LATE. DON'T DILLY."

"IT PROBABLY WOULD HAVE BEEN A NICE PARTY, BUT I RECLINED."

"THEY'RE ABSOLUTELY, DIABOLICALLY OPPOSED."

"EVERY WORD HAS AN ANTONYM AND A CINNAMON."

"YOU ARE ONE INDUSTRIALIST GAL."

She put the handwritten notes on the discard pile, remembering the photo on Joe's social media feed, showing him standing proudly behind his wife and their three children. They all had dark hair, and they all looked happy.

Honey emptied two cardboard boxes that day—but the memories always came with her. And from then on out, she didn't even have to pay to ship them.

~ ~ ~

When you never made friends as a kid, you hang on to them tight when you find them later. All the card and letter writers had received a wedding invitation. Rodolfo from Ramrod was there—showing photos of his grandbabies. Ashley from Atlanta attended, their hair now graying, like Honey's. Helen from Emma Brandt was in attendance, and Milana with Francisco, and Shane with his wife Brandy, and Nicole with Jimbo, who had mellowed, thank

God. Sir Stokes was there, from the Southern circuit, with the lovely Tisha, and Margo, and CeeCee, and even Jake Franklin from Jameson Ross, who came with his date, Jamal.

That day, everyone got a chance to turn their faces to the sun together. The wedding was a commemoration, really. A celebration of dreams that did come true.

Because she'd had so few of them growing up, Honey never let go of a friend. She always valued their stories, good or bad, and that impulse served her well—in more ways than one.

~ ~ ~

Many of our girl's longtime friends—and not just the women—came right back into her life to help her, when Honey took Trevor up on his offer and abandoned traditional employment. Many people from her past remembered Honey. They wanted to work with her, and they valued her counsel. So she took the plunge into entrepreneurship. Our girl was ready to build herself some efficient conduits. She was ready to take the risk.

Trevor started calling her "the Queen of the Multiple Income Stream."

Honey formed a Florida S corp called Affluent Advisor Outreach, Inc. that provided investment advisors and wealth managers with content for personalized client emails. All Honey needed was basic information about a client's interests, and she was off to the races. Your top client Ed likes golf? Here's a short note from you to Ed that includes the words, *Thought of you when I saw this*, with a link out to a story about a new driver design that's being considered by the USGA. Your wealthy client Patricia collects Limoges porcelain? *Thought of you when I saw this*, with a link out to a calendar of all the fine-porcelain shows in Patricia's part of the country.

It didn't take Honey much time to populate a healthy database of hobbies and interests, and not even two minutes to write the email copy. Her buddy Helen was retained to help with PR, and straight away *American Wealth Management* magazine interviewed Honey, then published a glowing assessment of her offering—Honey wasn't the only person to offer personalization, but she was the first. Even though her content strategy services carried a premium price, customers poured in. This was business at its most basic, she reminded herself. *See a need and fill it.* She never got the tat, but she did consider where she'd put it, if she did.

Honey's new business was profitable within 90 days, since startup costs were negligible, and the national press coverage brought eager customers. Over time, the construct proved profitable for other service providers, and soon enough Affluent had a staff of eight, who contributed remotely.

But when it came time to hire her staff, Honey didn't use the word-of-mouth, who-we-know method of selecting employees that was still common in her community. Looking back at her career, she regretted that she had been part of it. So Honey posted jobs for all to see on the TalentAlly site. She reviewed each resume that arrived. She'd moved through the world of business with advantages, Honey knew—but some of those had been unfair advantages. Old habits die hard, but die they must.

~ ~ ~

Honey handled all the details when her father passed away. He died hard.

Dad left this mortal realm all alone, living off government benefits in a double-wide mobile home in Seminole County, with not a true friend in the world, estranged from family. Honey was not honored to learn that it was her name and number that her father had left with the trailer-park manager, the man who'd called to tell her that Mitchell Malone had been taken away in a coroner's van.

Heart attack, they said. Dad's life, which had spawned so many rollercoaster feelings across the United States, had come to a sudden stop at the station.

Honey called her mom, who was vacationing on St. Bart's. She said, "Thanks for letting me know."

She called her brother, who just said "Oh, okay" and who'd laughed out loud at the idea of a memorial service. "Who'd come, though? Four sex workers?" As always, Max expressed himself succinctly: "Fuck him."

~ ~ ~

It was Honey who filled out the forms, who threw out her father's belongings, who orchestrated the sale of his musty mobile home and the disposal of his old beater car. She got an unexpected glimpse into her father's life when a series of elderly women stopped by during the two days it took to clear out his trailer.

The first old lady, a spritely little thing about five feet tall, arrived wearing a red skirt suit, sensible heels, and full makeup. She looked like the world's oldest Realtor. She stood outside the screen door and saw Honey cleaning out the refrigerator.

"Is Mitchell here? He owes me money."

~ ~ ~

The sound of an insistent car horn alerted Honey to the second visitor, a redhead in a leopard-print top who showed up a few hours later. This one didn't even get out of her Lincoln, just lowered the window, looked out across the discarded boxes and trash bags, and called over, *Where's Mitchell? I hope he's not dead, he owes me money.*

Mitchell's small place smelled of mold, but it looked tidy enough, for a bachelor pad. The walls were bare of decoration. In the living room, she could tell where Dad had sat to watch TV, from the one set of cushions on the couch that revealed the telltale dents. *He didn't leave dents on the furniture at home when I was a girl,* Honey thought. *He never stayed long enough to create them, there.* A nonfunctioning treadmill in the corner was draped with dirty clothes, and Dad's dining room table was stacked with girlie magazines and correspondence dating back six years.

Honey found a bank statement and his checkbook. She discovered a letter from a Seminole County maid service informing Mitchell Malone that because of his actions with Monique on the 23rd, he should find himself another service vendor. She found love letters from somebody named Cherry that had been balled up and then flattened again. Soon enough, Honey just swept armloads of paper into garbage bags, and called it done.

A neighbor man stopped by, asking for the abandoned booze, so that was helpful. The old guy brought along two empty cardboard boxes, also super helpful, and they filled each one with bottles of liquor, which her Dad had hoarded in multiples in case of a shortage, like during a hurricane or during a Sunday, when the liquor stores were closed in Seminole. Once all the bottles were transferred, Honey offered to help carry the boxes, but the old guy was motivated enough to do it himself. He had a handy way of balancing the cartons on his high-end wheeled walker, which waited patiently under the carport in the shade.

As she cleaned out her dad's place, Honey stayed alert for signs of melancholy that might spring up inside her. *This is just the sort of task that will bring it on, after all.* She went through her father's drawers and his closets, and waited to feel emotions like sadness, longing or regret.

One of Dad's closets was packed with expensive clothing that smelled of sour mash bourbon with an undertone of Pink Sugar perfume—but his refrigerator held little sustenance. He'd certainly been proud of those liquor bottles, which had their own lighted display case in the living room, but there was not a single photograph of his children. Honey had gone looking.

She inspected Dad's wallet, rooted through files and shoe boxes filled with ephemera. But no family photos existed in Mitchell's world. His heart might have been as empty as the walls that surrounded her, just an expanse of thin faux wood, void of life or connection. *It's like we never existed.*

She waited for the melancholy, but it didn't show its face. Edgy exhaustion was about all Honey felt. Our girl had never been one for examining "what might have been." *It is what it is, in the end.*

~ ~ ~

The third old girl seemed quite hopeful when she departed a taxi at Dad's address just before noon on Day Two, lugging a suitcase so ancient it didn't even have wheels. She was wearing a wide-brimmed straw hat and sunglasses, and there was a quickness in her step as she approached Honey, who had just stripped the bed and was tossing the bag of linens onto the pile curbside.

"Hello hello!" the woman chirped, "I didn't know Mitchell had a maid."

Honey looked over with hooded eyes. "Mitchell's not here."

"Are you sure?" The woman pushed up her hat brim and peered across to the trailer door. "We're leaving for the airport in ten minutes. He's taking me to the islands, St. Bart's!"

"Ouch," Honey said, feeling sorry for this stranger who thought she was about to embark on a romantic trip to the French West Indies, and who'd made it a point to purchase new Crocs.

Our girl picked up the suitcase and pointed to the carport. "Let's sit for a minute. Come on into the shade." Honey turned and started walking up the drive. The woman had no choice but to follow her.

They sat next to each other on a bench, looking out into the

275

blazing Florida sunshine, and Honey delivered the news about Mitchell. Instead of crying, which is what Honey expected, the woman leaned forward and looked up and down the street.

"Well, the cab's gone, now."

Heat shimmered up from the asphalt. From a window nearby, Country music, *These are sad times, world gone mad times* and it all just seemed so otherworldly.

"I can't call another one," the woman said, still not looking at Honey. "I'm out of money until my Social Security check comes in."

Trapped as she was in this Kafkaesque Geritol moment, with the scent of her dad's bedsheets still on her hands, Honey thought fast. She reached into the Tupperware container that held the few things that had seemed worth keeping.

"Here." Honey handed the woman a piece of paper and a key fob. "Take his car. It's yours, and it's got a full tank of gas."

"Get out." The woman's hat brim dipped as she looked down at what she held. "Really?"

"That's the signed title. It's all yours."

The woman stood, picked up her suitcase and started walking toward the rusty Toyota that waited like salvation at the foot of the drive.

"Well," she said, as much to herself as to Honey, "At least something good came out of this."

~ ~ ~

It was Honey who took her father's death certificate to the bank to close out his checking account, the one with a balance of $812.

It was Honey who composed and submitted to the *Tampa Bay Times* the obituary that her half-siblings might one day read, if they went looking.

Her Dad had not only paid for her college education, he'd given her a little thing called life. Honey felt like she owed him, for that.

A funny thing, perspective—just when you're sure you've got it nailed, life nails you, with another fast-moving curveball. Mitchell Malone had made millions in American business, and he'd spent most of it on other women, many of whom worked in the field of adult entertainment. The rest, his former wife eventually revealed, were his employees. They'd reported to him at work, like Honey had with Sugar Man.

Mitchell's lasting legacy would include her and Max and Oliver—but it would also include the lives he'd wrecked and the unclaimed progeny he'd left scattered in his wake, Honey knew. Maybe that's why they'd moved so often, a nuclear family fleeing one man's obligations. In any event, this particular businessman would hand off no wealth to the son and daughter who bore his name—but those two had never counted on it, anyway.

Mitchell's kids had discovered that you can't miss somebody who was never really there in the first place. They could summon no grief for their father when he passed away.

You're on your own works both ways, sometimes.

~ ~ ~

Honey turned her energies to a second income stream, one that came from her marketing peeps—folks she'd known along the way, most of whom had ended up in that field not by intent, but by happenstance. Honey had watched them blossom, over the years, and she'd seen their children mature even as their careers did. She'd praised their unfortunate haircuts, helped them find jobs when they needed them, and welcomed a phone call when they felt adrift. Many of them were top leaders across the country, managing huge budgets and thousands of people.

But they still needed advice. They still wanted somebody to bounce ideas off of, somebody whose counsel they trusted when the political, power-hungry aspect of American business was on full display. Honey formed Leader's Friend, Inc. She hosted monthly group calls, along with one-on-one sessions on demand and a running tally of best practices, bundled into one affordable annual fee.

Our girl had monetized the Leader's Friend template to a broader audience, too. LinkedIn delivered a steady stream of buyers who sought to replicate the informal, timely and valuable services that Honey's approach provided, and Leader's Friend proved to be especially popular with traditionally underserved groups, like Black businesswomen and corporate HR managers. The "softer side" of business was proving to be important to enterprise success, but the men who led most businesses fell short when they attempted to encourage and scale these dreaded soft skills.

A community that can truly communicate has a natural tendency to become more diverse—and just calling something a "community" doesn't make it one. If only business was that easy. Honey's solution was just what business leaders needed, sometimes, to get fresh perspective, to give their teams a lift. Everybody seemed to enjoy the Featured Speaker segment that was livestreamed in January every year.

As far as ROI, the money from Leader's Friend wasn't as good, but by then the money wasn't as important. Back at Touchstone, Casey had taught Honey that everybody needs a passion project. This one was hers.

Honey Malone had become an entrepreneur. She'd taken the risk, and the risk paid off.

And really, she'd never had a better boss.

~ ~ ~

Honey and Trevor got a puppy, and Honey wanted to name him Chomsky.

"That's a pretty odd name for a Catahoula hound dog," Trevor said.

"Noam Chomsky's linguistic theory is that every person's born with an innate ability to learn language. He was my hero when I was in school."

"Well, you sure know language now, don't you?"

She caught his implication. "Are you saying I talk too much?"

"Um," Trevor hedged, "How old were you when you started reading?"

"Three. I remember it like it was yesterday."

Trevor scoffed at that. "No, you don't. You were three years old."

"But I do. I do remember."

She told him the story, about how she'd had been a born talker, one who vocalized at top volume even before she knew how to form real words. Little Miss Chatterbox, they called her. It had been plainly explained to toddler Honey that all anybody had to do to get smarter was to read words, which even at the time seemed like a pretty awesome deal. Thus, it wasn't long before Little Miss became envious of her mother's ability to read.

Honey and her mother had been sitting at the kitchen table, and our girl was peevish because Mom was reading the newspaper.

"You're rude," Honey said.

Mom looked up, surprised and smiling. "How am I rude?"

"You're reading. I can't read. It's no fair."

"You want to learn to read?"

"Yes," Honey said indignantly. "I want to be smart, too."

"Okay, then," Mom said, "I'll teach you."

It hadn't been a week before Mom's instruction hit home with the blond-haired tyke. Our tiny chatterbox didn't know that she was predisposed to understand phonemes—how could she? She was three—and her mother had no knowledge of the crucial role that these smallest units of speech played in distinguishing one word from another. But one night at bedtime, snuggled in bed with Mom reading *Goodnight Moon* for the thousandth time, Honey watched as her mother drew back the bedroom curtain. Mom pointed to the sky, just above the horizon.

"What's that?" Mom asked.

"Moon."

Mom put her fingertip on the cover of the book. "This is the word for moon. Look at the four letters. See how *moon* has these two round O's? Two round O's means you say *ooh*. That's the *ooh* in *moon*. And look here, Honey. Look at the word *goodnight*. See those two round O's there?"

"Ooh," Honey said. She got it.

And just like that, in that one instant, a three-year-old began to understand written language. Even as a tiny girl, Honey had felt the magic—and the magical import—of the revelation. Mom remembered it, too. This had gone down in family history as "Honey's Helen Keller moment."

Now, hearing this story, Trevor nodded.

"Chomsky it is," he said. "At least no other pups will come running, when we call him at the dog park."

~ ~ ~

The money rolled in, but Honey wasn't busy enough. She was accustomed to leading a team, to stretch assignments and tight deadlines. Our girl still felt compelled to make a difference every day, and Trevor had to remind her sometimes to take it easy. Take a minute. Breathe.

He was right. She needed to redirect her energy, and to find a new pace. So Honey spent four months collating her photographs of blues musicians, from back in the day when she'd first met them at Tippy's Smokehouse, and then later, when she'd been a music reporter, and traveling with Sir Stokes. She called her book a memoir, and tried to explain how these blues artists' stories had affected her at a time in her life when she needed something vital, something every woman needs: a fitting way to scream. The women and men who were profiled in the book had taught her that it's okay for an undernourished white girl to lend her contralto to the chorus, if the spirit down deep rings true.

The Visceral Voice of the Southern Blues was self-published, to little notice or acclaim, though from the smattering of reviews it appeared that Honey was a better photographer than she'd given herself credit for—so there was that. Her heroic photo of Sir Stokes graced the cover, and she'd had big dreams of presenting each of the book's subjects with their big fat share of the royalty check, but little cash materialized. *Another passion project*, she griped to Trevor, and he just laughed. *You say that like it's a bad thing. I'm proud of you, Honey.*

~ ~ ~

Our girl had forgotten that, on a whim, she'd submitted her application for a 12-month contract position with a global tech company—solely because she'd enjoyed their test exercise for digital content strategists. By the time the recruiter responded, though, Honey had moved on, putting email aside as she travelled to Washington state to spend two weeks in the Cascade Mountains, her longtime vacation destination. Honey felt an affinity for soaring vistas, stark contrasts and jagged edges, and this landscape delivered. It was like the opposite of Florida, in a good way.

Her friend Milana had relocated to Seattle, so they spent a few days together. They stayed up late into the night telling old stories, reminiscing about their time together working in Florida business, laughing at their memories of Honey's seven suitors. The mountains were beyond beautiful, and they hiked for miles in the cool, crystal-clear air—though they made sure to stand aside on the path when younger feet sought to pass. Flatlander Honey left wondering if she and Trevor might consider budgeting for a vacation cabin in the mountains. Something higher up, where the lahar wouldn't reach it.

~ ~ ~

When she finally checked her email at the Seattle airport, waiting for her return flight to the heat-saturated muggy mop that was Florida in August, Honey saw that she'd missed eight emails from the tech recruiter—each offering a higher hourly rate. By the time she opened the most-recent email, Honey was floored at the income opportunity. She certainly had plenty of time on her hands, and she'd be able to work 100% from the comfort of home. This full-time gig would be bra-optional.

Technology, Honey thought. *Why not?*

She scored a one-year contract working on behalf of a tech behemoth that employed half a million people around the globe. Another organization with deep pockets. Another example of large, well-greased conduits of revenue. During that year, Honey made plenty of friends, and stayed plenty busy, but she never had a boss. Terms of her contract stated that she would never receive feedback—positive or negative—because those actions smacked of an employer/employee relationship, and enterprise Legal certainly couldn't have that. Her only feedback was an offer of contract renewal. Honey's was renewed nine times. No bosses ever surfaced.

~ ~ ~

Following their father's death, Honey and her brother began to phone each other more frequently. She and Max had grown closer when he'd flown down to Tampa to scatter their father's ashes. Conveniently, the Mons Venus was located just three miles from the airport, and the strip club's expansive parking lot seemed to welcome the gritty addition from a slowly moving vehicle that night, as a full moon kept its eye on the proceedings.

He's at home now, Max said solemnly, tapping out the ashes from his open car door. *He's with his people.* Trevor listened wide-eyed from the back seat as Honey and her brother dissolved in laughter, giggling like the children they still were, in some regard, even after all those years.

Catharsis is especially sweet for older people, Honey realized. People like her just weren't counting on that particular lagniappe, anymore. So when it happens, it's like an ice-cold wind from a Cascades glacier. It's enough to jolt a girl alive again.

The siblings reconnected after their dad passed away. They discussed at length how crucial their mother's love had been to them, as they'd rocketed like pinballs across the United States with Dad's thumbs on the paddles. They made a joint commitment to thank their mom properly, in every way they could, as long as she was with them.

Perspective, Honey thought, *the gift that keeps on giving.*

~   ~   ~

For many years, our girl was editor of Behemoth Tech's main landing page on the web, which gave her amazing access to the stories that made the business come alive as a brand. She learned about the company's product offerings, about the research and consultative sales divisions of the firm, and all she'd ever need to know about writing short. Because the corporate landing page was the "digital front door" to the enterprise, Honey's content skills were vaunted—though never publicly, of course, because Legal forbid any vaunting of contractors, lest they be seen as equal to full-time employees (who, Honey came to know, earned less, routinely got laid off, had to deal with office politics, and were expected to work a lot of overtime hours.)

Honey the Hired Gun outlasted dozens of full-time company employees during those ten years working on behalf of Behemoth Tech. The reason an enterprise retains long-time contractors, she came to know, is because these subhumans live in an HR-free zone. Not only was management feedback forbidden, but the rules of polite society did not exist on her agile team—nor were they expected. It wasn't pretty, locked away on the dark side of civility. It was no picnic, on those days when Honey's skills were diminished publicly, when the shame of even the smallest mistake was loudly broadcast to the full team on standup calls.

Agile methodology prioritizes cross-functional collaboration and continuous improvement—much like the Six Sigma methodology that had tickled Honey's fancy back in her print production days. This kind of approach divides projects into smaller phases, hopefully guiding teams through cycles of planning, effort and execution. A senior leader at Behemoth had become enamored of the agile approach for building web pages for one reason: the competition used it. Scrum meetings, software tools, and clear roles would work in concert, this leader believed, to help teams structure and manage their work.

But there was a fatal flaw in the leader's plan: at Behemoth, the agile teams had no control over how much work they were expected to produce. For this reason, the agile approach was doomed from the start, as priorities shifted in real time, and as the loudest voices got their projects delivered first. "Dumpster fire" projects were common as teams abandoned their plans in order to tackle a leader's whim. To make things worse, communication was fragmented, processes undocumented, and the labyrinth of antiquated, hodgepodge systems at the tech company required months of hands-on experience to learn. Constant corporate re-organizations created confusion as Honey's agile team sought to identify appropriate reviewers and approvers for the work that just kept coming.

Quantification of "quality" was a slippery slope that no leaders dared to climb, since each of the six divisions of the company claimed ownership of the "single source of truth" about product offerings. In this ill-fated environment, even the top-producing web production teams met few deadlines, so leaders put into place their solution: a meeting would be held monthly to compare the many floundering agile teams, so that one could publicly be named superior—the mostly-male contractor workforce called this "the Blondest Blonde Award."

It was more important to leaders to spend time creating unreachable KPIs (key performance indicators) than to address the issues that caused delay. As more meetings became mandatory and time-sensitive tasks took priority, the remaining projects missed deadline by weeks or months. Even though the organization was itself far from agile, the agile production methodology remained solidly in place. Honey's team of well-compensated contractors called this "job security."

~ ~ ~

During her tenure at the tech company, one colleague was especially triggered by Honey Malone. For some reason, she really got under his skin. Maybe she reminded him of a girl who'd been mean to him grammar school, or something—there was no way to know, with immediate knee-jerk reactions like his. They were both contractors, and they'd worked together for a few months before she'd joined Behemoth's home-page team.

But when it was announced that Honey had been selected to edit the tech company's high-profile corporate home page, Tony "Fitz" Fitzgerald exhibited public outrage that he hadn't been chosen for the role. It was Hissy Fit City for Fitz, there for a while.

Fitz might have felt diminished and slighted, since he had been a contractor longer than Honey, and probably felt that his skill set had been proven stronger than hers. Too bad leadership disagreed; Honey left Fitz and her initial team behind, and began to interact with leaders at the highest levels of the massive corporation. Her star rose, and Honey was far removed from the murky depths of product-page web production, where tech bros roamed free.

She'd almost forgotten what it was like, to work in the depths with Fitz. Then came the day when another corporate restructuring occurred, and a full-time employee was given the job of home-page editor. Contractor Honey was told that her presence was no longer required. They gave her plenty of notice, though, which they weren't required to do, and soon enough our girl was scooped up by her original web production team, down in the murk of the organization—but with no reduction in her quite exorbitant rate of pay.

Back on that production team, Fitz was waiting, his fin barely breaking the water as he circled his hapless prey. It was time for our girl's comeuppance. Vengeance is sweet, for some people. Honey had no idea whether Fitz just didn't like her as a human, or whether he'd been simmering in bile all that time, formulating a plan to punish her for what she was: a threat to his ego.

This sort of thing happened, she knew. She'd encountered it before, for sure, but she'd been an actual employee back then, not a less-than-human contractor in an atmosphere that was no-holds-barred, like the Wild West, with no sheriffs within a thousand miles.

Her nemesis Fitz pounced early, in the very first moment of Honey's very first day back on the web production team. A scrum master named Baron ran the meeting, and opened the call by announcing that a new person from the content discipline had joined their merry band.

"Honey, tell us a little about yourself."

Fitz said, "We don't have time for fucking pleasantries. Right, guys?"

The other men on the call said *Yeah!*

The three other women on the 20-person team didn't say anything, but they stopped sharing their video feeds on Zoom, Honey noted. She turned off her camera, too. Solidarity, of sorts, in the fetid netherworld of digital production at a 40-year-old company full of middle-aged men, many of whom had one thing in common: they seemed perennially pissed off.

Because scrum master Baron couldn't honestly say something like *Honey, you'll love it here*, he took another tack. "Sorry there isn't any formal onboarding, Honey. We could—"

Fitz was unrelenting. "—She'll figure it out. WE had to."

You got that fucking right, some guy muttered, and again a chorus of male voices said *Yeah*.

Honey said, "Baron, I'll get with you after this call."

"Are you still talking?" Fitz demanded of Honey. "We gotta get 43 updates to dev today, and you want to talk about yourself? Seriously?"

"Jesus," a guy said, "Who is this girl?"

~ ~ ~

There were no rules for the contractors. Honey was in a tank with the sharks, and survival required sharp teeth. But she tried to move forward with as much peace as possible, trying to smile with normal teeth. She worked to keep the mood somewhat positive, to keep the fractious team somewhat upbeat. Our girl had always said that she wanted to work with people who were smarter than she was—and Behemoth Tech delivered. Not everybody was like Fitz, thank God.

On her new team of 20, in that fast-paced environment, only the web developers were rewarded for turnaround speed. These folks were serious about efficiency. If you couldn't cater to the needs of the dev team, Honey soon realized, your days as a contract-based contributor would be over. They'd vote you off the island in a jiff.

After seven years of pay increases on the home-page team, her hourly rate was high, and Honey and Trevor had saved nearly enough money to purchase a decrepit little cabin in Washington State, so our girl was determined to keep the extra money rolling in. Motivated to succeed on her new team despite the thorn in her side that was Fitz, Honey learned all she could about page code, taxonomies, user experience strategy, alt text requirements and tagging for call-to-action buttons.

She kept a running list of the information that a developer would require, and she made herself available after hours, in case real-time cutting of copy was required due to some fluke in the firm's felicitous content management system. It didn't take long for word to get around in the tight-knit team of web developers: if you're coding a new page on deadline and your content writer is Honey, your turnaround time is sure to be low. You're that much closer to earning your performance bonus.

As the devs became aware that newcomer Honey added value, the rest of the team took note. Daily scrum meetings became a little less testy, and the developers began to stand up for our girl on the calls. In one meeting, Honey asked scrum master Baron where she could locate a certain asset that was required to begin her next project.

"I think Fitz has that link," Baron said.

"No, I don't," Fitz said.

"Well, you worked on it last," Baron said. "Just go look."

Fitz sneered, "I'm not helping her, if she's too stupid to find it."

He had just called Honey "stupid," the lowest blow on a team that valued intellect—and he'd done it so publicly that his fellow sharks fell uncharacteristically silent. The women on the team immediately messaged Honey directly:

Wtf, one wrote.
WTF??!! another wrote.
This motherF, the third woman wrote.

Then everybody on the Zoom call paid attention, because the lead developer came off mute—something he rarely did. "You better help her, Fitz. She's the only writer pulling her weight around here. She's eating your lunch, pal."

All four female team members went on camera. Instantly. No consultation was necessary, because after all they were members of the same pack, instinctively.

"Truth," another developer said, and on the video feed, Honey saw Fitz's face redden. He said nothing for the rest of the call. Maybe his pack members were Slacking him, too, in the background.

Fitz did send her the link she needed. But he also began to incessantly send short DMs.

Need a 1:1
Let's schedule time
Available today?
Available at 2?
Available today?

When she ignored him, the next message cycle started: *Join my vid call. Join my WebEx. Join my meeting.* Honey didn't respond, and his messages got increasingly volatile until she finally got one that read:

Get on my Zoom now.

Ooh, Honey thought. *That sounds like an order.*

She smiled and went back to her work. She had developers to please.

But Fitz blindsided her a month later. He'd organized a meeting for an innocuous improvement project, and Honey was just one of 10 people invited. Once she accepted, he cancelled the meeting for everybody except her, as she discovered when she connected to find just the two of them on the call.

"What is this, Fitz?"

"Well, you won't meet with me. And I have something important to bounce off you."

Doubtful, Honey thought, but she said, "What is it, then?"

Fitz began talking at high speed for several minutes, and she could tell from the vid stream that he was reading from a script on another monitor. From what Honey could discern, he wanted to form a committee of some sort, to address an arcane style issue that nobody cared about except him.

"And—I want YOU on the Serial Comma Reinstatement

Committee," Fitz said. He sounded super upbeat, like he was handing her the Hope diamond.

"Yeah, no," she said. "Gotta run."

"Why are you acting this way?"

Honey took a breath and thought, *Okay, you asked for it.* "Let me give you a little perspective," she said. "You've never been anything but hateful to me."

"But that's not true!" Fitz declared. She watched on screen as he touched his fingertips to his chest, like an innocent.

"You disparage me in front of others," Honey said.

"Never! That's not me." She watched his eyebrows twitch higher.

"You called me stupid."

"No! I would never do that." Fitz looked concerned. Genuinely puzzled.

"Are you gaslighting yourself?" Honey laughed. "That's rich."

"What's gaslighting?" he asked, so she told him, and it wasn't long before Fitz was the one who was anxious to get off the call.

~   ~   ~

Despite her colleague Fitz, Honey enjoyed working for Behemoth Tech. The pace of her new duties suited her. Not since Touchstone had she felt so engaged. Honey knew exactly how her actions contributed to corporate revenue, which felt good. When she explained it to Trevor this way, he finally understood why she expended so much of her effort on behalf of Behemoth. He still thought she worked too much—but he wasn't exactly the guy to throw shade on that behavior. Both of them, it seemed, enjoyed a challenge. And neither of them could resist the allure of human nature. They enjoyed people, who were charming or unpredictable or brilliant or frightening, or all of those things at once sometimes, and more.

~ ~ ~

In her tenth year as a contractor for the tech behemoth, Honey's content strategy skills were widely acknowledged, and she found herself pulled onto a new scrappy team whose goal was to prepare for platform change by reducing character count for the firm's digital product pages. This was an effort that was supported by upper management—or it wouldn't have happened, since leaders who were unfamiliar with digital still believed the core myth: more words are always better.

This was known as the dinosaur rationale: But we've got such a rich story to tell about the latest release of this obscure industry-specific hybrid cloud-as-a-service integrated enhancement software plug-in solution offering! A story like that can't possibly be told in fewer words, and buyers actually WANT to read long copy on web pages. How do we know? We know because we've been in this space for 30 years, sweetheart, long before this digital crap. What do you mean, user surveys? We've been in this business longer than some of these users have been ALIVE, by God. We know best what they want, and they want more words. Here's your paycheck, what do you care?

As the sole representative of the content discipline on the scrappy re-design team, Honey led the charge in cutting copy—which could only be accomplished through researching and articulating product benefits that would instantly resonate with the audience. And then she had to build a quick way to scale all that, because 200 products were on offer at Behemoth. Clear communication demanded that she create a 50-word value proposition for even the most complex technology offerings, articulate exactly how a product's features provided benefit, and put sound content strategy into place. There were five art designers on the team, but

Honey was the only person responsible for the words.

After a 10-month effort, her scrappy team revealed its performance stats: page engagement for the firm's 200 technology products had increased by 18% across the board, representing additional revenues of hundreds of millions of dollars annually. Everybody on the team was lauded by corporate executives in a public setting, and then promoted into the stratosphere, clutching a big bonus check.

Everybody, of course, except Honey. She was a contractor, after all. Her contribution went unrecognized and unrewarded, so when the firm sent their next contract at the same rate of pay, she didn't respond.

The phone calls started immediately, and they had a frantic edge. Honey's contracting rep reached out, wondering why our girl hadn't renewed, when in the past contract renewals had been automatic. Honey replied, "Because my hourly rate isn't high enough." Then the rep was calling every three days with offers that were higher and higher. "Still not enough," Honey said. "Tell them I've moved on." She knew that the contracting company took a percentage of her earnings, right off the top. They were motivated to keep her working at the tech firm. But they couldn't meet Honey's hourly-rate requirement and still make their vig, so the phone calls stopped.

She wanted to be fully rewarded for the skills and expertise that she'd fully demonstrated—not an unreasonable request. And at that point in her life, Honey wouldn't settle for less. She didn't have to, by then.

~ ~ ~

It was true that Honey felt a sense of agency in her business life. It was also true that her left hand couldn't properly depress steel guitar strings anymore—and the reason was arthritis. Honey dropped off her beloved Sigma at the middle school music department, lamenting the end to all the joy that the instrument had brought her, remembering all the people she'd met with that dreadnought slung behind her on its well-worn strap. Mourning the times she'd held it close, like a baby.

This was when our girl could admit precisely what was barreling toward her. There was a name for it, she realized: old age.

Okay, Honey thought. *Here we go with this.* But she wasn't caught unaware.

~ ~ ~

When you have a mother you're close to, you know exactly what to expect from old age. From Honey's perspective, if she entered her dotage half as engaged and alert as her mom, she'd be doing just fine. Samantha Malone, after all, was no slouch. She grew watermelons and pumpkins now, and had the pecs to prove it. She produced the boldest zinnias in town. Her income from interior design had never flagged, and she always had an eager client waiting in the wings. *I want to be like that,* Honey thought. *Without the outdoor part.*

The family gathered for Christmas at Mom's—and it would be a birthday celebration, too, since Samantha turned 75 just two weeks later. The big house in Tallahassee brimmed with voices: Mom, Honey, Trevor, Max, his wife Peggy and their little boy, Oliver. The scent of cinnamon and butter crust filled the kitchen as they sipped iced tea and caught up on each other's lives. Young Oliver seemed partial to the sugar cookies that had been stamped out in the design of stars.

Honey looked out across the kitchen at one point, watching them. *Dad could have been part of this, if he'd wanted to.* And then she thought, *His loss.* She'd learned that a man can change his behavior, if properly motivated—Shane McLane had proven that.

~ ~ ~

At nine o'clock on Christmas morning, coffee cups (and one sippy cup) in hand, the clan walked together into The Room of Many Gifts, where the soaring tree held gleaming ornaments in shades of silver, gold and bronze. Little Oliver fell asleep in his playpen as the festivities began.

Max handed Mom the first gift, as was customary.

"From me and Honey, and from Peggy and Trevor, too. Merry Christmas and happy birthday."

Samantha's hair was full-on white now, with no hint of the amber blond she'd been for most of her years on earth. Honey watched a lock of hair fall across her mother's cheek as she bent to pull the ribbon from a tiny box, the kind that might hold jewelry.

"Ooh," Mom said, "Looks like a bracelet—What? Is it the—" and then she burst into what are truthfully known as happy tears. Sometimes a gift is so special that no one blames you if your joy feels boundless. The givers even celebrate sometimes, when you're moved emotionally—because sometimes, they are, too.

Samantha pulled it from the box: her old starter charm bracelet—long forgotten in her jewelry box and filched by Honey last Christmas—now polished and hung with twelve gold charms.

A little boy, for Max
A little girl, for Honey
One ring fused from three links, for Peggy's and Trevor's connection to their family
A baby in diapers, for Oliver
An open book
A garden spade
A loquat fruit
A steering wheel
The I-75 road sign insignia
A paint roller

A disk that held a tiny swatch of chintz

The baby slept while the adults gathered close around Samantha. They all wanted to examine the charms, to postulate excitedly about what each bauble might represent, and to *ooh* and *aah* about the weight of the finished piece.

"Dang, you'll build muscle just lifting your arm, with this thing on it," Peggy said.

Mom grinned over at her. "I guess if I have to work out, I'd just as soon do it with gold as iron. But what's this one? What is this little thing?" She pointed to the final charm.

Brother and sister exchanged a glance, and Max said, "It's called a cavalier bicorne."

"It's a hat," Honey said. "You know, like musketeers wear."

~ ~ ~

Honey wrote a story for her mom.

The Prism in Lake Lure

When I was a little girl, my mother brought home a rod of polished glass. It was shaped as a triangle, with sharp edges. She said, "Honey, this is a prism. Let's see what happens when we put it into the light."

She drew the curtains almost shut, then held the prism in the shaft of sunlight that sliced through. And everything changed.

Rainbows appeared from nowhere, saturated and strong against the dark ceiling. Color bars sprang onto the walls and jumped across the floor. My sneakers rested in a pool of purest blue.

"A prism is something that is alive," I remember thinking. Nothing that wasn't alive could possibly possess such magic. I figured that the prism had a living heart, one that could hold within itself an immense power—a power as strong as the sun in my sky—and then release that power, transformed and concentrated. A way to change everything.

Years later, I'd stopped to take photographs on an autumn day at Lake Lure, in North Carolina. I'd intended to capture the brilliance of the sky and the foliage—the blues, the golds. The spectrum. I pointed my camera up toward the trees.

Instead, the camera lens was drawn downward. And once I looked through the viewfinder and saw the reflective surface of the water, my soul was drawn back to that moment with my mother and the prism.

I was hit with the realization that this one woman has created profound change—for me, and for anyone with whom she shares.

And that leads us to the lesson in this story.

You are the prism, and you possess the magic. Your heart is big enough to hold the immense power of what it means to be alive— and your heart can release that power in an instant, concentrated and transformed, to affect the lives of others.

Concentrate your power. Release it. Change the world.

HONEY'S NEXT ACT

Even when you live a full life, you can be surprised when it gets fuller. The Behemoth Tech leaders that she'd worked with for ten years reached out to Honey directly. Her expertise, it seemed, was urgently needed. *There's something new on the horizon*, they said. Something so new, they were now challenged to find an expert with an unprecedented set of skills. They needed someone with:

- Deep knowledge of their enterprise and its products
- Ten years of experience in the creative art of meaningful content
- An academic degree in the science of Linguistics

Linguistics? You bet. To help understand, train and market the greatest thing in technology since the Interweb: Artificial Intelligence. AI.

Honey was absolutely able to help them, through her new consulting corporation. This was the sweetest revenue stream of all, though the linguist in Honey was so seduced by the science behind AI that she felt like Oppenheimer, sometimes. She never really retired. She splits her time between Florida and Washington State, where she and Trevor restored a cabin high up on the mountain, with a patch of green for Chomsky, and a sweet little suite for her mom.

~ ~ ~

So that's our girl's career in a nutshell. Thanks to friends, family, colleagues—and seven bosses who were just doing their best—she'd been given ample opportunity to add value.

Was Honey Malone successful in business?

You could probably say she passed mustard.

ABOUT THE AUTHOR

Juli A. Herren works as a tech consultant, where she articulates value for AI products. Her job is to grab the attention of her audience and tell a fresh, compelling story in the smallest possible character count. She thanks you for being a reader.